White Fire by John Oxenham

John Oxenham was the pseudonym used by William Arthur Dunkerley for most of his fiction works including poetry. For journalism he went by the name of Julian Ross.

Dunkerley was born on November 12th 1852 in Manchester. He attended Old Trafford School and Victoria University, both in Manchester.

He married in America and lived they for a short time before returning to these shores, this time to Ealing in West London becoming both the Deacon and teacher at Ealing Congregational Church in the 1880's.

In 1913 he wrote a bestselling book of poems entitled 'Bees In Amber' followed by 'All's Well" in 1916. As a journalist he was a major contributor to Jerome K Jerome's Idler magazine.

In 1922 he moved to Worthing in Sussex and became the town's Mayor.

He died in Worthing on January 23rd, 1941.

Index of Contents

CHAPTER I - MISS INQUISITIVE
CHAPTER II - THE MAN
CHAPTER III - THE MAN'S MAN
CHAPTER IV - A SHAMELESS THING!
CHAPTER V - LEAP YEAR
CHAPTER VI - A SUDDEN WIDE HORIZON
CHAPTER VII - SOME ODD FURNISHINGS AND A HONEYMOON
CHAPTER VIII - GOING STRONG
CHAPTER IX - ARMS AND THE MAN
CHAPTER X - A BLACK OBJECT-LESSON
CHAPTER XI - TOO LATE
CHAPTER XII -THE FLAMING SWORD
CHAPTER XIII - THE MAN'S MAN'S MAN
CHAPTER XIV - CLIPPING A BLACKBIRD
CHAPTER XV - WHERE THOU GOEST
CHAPTER XVI - SAWDUST AND SHAVINGS
CHAPTER XVII - FIRST FRUITS
CHAPTER XVIII - SETBACKS
CHAPTER XIX - FORWARD
CHAPTER XX - MANY FORMS OF GRACE
CHAPTER XXI - MIGHT OF RIGHT
CHAPTER XXII - PAX
CHAPTER XXIII - THE SCOURGE OF GOD
CHAPTER XXIV - GAIN OF LOSS

CHAPTER XXV - THE LIFTING VEIL
CHAPTER XXVI - THE GENTLE MARTYR
CHAPTER XXVII - PEACE WITH A SPEAR
CHAPTER XXVIII - NO THOROUGHFARE
CHAPTER XXIX - THE ACT OF GOD
CHAPTER XXX - WIPED OUT
CHAPTER XXXI - REVERSIONS
CHAPTER XXXII - FROM THE BEGINNING
CHAPTER XXXIII - SALT OF THE EARTH
JOHN OXENHAM – A CONCISE BIBLIOGRAPHY

CHAPTER I

MISS INQUISITIVE

She was so dainty a little figure that the bare-armed women in the doors of the lands and closes turned and looked after her with enjoyment untinged even with envy. They scratched their elbows and commented on her points with complacent understanding.

"None o' your ten-and-six carriage paid in that lot, I'm thinking, Mrs. O'Neill," said one.

"Thrue for ye, Mrs. Macfarlane. Purty as a daisy, she is. It's me that wud like to be on tairms with her maw when she's done with 'em."

And a decidedly pretty little figure the small girl made, in her stylishly pleated blue serge, jaunty tam, natty leather belt, and twinkling brown shoes, and her absolute unconsciousness of anything unduly attractive in her appearance.

Her determined little face was set strenuously. She looked neither to the right hand nor to the left, beyond a glance now and again for landmarks. And above all, and most inflexibly, she never once looked behind her; for she was bound upon an adventure, and her reward lay on ahead.

"Past the cemetery gates," she said to herself. "Up a brae. Past a pond and up a cinder path. That's all right! That must be the woollen mill, and that's the paper-mill, and that splashing white must be the Cut."

As she took the cinder path, the gates of the two mills opened, and a flood of hurrying girls came down towards the town, mostly in bunches, laughing and joking, some with linked arms, some few solitary. Then followed boys and men, with dinner in their faces, and an occasional word fired at the girls in front.

The girls all fell silent, and resolved themselves into devouring eyes, as the dainty little figure stepped briskly past them. There were spasms of longing among them; they buried them under bursts of wilder laughter. The men and boys glanced at her out of the corners of their eyes, and did not understand why the sky looked bluer and the sunshine brighter than it had done a moment before.

She came, presently, to a dividing of the ways, where the roads branched to the two mills, made a short reconnaissance of the flashing chute she had seen from below, then turned to the right, past the paper-mill and the manager's house, past the clump of fir-trees, and came out on a footpath by the side of which the rushing brown waters of the Cut hurried down to the mills and reservoirs.

"O-o-o-oh!" said the small girl rapturously, and her face was an unconscious Te Deum.

And well it might be, for she had a great appreciation of the beautiful, and she was enjoying her first full glimpse of one of the finest sights in the whole of Great Britain and Ireland and the adjacent Cumbraes.

"O-o-oh!" and she sat down to enjoy it.

Below her to the right rose the smoke of the town and the ceaseless clangour of the ship-building yards. A movement would have hidden them from her. But she did not move; she neither saw nor heard them. Her eyes were fixed absorbedly on the mighty panorama beyond: the lovely firth, blue as an Italian lake, and all alive with traffic; energetic little river steamers racing with rival toys; slow coasters toiling along like water-beetles; a great black American liner at the Tail of the Bank; the great grey guardship with its trim official lines and hovering launches; and farther out, near the opposite shore, the white sails of yachts flashing in the sun like seabirds' wings. And beyond—the hills, the mighty hills of God. She had known the hills in a general, wholesale way for long enough; but she knew now that she had never known them before. From this lofty vantage point she saw them now for the first time in all their grandeur and beauty, and they overwhelmed her.

Such a mighty array of giants: green, rounded hills; rugged brown hills, flushed with the purple of the heather; grey mountain peaks piled fantastically against the unflecked blue sky; bosky glens; dark patches of forest land; and all about them, down below, the silent strength of the sea, lapping the feet of the recumbent giants, creeping up among their sprawling limbs, and cradling the mighty bulks with tender caresses!

The girl sat for a long time drinking it all in, to the tune of the swirl and bubble and tinkle of the swift brown water behind her. Then she got up and went on along the path, which disclosed fresh beauties of the larger view at every step. She went on and on, heedless of everything but the wide, vast prospect and her own mighty enjoyment of it. She had some lunch in her pocket; she forgot it. The air was so sweet and strong that she felt no fatigue. She had walked for over an hour in this new heaven of delight, when she came tumbling to earth in truly feminine fashion.

The path followed the Cut round the folds and wrinkles of the hillside. At times, on in front, it disappeared into the sky. She was nearing one such sharp turn, when a pair of mighty horns came wavering round it, and behind the horns an evil monster all in black and with baleful eyes. At sight of her it gave an angry bellow and pawed the ground. Alongside her was a small stone erection like an unfinished hut, on a little platform, below which white water trickled down a glen full of ferns and trees. She clasped her hands, gave herself up for lost, and dropped out of the monster's sight behind the one end wall of the hut.

Then a boy's voice rang out full and clear—

"Ah, beast! Bos ferocissime! Get out o' that, or I'll do for you. What's taken you to-day, you old villain?"

Then followed more forcible argument in the shape of stones, and, with grateful twitches of her clasped hands, the small girl saw her discomfited enemy go crashing down the hillside among the whins and ferns and rolling rocks.

The beast was evidently possessed of an unusually perverse disposition that day. It looked up once at the girl behind the wall, and made some spiteful remark, which elicited a dissuasive "Would you?" and another shower of stones from its keeper. Then it went galloping away on the sides of its feet along the steep hillside. The boy, with an exclamation, sprang down after it, and the girl caught sight of him for the first time—a sturdy little figure, with light hair and unlimited energy. He chased the beast with boyish objurgations, which broke out with new vigour when the chase led through a piece of black swamp, with the natural results to the pursuer.

He came back presently, hot and muddy, whistling like a blackbird.

She was just about to get up and go on, when she heard him jumping down into the little glen below, and she craned over to see what he was about.

He scrambled down to a small round natural basin in the rock, threw off his jacket and waistcoat, unbuttoned his flannel shirt, and proceeded to a mighty wash.

He seemed to revel in it so exceedingly that the girl sat and watched him with enjoyment. He had no towel, so did not waste any time in drying himself, but allowed the sun and wind to do their duties. Then he came clambering up the slope again. There was a large flat stone in front of the embryo cabin. He came and sat down on it, and remained there so long and so quiet that at last she moved slightly and peeped round to see what he was doing.

And what he was doing was so very astonishing that she gave an involuntary gasp of amazement.

He was lying flat on his stomach, with a tattered book open in front of him. On the flat slab was a diagram drawn with the chunk of chalk he held in his hand, and he was studying it so intently that he did not hear her till her shadow fell across his work.

"Hello! Where did you come from?" and he jumped up and stood staring at her. He was not aware of it, but he was dimly perceptive of the fact that she was very nice-looking. He remembered later—when her face evaded him—that she was very prettily dressed.

"From behind there," she said. "That nasty bull frightened me."

"He's a stupid beast." And then, suddenly bethinking himself, "Have you been there ever since?"

The girl nodded. She liked the look of him. His jacket and trousers were rough and well worn, but his face was wonderfully bright and clean. She did not know when she had seen a boy's face she liked so much. There was such a glow in it, and his blue eyes were so fearless and looked at her so very straight. She did not know very many boys, and did not care much for any of those she did know. They were always either teasing or silly, and always abominably selfish. Somehow this boy did not seem any of those things.

"You'd no right to watch a gentleman washing himself."

"You're not a gentleman, and I couldn't help myself. At least—"

"You're not a lady, and you could have gone away quite well. It's a good thing for you I didn't have a bath in the big pool there. You'd have watched just the same, I suppose, Miss Inquisitive!"

"Oh!" she said sharply. "You rude thing! How did you know?"

"Know what?"

"That! Miss— what you called me just now."

At which he laughed out loud, a great merry laugh that did one good to listen to, and showed a set of sound white teeth and a quick apprehension.

"Is that what they call you at home?" he asked, with a mischievous twinkle.

"My aunties call me that. Father says 'Want-to-know gets on.'"

"He's right," said the boy, with a blaze in the blue eyes. "I like your father better than your aunties. Where were you going when the beast stopped you?"

"Right along there," she nodded.

"All the way to the Sheils? It's a gey long way for a bit lassie like you."

"I'm not a bit lassie. I'm thirteen."

"Really! You're young for your age!"

She was somewhat doubtful about this remark, but it felt like a compliment, so she let it pass.

"What's your name?" she asked.

"Kenneth Blair. What's yours?"

"Jean Arnot. How old are you?"

"I'll be fifteen next July." This was August.

"What's that you were drawing? Is it a windmill?" staring intently down at it.

"A windmill!"—with unutterable scorn. "And you say you're thirteen! That's Euclid—Prop. 47. It's a thumper too."

"I haven't begun Euclid yet," she said meekly, and regarded him with a face full enough of questioning to amply justify her nickname. "Will you please tell me something?"

He began to laugh, and she knew that "Miss Inquisitive" was on the tip of his tongue. He only nodded, however.

"Do all the herd-boys about here do Euclid?"

"I d'n' know. There's nothing to stop them if they want to."

"Why do you speak so differently from most other boys? You speak almost as well as I do."

A smile flickered in his face for a second, but died out, and he said quietly—

"That's easily told, anyway. My father was schoolmaster at Inverclaver. He taught me."

"And does he teach you still? Where is he schoolmaster now?"

He looked at her a moment in silence, and then said—

"I don't know. He's dead."

"Oh! But he can't be a schoolmaster anywhere if he's dead. I'm so sorry. And of course he can't teach you either."

"I don't know," said the boy slowly. "I think sometimes—"

But she was off on another scent.

"What are you going to be when you grow up?"

"Ah!"—with animation. "I'm going to be a big man."

"You can't make yourself that. You're not very big now."

"I've not done growing yet, and I'm very strong, and I've never been ill in my life. Besides—"

"I've just had measles and whooping-cough. That's why I'm here."

He nodded, as much as to say, "Yes, that's just the kind of thing girls would have"; and went on, "And then I'm going to be an explorer."

"O-o-o-h!" with snapping eyes. "Where?"

"I don't know where. Anywhere where nobody's ever been before."

She devoured him with hungry appreciation. His face was so very clean, so radiantly bright, and the sparks in his blue eyes kindled answering sparks in her own. For she too possessed a lively imagination, and a spirit many times the size of her body.

"But will you be able to? Are you very rich?"

"Rich? No, I'm not rich, but I'm not that poor either—not just now. I bought this last week," with a touch of superior pride, as he hauled out a Latin grammar, sixth-hand, but still boasting covers. "When I've finished it I'll feel poor till I get the next. But that's not yet."

"Wouldn't you like to be very rich?"

"I d'n' know. I never tried it."

"My father is very rich."

"Is he? And what are you going to do when you grow up?"

"Oh, I'm going to be a lady."

"Yes, that's about all you can be, I suppose," he nodded, and looked really sorry for her.

"I shall be very rich, and I shall do just what I like—except darning and needlework. They're hijjus!"

"Hideous," he said, with a touch of pedantic reproof which consorted oddly with his jacket and trousers.

"I always say 'hijjus' when it's quite too awful and past words. How would you like to be a manager of one of my father's mills?"

"I don't know," he said, regarding her doubtfully. "I'm thinking perhaps I wouldn't make a very good manager. Not yet."

Then her hand happened to touch her pocket, which reminded her of her lunch.

"Are you hungry?" she asked. "I'll sit down here and you shall have some of my lunch, and you shall tell me the names of all those hills and lochs opposite. Aren't they splendid?"

"Ay, they're grand. I've been watching them for a year now."

She wrestled her dainty little packet out of her pocket, and sat down on a rock looking out over the wonderful panorama in front. The boy sat down on another rock and hauled out a piece of newspaper in which were wrapped some broken pieces of thick oatcake and some rough fragments of cheese.

"Do you like oatcake and cheese?" she asked.

"Rather!"

"Won't you have some of my sandwiches?" she said politely, but not without anxiety.

He looked at the delicate provision, and said stoutly—

"No, thank you. I like this best."

And, as the little lady possessed the dainty but vigorous appetite of the fully-restored-to-health-and-got-to-make-up-for-lost-time, and as she was only thirteen, she was not rude enough to press him unduly.

"Now tell me the names of all those hills and lochs," she said, and he proceeded to tell her all she wanted to know.

"Yon's Dumbarton,"—between bites; "you can see Glasgow some days," and she regarded him doubtfully.

"And yon's the Gare Loch. That big fellow with the shoulders is Ben Lomond. The one humped up like this is The Cobbler. That other big one is Ben Ihme. That's Loch Long and a bit of Loch Goil, and yon's Holy Loch and Ben More."

When she had eaten her tiny sandwiches, and her two small cookies with jam inside, and her two biscuits, and had learned the names and personal peculiarities of all the hills and lochs, and he had finished the last crumbs of his oatcake and cheese, he convoyed her past the black menace down below, as far as the next stone dyke, and told her how she could shorten her journey by cutting across some fields, and so get down to the Inverkip road, and eventually to Ashton and the "caurs."

He watched the sprightly little figure, with the gleaming mane of hair and swinging skirts and twinkling brown shoes, till she reached the next distant corner, waved his hand to her, received an answering wave from her, and turned back to his life—his unruly beasts, his treasured Euclid and Latin grammar, his dreams, his hopes, and ever so much more than he knew.

But Prop. 47 was not amenable that afternoon. He smiled at thought of the windmill, and looked up to see her standing before him with her sweet childish face and questioning eyes. He thought much of the winsome little lady, both then and for a long time afterwards. He scanned the winding path by the Cut each day in hopes that she might come again. But she was away home to London, and at last only a memory of her remained, and that growing dimmer and dimmer till it was little more than a sentiment—simply the warm glow of a pleasant impression.

And she? Ah, she wrought better than she knew that day.

For when she got home from her great adventure, and had been duly scolded by her aunts for undertaking so much, when they had only expected her to go up to the Cut and down again in a couple of hours or so—when she reached home, old Mr. MacTavish, the minister, was there, and he rejoiced in her prattling tongue, and delighted in drawing her out.

She enlarged upon the very uncommon herd-laddie she had met up on the Cut,—on his satisfactory looks, his unique cleanliness, his fearlessness in the matter of wild beasts, his understanding, and his aims in life. Her thoughts were full of him, and when Miss Jean Arnot had something on her mind her little world was by way of hearing of it.

Old Mr. MacTavish had been a herd-laddie himself in his time.

Suffecit!

CHAPTER II

THE MAN

Ten years later Miss Jean Arnot was visiting her aunts in Greenock again. Not but what she had been there many times in between, but this is the only occasion of which we need take note.

There had been many changes in these ten years.

For one thing, Jean's father was dead, and she was a very wealthy young woman. In many respects she was still very like the little Jean of earlier times. Her face was still the sweet, long oval of her childhood, though the features were more pronounced and matured. But the chief impression it left upon you was still that of eager questioning, a great longing to know, tempered somewhat by years and freedom from all material care. "Want-to-know" was getting on in years—twenty-three, a great age—but there were still mysteries of life which she had not solved, wherein she found matter for surprise at times.

But life ran very smoothly and pleasantly with her. She went out a little, and entertained a little in return, travelled much, and was not wanting in good deeds and charity. Her income was about ten times as large as was really good for her, and if she gave munificently she never missed what she gave, so that the recipients were the sole beneficiaries of her giving.

She had hosts of friends, phalanxes of admirers; could have had hosts of aspirants to a still closer relationship, but so far would have none of them. She was enjoying herself exceedingly, and fulfilling in their entirety the aspirations of her childhood. She was a lady, she was rich, and she was doing as she liked—and she had not touched a needle since she came into her kingdom.

That was the natural rebound, for Aunt Jannet Harvey, a famous needlewoman and housewife herself, had rigorously insisted—so long as she was in power—on her niece learning the minor as well as the major accomplishments of a gentlewoman, such as had obtained during her own long apprenticeship to that high estate. And that is how it came to pass that Miss Jean Arnot, wealthy heiress and society lady, really knew a very great deal more about some things than you would have imagined from the casual sight of her at dance or opera.

The moment she was free, and a woman of herself, she relegated the "hijjus" things to what she considered their proper place in the economy of her life, and, later, dug them up out of their dusty corners gratefully, and Aunt Jannet was justified.

Aunt Harvey—Aunt Jannet Harvey, to distinguish her from Aunt Lisbeth Harvey—had lived with them and mothered her since her own mother died, when she was a very small child indeed. Aunt Jannet was really her mother's aunt, early widowed and childless, a wise and placid old lady—old, that is, in the eyes of effervescent three-and-twenty—with somewhat rigid ideas of right and wrong, toning slowly, by course of time and easy circumstance, into a tolerant acceptance of things as they came. Her husband had been a professor in Edinburgh, and the society he and she had enjoyed in the modern Athens, thirty years before, was her standard of what society ought to be. She was, however, each year becoming more reconciled to the disparities of the lighter age with which John Arnot's great success in life had forced her into contact. And Jean had been to her as her own daughter would have been, if she had had one, since the day she first took charge of her and began to endeavour to answer some of her questions, and quietly to shelve others for more suitable occasion of discussion. For little Jean Want-to-know had a most active brain and an insatiable curiosity, and never hesitated to ask for fullest details of anything she did not understand; and the wonderings and questionings of such a child have no bounds at times, and are almost impossible of control, either from the inside or the outside.

Jean made a point of spending a part of each year in Scotland, wherever else she and Aunt Jannet might wander at other times. On such occasions Aunt Jannet went to Edinburgh and lived again in the past, but in a yearly narrowing circle, so far as the personal element was concerned, and Jean went to Greenock and queened it over her aunts there.

She was a great enjoyment, a continuous ripple of excitement, to their ordered household; and since they no longer sat upon her and answered her erstwhile inconvenient questions by gentle snubs and nicknames, the times she spent with them were times of great enjoyment to her also.

She rather patronised them, of course, which was perhaps inevitable; for she lived twenty to their one, and, moreover, possessed the means to do it and a will that carried all before it.

She insisted, for instance, on paying for her board and lodging, and on a tariff of her own fixing, whenever she came to stay with them, and flatly declined to come on any other condition. They were independent-minded, and declined to be dictated to in such a matter by a small thing whom they had known in frocks with skirts only thirteen inches long. She promptly scandalised them by going to the Tontine and putting up there. Then they gave way, and she had them. After that she was capable of anything, and they submitted to all her whims, which were always pretty and thoughtful ones, and—she assured them, just as they had been wont to assure her in the days of the thirteen-inch frocks—entirely for their own good and happiness. She salved the cicatrice of the Tontine wound by carrying them all off en masse to the Riviera for a month; and Aunt Jean, after whom she was named, gravely suggested the advisability of frequently opposing her ideas, since the outcome was so eminently agreeable.

Then she was always making them presents, at which their independency kicked, but in which, nevertheless, they could not but own to enjoyment.

But the girl was right, after all. She had much too much, and they had only enough, and that only with clever handling; and they would no more have accepted bald gifts of money than they would have burned down their house and claimed double the value of the furniture.

Jean and her visits, and their visits to her, and with her to hitherto unattainable places, were the high lights of their lives. They loved her dearly, rejoiced in her greatly, were proud of her, and wondered much when it would all come to an end in the centering of her thoughts and affections on one sole and—they fervently hoped, but were not without misgivings, because of her wealth and her impulsiveness—worthy man.

They made ingenuous little attempts at sounding her on that subject, but she was much too clever for them, and skilfully eluded all approaches which might tend, even remotely, to any self-revelations. That there were no revelations to make only added piquancy to the game, from her point of view, since it kept the aunts in a state of perpetual mystification, and held no pitfalls.

Among many other changes she had seen in the last ten years, old Mr. MacTavish had retired long ago, and a younger man occupied his pulpit, and, strange to say, gave satisfaction in it.

The Rev. Archibald Fastnet was so exactly the opposite of his predecessor that it might have seemed impossible that where the one had pleased the other should do so. Mr. Fastnet was young, and he believed in—as he put it—making things jump. And he made both things and people jump at times. He was full of enthusiasms which were generally at white heat and—which is more unusual—remained so. The older generation said he kept them on the perpetual "kee-vee" to see what he would do next; the younger people enjoyed him and the service he exacted from them. And on Sundays they all, old and young, always turned out both morning and evening, since it invariably came to pass that, if they missed a service, something happened which made them feel out of the running for the whole of the following week. When Jean Arnot was at Greenock she did as good Greenockians do, and went to church twice every Sunday and one evening in the week as well.

The Rev. Archibald never failed to furnish her with a certain amount of quiet amusement, and, apart from other feelings, she always went in expectation and was rarely disappointed.

On this particular Sunday morning Mr. Fastnet had prepared a little surprise for his people, which turned out, as his arrangements generally did, a perfect success. It also afforded Jean Arnot the surprise of her life, and she never forgot it.

You can forget many things in ten full years. If, for instance, you yourself had met a person informally ten years ago, and spent half an hour with him, just incidentally hearing his name, it is doubtful if you would recall him very distinctly if he presented himself suddenly before you after the ten years had passed.

Jean felt a rustle of surprise among her aunts in the pew, and she saw that two men passed up into the pulpit where the Rev. Archibald lorded it alone as a rule. The voluntary ceased, and he stood up, beaming all over, as usual when he had something unusually delectable up his sleeve for them.

"Instead of speaking to you myself this morning," he said, "I have asked our friend Mr. Blair to say a few words to us. We all take a fatherly and motherly, and I may say a sisterly and brotherly, interest in Mr. Blair. Perhaps some of us regret that none of us has taken a still nearer and dearer-than-all-otherly interest in him"—at which Fastneticism a smile rippled round. "Our young friend leaves this week to begin his work in the South Seas, where, as you know, he is about to join that valiant bearer of light into outer darkness, John Gerson, in his noble work. You will, I know, appreciate with me this chance—it may be the last chance—of hearing our young standard-bearer's voice before he passes beyond the fringes of the night."

Then he came down, and took his seat in a front pew and enjoyed a preacher's holiday.

And, after a pause, and very quietly, young Blair rose in the pulpit and gave out the hymn.

So far Jean Arnot had been only interested and amused. But the sound of his voice, clear and round and full as an organ tone, made her jump with surprise. He had spoken quite naturally, but there was a ring in it that told of immense possibilities behind, and there was something in it that plucked at some hidden chord of Jean's memory and set it humming as a harp-string responds to a bugle note.

She stared at him eagerly. Had she ever by any possibility met him before? She could hardly have forgotten it if she had, she thought. For he was a young man of most striking appearance. Tall, square-shouldered and broad-chested—a commanding figure in truth. It occurred to others besides Jean that if the natives needed more forcible arguments than words for their conversion, here was a likely man for the work. Light-haired and clean-shaven, his face seemed to glow with an inner radiance—a masterful face, and grave. His eyes were wonderfully magnetic; fearless and steadfast, they made you jump as their glance crossed your own. Jean had just jumped, so she knew.

Now who was this? Surely she had met him before somewhere.

Remember it was ten years since she had seen him, and then only for half an hour, and under very different conditions, and she had never heard his name since.

She ordered her brain, or her heart, or whichever of her inner servants it was that held the key, to go find it, and sat gazing at him to give them such light as that might afford. But the clue evaded her till he was near the end of his quiet, forceful talk.

He had told them of his hopes, and the plans he and Gerson hoped to carry out—"The grandest man I have ever met, a most noble Christian gentleman," he said, in a burst of enthusiasm. He asked them for their help, their prayers, their sympathetic remembrance, their money—since the work had to be maintained from the outside, and even missionaries must live.

He spoke very simply, with no ornate periods or calculated sentences; but his voice was like a trumpet, and his eyes were like stars, and his words were illuminating and full of power, and now and again were flung out white hot from the glowing heart within. Though he spoke for the most part so restrainedly, now and again the brake would slip, and the sweet, white fire of a great, enthusiastic soul would flame through.

Perhaps he was a trifle over-confident of success—that is one of youth's glories and pitfalls; but there was no doubt that his whole heart was in his work—that here, for once at all events, a square man had found his own square hole.

"It was always the great hope and desire of my boyhood to go out into these unknown lands," he was saying. "Though perhaps at that time the inducement was chiefly the unknown, and the inhabitants, I fear, appealed to me more as possible hindrances than inducements. When I tended my uncle's cattle on the hillsides of the Cut—"

And then she knew him, and she sat up with a jerk, and stared at him as though she had only that moment awakened to the fact that he was speaking.

And such, to some extent, was the fact. She had been interested and puzzled. Now, in a moment, it was a new man she was looking at and listening to—a new man, but an old friend. And she was sitting on one piece of rock eating cookies, and he was sitting on another munching oatcake and cheese, and he was saying, "I'm going to be an explorer."

It was very wonderful—though she remembered that she had recognised him, even then, as a boy of different texture from most other boys. And so he had got what he wanted—the greatest prize a man may win, she supposed: to desire vehemently a certain lofty course in life, and to attain to it.

And she? Yes, she remembered. She was going to be rich, and a lady, and do as she liked. Truly hers was but a poor attainment compared with his.

She did not hear much more of what he said, though she was gazing fixedly at him all the time. Her mind was away back to the hillside by the Cut, and it was only when they stood up to sing the last hymn that mind and body came together again.

Mr. Blair came down to shake hands with his many friends, and most of the people went forward for that purpose, Jean's aunts among them, and she with them; and as they sat at the back they were among the last to reach him.

She was shaking hands with him, and the straight blue eyes looking into her own set her heart jumping.

"Ah!" said the Rev. Archibald, all one vast beam of satisfaction at the general enjoyment of his little surprise. "Now we have you, Blair. This lady, at all events, you can't claim as an old friend, though I am quite sure she is a well-wisher."

Blair still held her hand and looked steadfastly into her eyes.

"This is—" began Mr. Fastnet, and was stopped abruptly by a peremptory gesture of Miss Arnot's other hand.

"Yes—I think so," said the young man, breaking suddenly into a smile of enjoyable reminiscence, "Miss—Jean—Arnot? Or possibly now Mrs.—?"

"Jean Arnot is still good enough for me, Mr. Blair," she said brightly. "How wonderful that you should remember me all these years!"

"Why more wonderful than that you should have recognised me, Miss Arnot? We are both a good deal changed since last we met."

"Why, what's all this?" said the Rev. Archibald jovially. "I had no idea you knew Miss Arnot, Blair."

"We met once, ten years ago, up on the Cut—and had lunch together," said Blair, with a smile. "I was keeping Highland cattle from goring little girls, and Miss Arnot was exploring. We have both travelled far since then."

"You much the farthest," she said quietly, "and going still farther. I congratulate you very heartily. It is what you desired then. Do you remember telling me?"

"Yes. I am very grateful."

Blair's thoughts were full of her. As they went home he quietly led Fastnet on to speak about her, and offered him the best inducement to plentiful speech in the appreciation with which he listened.

Fastnet enlarged upon her great wealth and generosity, her cleverness and culture, her independence of thought and deed, and incidentally mentioned that he had seen or heard some rumour of her possible marriage with Lord Charles Castlemaine, second son of the Duke of Munster, but he could not say what truth there was in it.

As a matter of fact, Jean Arnot would as soon have thought of marrying the ticket-collector at Monument Station as Lord Charles Castlemaine. The gentleman with the snips at Monument Station is doubtless a most worthy individual, but I know absolutely nothing whatever about him. Jean Arnot knew exactly as much, and one does not, as a rule, marry a man one knows absolutely nothing about, nor—a man about whom one knows considerably more than is to his credit. Jean Arnot knew a good deal about Charles Castlemaine, and there was not the slightest danger of her marrying him.

"Is he a good sort?" asked Blair.

"Much what dukes' younger sons mostly are, I imagine. The elder brother is not strong, so if it comes off you may perhaps count among your well-wishers a duchess sooner or later."

"Miss Arnot's good wishes would weigh more with me than those of all the duchesses in the land," said Blair quietly. "There is something very taking in her face—it is so bright and eager." Then he laughed at his thoughts. "I remember, that day up on the Cut, I quite accidentally hit upon a nickname they used to her at home—Miss Inquisitive—and she flared up at me like a rip-rap. She was always wanting to know, I believe."

"She is still," said Fastnet, laughing, "though she must have learned a good deal in all these years. She told me once that she was born curious, and that she was especially curious to know all about what came after this life. She said she thought the thought that she was going to solve that greatest of all puzzles would take away all fear of death when the time came. That was just after I came here. She must have been about fifteen then."

Blair's time was very short. He left that afternoon for Edinburgh to spend his last two days with his old friends, Mr. and Mrs. MacTavish. He was to join Mr. Gerson in London on Wednesday and sail on Thursday.

Mr. MacTavish had been a father to him from the time he walked along the Cut—the very day after little Jean Arnot's prattle had set him on the boy's track—and found him, prostrate on the flat stone, still wrestling with Prop. 47.

He had been just there himself when a small boy, struggling against the retarding clay of a narrow agricultural home. He knew the sturdy independence that would be in the boy; and, in his own full knowledge, went to work warily. The slightest hint of charity, and the shy, proud one would be off.

So he never mentioned Jean, met the boy on his own ground as a perfectly new acquaintance, gradually won his confidence and his heart, guided, led, and finally enabled him by his own exertions to obtain a bursary and proceed to college. With that, nothing could keep him back. His heart was in it, his aims were high, and his course was a triumphal progress. He had learned, as a boy, that greatest of lessons—how to learn. The rough experiences of his boyhood on the hillside had given him splendid health and a body that never tired. He was tough as wire, and, among other things, was known at college for that passion for personal cleanliness which, in its earlier days, had helped to introduce him to Jean Arnot on the hillside. He had, quite early—as soon, indeed, as he perceived the possibility of attaining to it—fixed on the mission-field as offering what his soul yearned for. Perhaps at first it was the unknown that drew him. No matter. By degrees the known outrivalled the unknown, the greater absorbed the less, and his heart was fixed on the highest of all high work.

In these ten years he had learned mightily. Head, heart, and hand had toiled incessantly, and never felt it toil, since it was only the natural satisfaction of a great heart-craving. Then he had come across Gerson, home on leave for the first time in twenty years. Their hearts and eyes struck sparks the first time they met.

"That is a man!" said Gerson, "and I'll have him if I can get him."

"That is a saint and a hero!" said Blair. "I'm his man if he'll have me."

After that no power on earth could have kept them apart, and on Thursday they were to sail together for the outer fringes. Gerson was busily bidding his friends goodbye.

"You may hear of me from time to time. You'll never see me again—this side the veil at all events. We'll hope to meet on the other side," he said heartily, and grudged every day that lay between him and his work.

Blair, in telling Mr. and Mrs. MacTavish of his reception at the Greenock church, incidentally mentioned Miss Arnot, but doubted evidently whether they would know anything of her.

But the old man laughed gently, and said, in his quiet, old-fashioned, precise way, which was the very antithesis of the Rev. Archibald's jovial utterances: "I will explain to you now, my dear boy, what at the time I deemed wisest to treasure within the repository of my own heart. It was from Miss Jean Arnot that I first heard about you. It was in consequence of her delighted account of her meeting with you, and the Euclid and the Latin grammar, that I sought you out on the hillside and tendered you the helping hand of which you have made such excellent use."

"It was Miss Arnot?" said the young man in amazement.

"Truly, yes! Though I do not for a moment suppose she knows anything whatever about it. I certainly never told her, and I never told you, because I had been a studious herd-laddie myself, and I knew what shy and hypersensitive colts they are, and the delicacy necessary to their proper handling."

"I thank you for telling me now, sir. It is as I would have it."

"I believe it would please her to know what you told me, sir," Blair broke out abruptly a little later on, and the old gentleman smiled at the evidence of the track of his thoughts.

"I will write and tell her, if you like, if you really think the knowledge would afford her any gratification."

"I think it would, sir."

And so Jean Arnot received two notes which gave her very deep pleasure. And the shorter one of the two said simply:—

"You will have learned by this time, from my dear old friend and second father, what I myself only learned three days ago—that it was your unconscious hand that set my unconscious feet on the ladder. I rejoice to know that it was so. The knowledge of it would be an additional spur, if any spur were needed. Time may come, however, when the remembrance of your kindness and all it has done for me, unconscious though it was, may nerve me for some critical passage in the life in front, for we are going among perilous peoples. It is not likely we shall ever meet again, but, having learned how this matter stood, I could not leave home without tendering you my most grateful and hearty thanks.

"That your life may be a wide, and bright, and beautiful, and happy one will be the prayer of

"Yours faithfully,
"KENNETH BLAIR."

"He is a good man," said Jean thoughtfully, as she folded the letter and put it carefully into a special corner of her desk, and then immediately took it out again and re-read it. "May God go with him also!"

She read in the papers next day of his sailing in company with John Gerson, the prophet of the Dark Islands, and was surprised to discover in herself a curious feeling of loss, as though something had gone out of her life. Which, considering all the circumstances of the case, was distinctly odd, you know.

She had only met him twice in her life; for ten years she had hardly given him a thought; and yet his going left a little blank in a life which was quite unaccustomed to anything of the kind.

But the sudden sight of him in all his quiet strength of attainment, and the knowledge of what it all meant to him, together with this new understanding of how it had all come about, and of the share she herself had unconsciously had in the making of him—well, perhaps after all it was not so odd. For she had felt a sudden glow of participation in his triumph, a sudden sense of increase such as no procurement of her wealth had ever brought her—and now it was as suddenly gone, and a blank remained.

She caught herself thinking of him oftener than she had ever thought of any man before, and she said to herself in surprise—

"Goodness gracious me! why does that herd-laddie stick in my brain so?"

A quite dispassionate dissector of the emotions and their origins might have come to the conclusion that it was, after all, only a case of the heart performing its natural function of feeding the brain. For the heart is the life.

She laughed at herself; but the herd-laddie remained in her thoughts, and one day, before she went south, she actually found herself sitting on that very same piece of rock where she had sat ten years before, and in imagination he sat on the adjacent rock, munching his thick oatcake and broken pieces of cheese.

"What a greedy little pig I was!" she said to herself, as she sat leaning forward with her chin in her hand. "But I don't believe he'd have taken a bite from me, however much I'd wanted him to."

She looked at the slab where the windmill had been, and at the pool where the gentleman had washed. He looked as if he had been strenuously washing ever since. What a radiant face he had! It did not come from much washing, she knew; but somehow the two things linked themselves in her mind. It was the white fire inside that lit up the outside: a real man—a man to trust infinitely—a man to—

She sat looking out over the mighty panorama of hills and lochs and mountains opposite—"Gare Loch, Loch Goil, Loch Long, Ben Lomond, Ben Ihme, The Cobbler, Holy Loch." She knew most of them still. How the sight of them all brought him back to her! And, in all probability, he would never see them again. "We are going among perilous peoples."

Well! he had done very wonderfully; he was fulfilling the highest aspirations of his boyish heart.

And she? She was a lady, and very rich, as she had said she would be. And she remembered the touch of scorn with which the herd-laddie had said, "Yes, that's about all you can be, I suppose."

Close behind her the swift brown waters of the Cut hurried headlong to the town—one long, unceasing blessing. "Men may come and men may go, but we go on for ever," sang the bubbling waters against the rough rock walls of their narrow way.

"Surely I am one of the most useless of God's creatures," said Jean Arnot, as she wandered slowly back towards the paper-mill and home.

CHAPTER III

THE MAN'S MAN

Unflecked blue sky above, with a blazing white sun in it. A mighty mountain peak, with bald summit, seamed sides mantled with greenery, and round its waist, where it sat in the water, a narrow band of gleaming white sand and tufted cocoa-palms, like an Island woman's girdle. A smooth, dark, ruffled mirror of lagoon; and farther out, with gaps here and there, a barrier reef on which the hungry sea chafed and roared in ceaseless thunder. Two white men and a menacing crowd of brown ones.

"Ready?" asked the elder of the two men.

He was tall and thin, white-haired and grey-bearded, and his eyes shone like stars. His face was bronzed with much sun. There was a glow in it which did not come from the sun, a mighty determination which did not come from mere strength of will, a sweet white soul-fire which had made him a power throughout the islands of the Southern Seas.

"I am ready," said the younger man.

His face was brown also, but not bronzed. There was a lighter patch of tightened skin above each cheek-bone. His jaw was set so grimly that it looked aggressive. His lips were tightly closed. His eyes were unnaturally wide at the moment. He looked slightly raised—fey, in fact, as a man looks when he and death meet face to face in a narrow way.

In front, the crowd of Islanders stood waiting for them at an angle of rock where the white beach curved round into the land. They carried clubs and spears, and swung them restlessly. Behind, on the smooth reflexive swell of the lagoon, a white boat, just pushed off from the shore, rode like a seabird with wings outstretched for swoop or flight. Farther out a waiting schooner, whose white sails shivered softly to a head breeze.

"Remember, my son," said the elder man quietly, "one sign of flinching and it is finished. Now let us go." He bared his white head and said softly, "In the name of the Father, and of the Son, and of the Spirit," and went up towards the dark men like the courteous Christian gentleman he was. The younger man did the same.

The natives drew back round the rock; the white men followed. The men in the boat watched intently, and then listened and gazed at the angle of the rock. Their orders were to wait.

The two men passed out of sight, the elder, quiet and calm, as if going for a stroll in his mission garden, the younger, strung to martyr pitch, ready to endure to the utmost. The islanders retreated foot by foot; the white men followed steadily. Then, suddenly, clubs whirled and spears bristled, and the brown men turned and rolled on the white like a flood, and parted them.

The elder man stood and eyed them steadfastly. He had been through it many times before. Death and he had been old friends and fellow-travellers for many a year, and the passing of The Gate was to him but the entrance to a larger life. He spoke to them in words he thought they might understand. For a moment the two men were like two white rocks in a foaming mountain stream. Brown arms, clubs, spears whirled about them. Not one man in ten thousand could have stood it unmoved.

The white-haired man was such a one. He stood. The younger man's face broke; the strings had been drawn too tight. He cast one swift glance round.

In an instant the silvery crown beside him ran blood, and disappeared. With bent head inside his folded arms the younger man dashed at the throng, and sent the brown men spinning, as he had sent men of a brawnier breed spinning on the football field at home. He burst through them in spite of blows and cuts. He was close up to the wild eddy under which his old friend lay when a well-flung club caught him deftly in the neck and brought him down in a heap. The brown men danced madly, and let their shouts go up. They took the younger man by the heels, and dragged him to where the body of the elder lay, and flung him down on top of it. Then the sailors from the boat burst on them with a yell, and sent them scattering.

It was days before he recovered consciousness, weeks before he could lie in a chair on the verandah of the distant mission-house—weak from loss of blood, weaker still in other ways.

They tended him lovingly. There were gracious women there who ministered to him like angels. To them he was hero, saint, martyr but once removed. To himself—!

He was almost too weak to think about it yet. He was hacked to pieces, and bruised to pulp. When he tried to move, it seemed to him that not one sound inch of flesh was left him. When he tried to think, all the little blood that was left in him rushed up into his head and set it humming and buzzing, and dyed his face crimson under the partly bleached tan.

His mind was still in a state of confusion; his thoughts were almost as broken as his body. He remembered facing the bristling brown men. He could see their shaggy heads and twisted faces, their white teeth, their gleaming eyes, and the whirl of their brandished weapons. After that all was blurred, and broke off into sudden darkness. He had a dim remembrance of intense strain and a sudden snap. He groped for the ends of the broken threads, but they were hidden in the outer void. He was still very weak.

He accepted gratefully all that was done for him, but for the most part lay in silence. His sufferings were great, but no word of complaint ever passed his lips. If he had permitted himself any such, it would have been that he still lived when his leader died. To all he was a monument of patient resignation.

So great was his depression, and so slow his recovery, that it was decided at last to send him home, as the only hope of full recuperation. He acquiesced, as he had done in everything they suggested, but in this matter with evident reluctance. He thought it unlikely he would ever return. His heart had been in the work, but he had been tried and found wanting. The work, he said to himself, was for abler and more faithful hands.

So the mission schooner carried him to the nearest port of call, and in due course he was lying in a deck chair carefully swathed in plaids, and the great steamer bore him swiftly homewards.

The story of the martyrdom and of his heroic defence of his old friend: how they two had gone up alone to the peaceful assault of an island of the night; how he had fought for his leader till he could fight no longer, and had fallen at last wounded to death across his dead body,—it had all preceded him. The very sailors were proud to have him on board. The officers made much of him in an undemonstrative way. The ladies fluttered round his chair like humming-birds, and loaded him with attentions.

And he suffered it all in silence. He was still very weak. How could he turn his sick soul inside out to these strangers, and what good to do so?

He had not yet decided what course to take when he got home. He had thought and thought, till he was sick of thinking, sick of himself, sick of life. Ah! why had he not died with the brave old man out there on the shore of the creek behind the rocks? Why had his nerve given way at that supreme moment? Why had this bitter cross been laid upon him? Far better to have died—far easier, at all events. But easier and better run opposite ways as a rule, and have little in common.

Should he confess the whole matter, and retire from the field and find some other way of life? Truly he felt no call to any other work. This had been the one desire of his life; he had grown from youth to manhood in the hope of it. He believed he could still be of service when once he got over the effects of his present fall. Should he not rather bury the dead past, with God as only mourner, and start afresh?— to fail once more when the strain came again, he said to himself with exceeding bitterness. He grieved over his lapse as another might grieve over a deliberate crime. But he postponed any final decision as to the future till he should feel stronger in mind and body.

There was a noted writer on board, a realist of realists. He sought impressions at first hand. He cultivated the sick man's acquaintance, greatly to his discomfort.

"Mr. Blair," he said, sitting down by his side one day, "I would very much like to know just how you felt, and what you thought of, when you were fighting those brown devils. Won't you tell me?"

And the sick man roused himself for a moment, and looked at him with that in his eye which the other comprehended not, and said slowly, "I felt like the devil and I thought of the devil," and not another word would he say. And the writer pondered much on the saying, but never got to the bottom of it or knew how true it was.

His people met him at the landing-place, the reverend father and the white-haired mother, proud to be known even as the foster-parents of such a son, grateful for one more sight of him in the flesh. How could he break their hearts by telling them what a broken reed their trusted one had proved? They rejoiced over him greatly, and said to one another that as his strength came back the cloud that lay on his spirits would be lifted. Their gentle encomiums stung him like darts.

But, by degrees, broken body and broken spirit were healed. Slowly and thoughtfully he made up his mind that the past should be past. He would go out again. He would take his stand in the forefront of the battle in the hope of an honourable death—for he held his life forfeit to the past.

Decision brings a certain peace of mind. He was happier than he had been since he leaped out of the white boat on to the shore of the Dark Island that morning—so long ago that it seemed to belong to a previous life.

The old people said God-speed to his decision. They had possessed him once again after giving him up for good. It was more than they had ever hoped for. They were thankful.

All interested in mission work hailed his decision with enthusiasm. He was common property and too big to be monopolised by any one sect. They had not been able to make one quarter as much of him as they had wished. He had quietly declined to be fêted and lionised. They considered he carried his modesty to too great an extreme. They would have made capital out of him and kindled fresh enthusiasms for the cause by the sight and sound of him. It was with the greatest difficulty that he avoided it all, using the plea of ill-health till his bodily appearance would no longer countenance it.

Once his decision was made known, however, they decided to drag him out of his retirement, and by dint of persistent importunity prevailed on him at last to appear at a public meeting. He consented with reluctance, and only because it was represented to him as a matter of duty.

As the time drew near he began to fear that he was in for more than he had expected. But he had given his word, and he would not draw back.

There were clever men at the head of the movement. Thousands of interested men and women were hungering for a sight of the almost-martyr. They had seen his portrait in the illustrated papers—how joyously the old mother had responded to the many requests for it!—but they wanted to see him with their eyes and hear him with their ears, and the younger folk were to remember all their lives that they had done so. And so, without going into details with him, the leaders of the various societies quietly arranged matters on a generous scale. There were men of imagination among them too, and they prepared a dramatic touch for the meeting which they calculated would make it go with a swing. It went beyond their expectations.

When the young missionary stepped on to the platform he stopped short, and for a moment looked almost as fey as he had done when he leaped out of the white boat that morning on the beach of Dark Island. But there must be no drawing back. He had flinched once—never again!

The chairman of the meeting was a philanthropic Cabinet Minister. As he welcomed the hero of the hour the great audience rose and waved and shouted.

The young man clasped the chairman's welcoming hand as though he were a drowning man, and that hand the one only hope of safety. Then he sank into the chair provided for him, and dropped his face into his hand.

All this was torture to him. Why could they not have let him go out quietly to his work, to his death? No bristling mob of savages that ever could confront him was half so appalling to him as that great well-dressed crowd of enthusiastic men and women and children, gathered to do him honour. Honour! And he before God a dishonoured man—a man who had failed when the pinch came. He groaned in his heart, and wished that he had not come.

But the chairman was speaking, speaking of him, and what he had done—what he was supposed to have done—in warm, appreciative words and flowing periods, and the audience was as still as a flower-garden on a summer afternoon. In the young man's soul there was a great stillness also, a stillness equal almost to that which had fallen on him when he came out of the shadows and lay in the verandah of the mission house.

His eyes wandered unseeingly over those solid banks of faces, all turned on him in eulogy of what he had not done. Those thousands of eyes seemed to pierce his soul.

One face caught his attention and held it, the face of a girl sitting in the third row from the front. Even in his agony he recognised it, as how could he help when it had been so constantly with him in his thoughts. The smooth white brow, like a little slab of polished ivory; the level brows; the large dark eyes looking up at him with something akin to reverence—the beautiful eyes with lustrous points in them; the sweet oval of the lower part of the face; the firm little chin and slightly parted lips, emphasising the old inquiring look which he knew so well: it was a face any man might remember with gratitude for the mere sight of it. It was the face he had at once longed for the sight of and feared to meet, since ever the thought of coming home had been suggested to him. And now here it was, more beautiful than even his dreams of it—inquiring, hopeful, trustful. And he must satisfy the inquiry—and dash the hope, and shatter the trust for ever. Oh, it was hard! It was grievously hard! His life laid down then and there would have been a small price to pay for the confirmation of her belief in him. And he must destroy it and still live on!

But what was this? The chairman had turned to him in his speech, the flower-garden in front had suddenly become a fluttering snowbank.

"Mr. Blair does not happen to belong to that particular section of the Church to which I belong, and which, as the State Church of the realm, retains, and rightly retains, within its own hands the appointment of its own high officers. There are some of us who, as we grow older, and perhaps wiser, regret more and more that any differences should remain among the followers of Christ. We would fain see them done away with. We would cast down all fences and walls of partition, and meet our Christian brothers and sisters on an absolute equality, on the common platform of love and service to the one Master.

"This meeting to-night, of many sects with one common object, is one step in the right direction—a great step. And here is another. The necessity for a supreme hand and head in the guidance of the mission enterprises of the Outer Islands is apparent to all. For such a position we require a man of tried courage and endurance, a man who can look death in the face without flinching, a man who holds his own life of small account, and who is ready at any moment to lay it down in the service of the cause he loves. Of such stuff martyrs are made. That the man who has given us such signal proofs of his fidelity and courage should be chosen for so onerous and so honourable a post is a matter of great satisfaction to us all. Mr. Blair, as all the world knows, has proved his fitness in a time of grievous danger and perplexity.—a time which I do not hesitate to say would have tried the nerve of any man to breaking-point, under a strain which might have broken any ordinary man, and small blame to him. But here"—and he laid his hand upon young Blair's shoulder—"we have the one man who did not break down, and it is this man whom we would rejoice to recognise as the first bishop of the Outer Islands. I am authorised to request Mr. Blair's acceptance of this arduous and honourable post, without reference to any question of form or creed. And that request is made, not in the name or on behalf of my own Church only, but in the names and on behalf of all the Churches represented by the missions to the Outer Islands. It is a common point of union. Mr. Blair's acceptance of the post will, perhaps, be one step towards that greater union of the Churches to which we look hopefully forward, and I earnestly hope that he will see fit to accept this joint and unanimous request of the Churches." And he sat down with glowing face amidst thunders of applause.

And Kenneth Blair? Oh! why could they not have left him to work out his redemption in quietness and silence? Now it was not possible. Those thousands of eyes burnt into his soul. The words he had listened to pierced him like two-edged swords. Silence was no longer possible. To accept all this, as if it were his rightful due, was to hang a millstone round his neck which would drag him down to perdition.

When the tumult died at last into silence, the young man got up and stood and gripped the railing of the platform.

His face was white and set. "A man of indomitable will," they said.

His eyes burnt with a gloomy fire. "He has seen strange and terrible things," they said.

He swayed slightly once or twice before he found his voice. "He has been very near to death," they said.

And then he began to speak, quietly, as one who might need all his strength before he was done; but there was a timbre in it, born of outdoor speaking, which carried to the remotest corner, and a thrill in it which found its way to every heart. And, of all that great assembly, the only face he saw with any distinctness was the face of the girl in the third row, with its calm brow and its lustrous up-glance. He spoke to it. He watched it. If he could convince that one face of all that was in him, he felt that it would be well with him.

In his emotion he overlooked all formalities. He found his voice at last, and said, "My friends, the words I have just been listening to have been to me as sword-thrusts through the heart."

The silence was intense. Every ear and every eye was upon him. He saw only the calm, sweet face of the girl in the third row.

"I have a very terrible confession to make to you. Had I known what was intended this evening I should not have been here, but no slightest word of it reached me. My sole desire has been to get back to my work out yonder, and to lay down my life in it. I have been told that I am a man of courage and endurance ... of tried nerve ... of unflinching fidelity. There was a time when I too believed this of myself." He spoke very slowly and with a solemn impressiveness which those who heard it never forgot to the last day of their lives. "But between that and this there is a deep gulf ... and at the bottom of that gulf lies the dead body of my dear friend and chief. His death lies at my door."

An almost imperceptible movement ran through the audience, as though a cold breath shook it with a simultaneous chill. The face of the girl in the third row remained steadfastly calm. If anything, it seemed to glow with a deeper intensity of hopeful inquiry. "Say what you will, I believe in you!" it said.

"The whole truth of what happened on that dreadful day has never been told. I will confess that I had dared to hope that it might never need to be told—that it might lie between myself and God—that I might be permitted by Him to work out my redemption on the field of my failure, chastened, and perhaps strengthened, by what has passed. For, at a vital moment, when the flinching of an eyelid meant disaster, I ... flinched.

"This is what happened. As we went up towards the savages that day, my dear old friend asked me if I was ready. I was ready. I said so. He said, 'Remember, one sign of flinching and it is finished,' and we went up and round the corner. We were going, as I believed, to certain death, and I was ready—at least, and truly, I believed so. When the savages rushed in upon us, the horror of it broke upon me like a deluge. I glanced round to see if there was no possible way of escape for us. But there was no way. My dear old chief's head was crimson already with blood, and he went down among them. I burst through—and I know no more. They tell me my body was found on top of his. It may be so. How it got there I do not know. What I do know is—that at that supreme moment, when I believed myself to be strong, I found myself weak. When I believed myself ready for a martyr's death, I tried to escape by shameful flight. I was weighed and found wanting, and the remembrance of it has seared my heart like molten iron, night and day, since ever I came to myself. Whether we should have won through if I had remained firm, God only knows. But—I flinched and fled. It seems to me now that I would sooner die a hundred such deaths as I fled from than stand here before you all and confess my default. I can accept no honours. Honours!" with a despairing lift and fall of the hand. "I can accept no position based on so terrible a misconception. All I ask, and I ask it with the deepest humility, is that I may be allowed to go out there again. My life is forfeit to the past. It shall be spent—if it be God's will, it shall be laid down joyfully—in the service to which I believe He called me, and from which I do not believe He has expelled me."

He sat down and covered his face with his hands. There was a momentary silence. The chairman did not quite know what to do. The face of the girl in the third row was ablaze with emotion; the dark eyes were swimming. She glanced restlessly about to see what was going to happen; she looked like springing up herself with flaming words. But another did it. A tall, white-haired man, with a flowing white beard and a face like brown leather, stood up on the platform, and said, in a voice that went straight to all their hearts—

"My friends, we have all heard. Some of us understand, because we have passed through that same dark valley as our young friend. Dare I, in all humility, remind you that a Greater than any shrank from the supreme moment, and prayed, with agonies no man may conceive of, that His bitter cup might pass from Him? I tell you, gentlemen," he cried, in a voice that rang like a trumpet, "that in doing what he has done here this evening our friend has proved himself a man among men. He has said that a hundred savage deaths appear to him less terrible than the confession he has just made. And it is a true saying. Ask your own hearts. I could prove to you that no man can answer absolutely for himself at such a moment; but I will not even argue the point. Our friend has been through the fire. He has been through God's mill. He has been hammered on God's anvil. I tell you that he is true metal. He has proved it here and now. I hold it an honour to grasp his hand and bid him God-speed."

He stretched a sinewy, leather-brown hand to Blair, and the young man gripped it with a new light in his face, and the two stood facing one another.

Still holding the young man's hand, the old one turned to the front again.

"If you agree with me that this is the man we want for the work out there, rise in your seats."

His voice had rung like a bugle-call through the outer darknesses of the earth; his name stood but little lower than God's to tens of thousands who dwelt there, and was held in reverence wherever the English language was spoken. That great audience rose to his call as if a mine had exploded beneath it. His eyes shone with the light the black men knew and loved.

"Let us pray," he said; and the young man fell to his knees beside his chair and dropped his head into his hands again.

CHAPTER IV

A SHAMELESS THING!

The night that followed that meeting at Queen's Hall was the most tempestuous time Jean Arnot ever passed through.

The dramatic events of the meeting had shaken her hidden soul out of its sanctuary. She was thankful to get home intact—so far, at all events, as outward appearances went.

She went at once to her own room. She locked herself in, and paced the floor till she could pace no more.

She could order her steps, but not her thoughts, and her thoughts took wings and climbed lofty heavens of white-piled clouds, and the white-piled clouds were all rosy-tipped, because the thoughts that scaled them came straight from her heart and were tinged with the rosy gold of her heart's desire.

Oh, wonderful! wonderful! The great big soul of him! Was there a nobler man on earth?

How easy to have let it pass! to have kept it between God and himself only! to have worked out his redemption in secret! But he could not, because he was a true man—the truest man ever born, and the bravest. Oh the great, big, noble soul of him!

To and fro she paced, and, no matter where she looked, his white, set face and blazing eyes looked out at her in that agonised strenuity of appeal which had stirred her so in the hall, stirred her to the depths till she had had difficulty in sitting still. It had seemed to her as though he lost sight of all those straining thousands and spoke only to her—as though they were all nothing, and she the whole world. Had he recognised her, she wondered, or had he perceived, in spite of the disguisement of her steady face, the intensity of her sympathy, and had clung to it as to a one and only hope?

And as she paced, and sank down into her chair, which had lost all its ordinary sense of comfort, and started up and paced again, there sprang up in her heart a great golden-glowing purpose—a purpose that trapped her breath and set her gasping when first it peeped out, but which grew like an escaped genie, and filled the world of her thoughts before she knew, and was never to be confined within bounds again.

An unheard-of thing! An incredible thing! A shameless thing!

Nay, not that—and yet—yes! yes! Shameless indeed, for shameless meant without sense of shame, and no sense of shame had she—glory rather.

An unmaidenly thing, then! That without doubt, but not without precedent, and circumstances make laws unto themselves.

But, whatever it was or was not, it grew and grew, stronger and stronger, and ever brighter in its glowing, golden rose.

As she paced to and fro it seemed to her that her path in life had suddenly flashed out before her on the darkness of the night. It was limned in lines and letters of fire, and they cried to her to follow, follow, follow.

And now, as she thought it all out, with tightened lips, and crumpled brow, and eyes that shone, it came home to her, like a revelation, that all her life had been working up to this starry point.

She thought long and deeply, and then turned up the light and sat down to her writing-table with a purposeful face. It was done in a moment—a couple of lines. But a single word has changed the destiny of a nation before this. Weighty things, words, at times! Live shells are playthings to them.

She folded and addressed her letter, and then pondered the best way over a difficulty. She wrote two more lines and enclosed them with her original letter in a larger envelope, and addressed it, and then she laid her white forehead on the packet for a moment as it lay on the table. And then, like one whose ships are burned, or whose golden bridge is built, she altered the indicator outside her door, so that her maid would call her at seven, and went to bed. Once, before she got to sleep, she smiled to herself and almost laughed out, as she suddenly remembered that it was Leap Year. Then she cooled her burning cheek on the other pillow and went to sleep, and slept soundly, for she had been living at high pressure these last few hours, and the morrow would need all her strength.

When the maid brought up her cup of tea in the morning, she handed her the letter which had stood on the table by her bedside all night, with these precise directions: "Tell William"—the groom—"to ride into the city and deliver that letter. The answer he will take to whatever address may be given him."

She got up and dressed, and went out for a quick walk in Kensington Gardens. At breakfast Aunt Jannet Harvey commented on her appearance.

"Why, child, what a colour you've got! What took you out so early?"

"I've been bathing in dew and early sunbeams, auntie."

"I couldn't sleep all night for thinking of that young man and his savages. It appears to me that that is a very great man, Jean. If he lives he will do very noble work. It needed a big soul to face that crowd and tell that story as he did it."

"Yes," said Jean. She had never discussed Kenneth Blair with Aunt Jannet Harvey, not to the extent of one single word.

After breakfast she found it difficult to settle down to any of her usual avocations. She could neither read nor play, and she declined to go out. Aunt Jannet Harvey expressed the opinion that such early rising did not suit her, and Jean confirmed her views by going upstairs to her room and wandering about there at a loose end and doing nothing—nothing but think, think, think.

Her maid brought her word that William had returned, having executed his mission in full; and please would Miss Arnot ride in the afternoon?

Miss Arnot would neither ride nor drive that afternoon, nor would she require the brougham in the evening. Mary would please ask Mrs. Harvey if she wished to drive in the afternoon. If not, the men's services would not be required.

CHAPTER V

LEAP YEAR

Kenneth Blair received Miss Arnot's note as he sat at breakfast in the pleasant room of the quiet little hotel overlooking the Embankment, where he was staying in company with Mr. and Mrs. MacTavish. He was to them as one come back from the dead, and they grudged every minute he was out of their sight.

The incidents of the previous night had been rather wearing on them all, and they were later than usual that morning, and, at that, dallying over an enjoyment that would soon be of the memory only.

The rare colour filled his pale face as he read the two lines of Miss Arnot's note, and he read them several times, as though frequent perusal might provoke interpretation.

"DEAR MR. BLAIR,—

"I have an urgent wish to speak with you. Will you do me the favour of calling here at 3 p.m. to-day?

"Yours sincerely,
"JEAN ARNOT."

"I wonder what she wants?" he said meditatively, and handed the note to the old people. "I don't think I want to see anybody."

"I think you must comply with her request, my boy," said Mr. MacTavish. "She has more than ordinary claims upon your consideration, you know."

Blair nodded, and winced involuntarily. It went a good deal deeper than the old man knew, and after last night he did not feel quite himself again yet. He had a morbid dread of hero-worship, and though the outward man was healed and shaping well again, the inner man still felt woefully sore and bruised and humbled.

"She was there last night; she sat about three rows from the front," said Mrs. MacTavish. "I wish you could have seen her face while you were speaking, Kenneth. It was like the face of an angel."

Kenneth had seen it, and nothing but it, and the thought of it made it none the easier for him to comply with her request.

He said quietly: "Well, I'll think about it, and see how I happen to be situated for three o'clock. I have to see Mr. Campbell at eleven in Moorgate Street. If he has any appointments for me, I might be unable to go, in which case I'll send Miss Arnot a wire."

But Mr. Campbell knew how short his time was, and so occupied as little of it as possible; and three o'clock found him at Miss Arnot's dainty little house in Knightsbridge, overlooking the Park.

He had hesitated—as an intelligent moth might flutter warily just outside the heat radius of a candle-flame—strongly tempted, desirous, but doubtful.

For she had occupied much, very much, of his thoughts—too much, he had angrily said to himself at times—since ever he learned the part she had had in the making of him. And quite apart from that, she was so very charming in herself. It could hardly be in the power of any man, he thought, to be much in her company and not have longings for still closer acquaintance and companionship—and such things were not for him. His way lay among the shadows of the outer night, and it must of necessity be, outwardly at all events, a somewhat lonely way. Companions he would doubtless have, and the best of all high company. But home, wife, child—these were not for him. In his mind's eye he saw the white beaches, and towering cliffs, and black bosky gorges of the Dark Islands, and the thunder of the surf was in his ear. And in his heart he said bravely, "My home, my wife, my children!"

But his thoughts were never far from her, and now that, in spite of himself, he was to meet her face to face, they gathered head and had their way in spite of him.

He had often wondered why she had not married. She was still young, of course; but, after all, twenty-five was not so very young for an unmarried lady of such unusual possessions of mind, body, and estate.

She possessed, he could well believe, an independent spirit. Had she not, even at thirteen, told him that one of her aspirations was to do as she liked?

He had recognised her instantly, and with a start, the previous night. That was before the drama became exciting. And he had wondered then if she had changed her name since last he saw her, or whether "Jean Arnot was still good enough for her."

And what could she possibly want to say to him?

Possibly—quite likely—in the excitement of the evening's proceedings she had felt an impulse to do something more for the mission cause than she had done hitherto.

That was it, no doubt. Well, they could do with Miss Arnot's assistance. Funds were never too ample for the work that cried aloud to be done.

He was evidently expected. The maid led him along the hall, through green baize doors, down a passage, into the library, a beautiful and cosy room such as he had imagined wealthy people might possibly possess, if, in addition to all their other possessions, they possessed a love of books. It overlooked the garden and the Park, and was as bright and secluded a little holy of holies as the most devoted worshipper of the sacred flame might desire. The Island Mission houses were—not exactly geographically perhaps, but in every other attribute and particular—the absolute antipodes and antithesis of this charming little sanctum. The walls were lined with bookcases full of richly bound books, the table was strewn with books and magazines, among which, and queening it over them all, stood a great night-blue bowl of white lilac, filling the room with the perfume of the spring. There was a cheerful little fire of mixed peat and logs on a flat hearth, with brass dogs and chains. A sudden whiff of the peat, as he passed the hearth, carried him in an instant back into his boyhood.

He glanced at the bountiful shelves, with the hungry look of the student whose pocket had never at any time been able to keep pace with his appetite. For knowledge of books is good, and possession of books is good, but knowledge and possession combined are still much better.

He was standing looking out into the garden whence the lilac had come, when Miss Arnot came quietly in.

He turned and bowed. He had made up his mind to hold himself tightly, but her welcoming hand drew forth his own, and carried his first line of defence in a walk-over.

"It was good of you to come," she said impulsively, "and I thank you. I know your time is very short, and you must have much to do."

"Yes, there is much to do," he said very quietly. "But I am grateful to you for, at all events, affording me another opportunity of thanking you in person—" But she stopped him with a peremptory little hand.

How beautiful she was, with her wistful face and commanding little ways! There was even more than usual of strenuous inquiry in those shining eyes of hers.

"You are going back on the first of May?"

Her speech was more rapid than usual. He saw that she was excited. Probably the remembrance of last night's meeting still held her, he thought.

"Yes, on the first of May. And then—I hardly think it likely I shall ever return to England."

"But why?" she jerked, in her old, quick, want-to-know way.

"Well—you see—I really feel as if I had no right to be here at all. By rights I ought to be lying under a cairn on the beach of Dark Island."

"Oh, but that is simply morbid, and the result of your long illness. You will not feel that way long."

"I hope not. The work is crying to be done. Perhaps, after all, I shall be able to help it more above ground than below."

"Of course you will. Don't you find it dreadfully lonely out there, with none but black people about you?"

"They are very fine people, some of them. And the loneliness only nails one the tighter to the work. Besides there are—"

"Has it never struck you that you might possibly help it quite as much by remaining here as by going out again?"

Oh, Jean! Jean!

"Never," he said, with a slight flush. "My work lies there, and I hope to give my life to it, and to give it up for it if need be, as my dear old friend gave his."

"But there are others who could do the work just as well, are there not?"

"Many, I hope. I hope many will."

"And, if I understand aright, Missionary Societies are always short of funds, and the work is hindered, or at all events progresses more slowly, in consequence."

"I have my own views as to that," he said quietly.

"Won't you tell me what they are? I am greatly interested."

"They are not shared by many of my friends, and I do not obtrude them. I believe that the work is God's work, and when He sees fit to provide larger ways and means, larger ways and means will be forthcoming. If we had all the money we wanted, we might lose our heads, and go ahead too fast—scamp the work perhaps, and prove but jerry-builders in the end. One cannot forget that it has taken Christianity eighteen hundred years to arrive at its present position, and that for long periods it lay almost dormant; whereas, if the Founder had deemed it best to accomplish the work at one stroke, He could have done it."

"Yes," she said thoughtfully. "I don't think I ever looked at it in that light before. And you are quite determined to go back?"

"Quite determined—only too grateful for the chance."

"And nothing would keep you here?"

"Nothing that I can imagine—except absolute incapacity for the work."

"You would not stop even if"—and she bent forward, with hands tightly clasped to prevent them jumping visibly before him, and eyes that shone like stars. God! how beautiful she was!—"if I begged you to do so?"

He jumped up hastily.

"If you—? If you begged me to—what?"

And her bright eyes, fixed intently on his lean face, caught the sudden fierce clench of the teeth inside, which threw the cheek-bones into bolder prominence. She noted it—she could almost hear the grinding of his teeth; and the game was in her hands. She had the advantage of understanding what the game was, while he was completely in the dark.

He stood gazing down at her for a moment, and then said more quietly—

"I'm afraid I don't quite understand. Perhaps my illness has dulled my brain somewhat."

"No, it hasn't, Mr. Blair. I was asking you in cold blood if you would not stay in England and marry me, and use my money from here for the furtherance of the cause out there."

He stared at her still with all his great heart in his eyes—all of it that was not jumping in his throat like a baby rabbit.

He gazed down at her for another moment, then bent suddenly before her and took her hand and kissed it, and said huskily and in jerks—between the rabbit-kicks—

"You will think no ill of me—if I go—at once. I dare not stop—"

But she had gripped his hand and held it tight, and stood holding him, and her face shone and her eyes.

"Then—will you take me with you, Kenneth?"

"Take you with me?" Her rings cut into her next fingers under the fierceness of his sudden grip, and she could have sung aloud, for the grip came right from his heart and told his tale to her. "Do you mean it—Jean?"

"Surely."

And yet he had a doubt. You must bear with him. You see, he had been half inside the gates of death, and—well, the proceeding was distinctly out of the common run of things.

"Is it myself—or the work?" he asked almost fiercely. For the thought had flashed across him—and not unnaturally—that this was but one more result of the excitement of the meeting last night. She had been shaken out of her usual discretion and decorum, had probably lain awake all night, and—

But her eyes were steady as stars, and as bright, as she said—

"Both! But yourself first. I liked you the first time we met. I loved you the second. I have never ceased to think about you. Your going away left a blank in my life. After last night I love and trust you more than ever, if that be possible. Last night my way was made clear to me."

"Now, glory be to God!" he cried, and kissed the wistful lips that looked as if they had been waiting long for just that seal to the compact. And then he sat down suddenly and covered his face with his hands, as though what was in him was not even for her eyes.

She sank down on to a footstool beside his chair, and noticed how white his hand was compared with the great, strong brown hand which had held hers that day in the Greenock church.

He was himself again in a moment—or suppose we say he came back from where he had been—and his face was full of the old radiant glow as he raised it to look at her.

"It is real, isn't it?" he asked in a light-hearted, boyish way.

"I'm real," she said, smiling back at him. "You seem not quite yourself."

"Did you ever try to imagine what it would feel like to have every single desire of your heart suddenly granted to you all in a lump?"

"I don't think I ever did. It sounds as if it might be too much for one."

"It is—almost. And you wonder if it is real and true, or only a vain imagining. Jean, is it true that you care for me?"

"No—love you, Ken,—dearly—every inch of you."

"And that you are going to marry me?"

"If you ask me properly."

"Jean, will you marry me and come out with me and share my work?"

"I will!"

He gazed at her steadfastly, and said softly—

"Thank God! it is true!"

He enjoyed that full sunshine of felicity for close on five minutes, and then said more soberly—

"Do you quite understand, dear, all that you are giving up? Life out there—"

"It is enough for me at present to realise what I have gained. Can you not understand, dear, that to a woman the time comes when the heart's love of one man is more to her than all the rest of the whole wide world? Life touched its highest with me when you made my fingers bleed a few minutes ago."

"I made your—" and he snatched her hands and saw the tiny wounds. "Oh, forgive me! I did not know—" and he kissed them tenderly.

"Sweet wounds!" she said. "They told me more than all you have forgotten to tell me—all that I was aching to know."

"And you really care for me like that, Jean? For me! Is it possible? I wonder why?"

"Perhaps God had something to do with it. It is so very good that it must be from Him."

"Yes," he said emphatically.

"And now—when are you going to tell me that you care a little for me, and are not just taking me because I threw myself at your head and you could not help yourself?"

"Oh, Jean! Jean! you knew—though how I cannot tell. You have been shrined in my heart since that second time we met, but I knew it was hopeless—"

"Clever boy! And you hardly knew me then."

"I knew your eyes the moment I looked into them, and they have never left me since."

"Such common brown eyes! But you didn't know what lay behind them?"

"The most beautiful eyes in the world."

And by degrees they settled into quiet talk of the future.

He still feared she did not fully understand all she was giving up, and conscientiously endeavoured to make it clear to her.

She listened to please him, and because it was sweet to hear him, for all his thought in the matter was for her and her well-being.

So she let him go on; and when he had exhausted all his arguments, she said quietly—

"It is all nothing and less than nothing, dearest, compared with the rest. Where you go I go. Your work shall be my work, and your people my people, and nothing but death shall part us."

And with a heart that seemed like to burst for very fulness of joy in her, he said, "Amen!"

CHAPTER VI

A SUDDEN WIDE HORIZON

"Mr. Blair! The young man who spoke at the meeting the other night? Why, I didn't even know that you knew him, Jean!" said Aunt Jannet Harvey, gazing at her in wide-eyed wonder.

"Oh, I've known him since I was thirteen!"

"And you never spoke to me about him! Why I don't remember your ever even mentioning his name!"

"I don't believe I ever did. We will make up for it now, auntie."

"And he has really had the audacity to ask you to marry him?"

"Yes, auntie,"—very meekly.

"And you've said 'yes,' and you're going out with him to the South Seas?"

"Yes, auntie."

"Well, child, let me tell you what I think about it. I think you might have looked much higher, and fared very much worse. He struck me the other night as a very noble young man indeed, and I wondered then why he hadn't made some woman happy. I believe you will be very happy, Jean, unless those cannibals kill you and eat you."

"If they eat us both at the same time I don't care," said Jean boldly. "Yes, I shall be very happy, auntie, for he is the best man in the whole world."

"And when do you go?"

"Our marriage will make some changes in his plans, of course, and he is seeing the Society people to-day about an extension of leave. We discussed it all yesterday—at least, all that we had time for. He is full of plans—such glorious plans! It is a grand thing to be a man, and to be built on a great big scale, and to have glorious ideas—"

"And the means to carry them out! And when did you say you'd be going?"

"In about six weeks probably. You see, he wants to buy a steamer for his work among the Islands, and we shall go out in her."

"I shall be quite ready," said Aunt Jannet Harvey "I shall want two or three new dresses suitable to the climate—"

"You, auntie? You will go too?"

"Why, of course, child! You'll need me more than ever out there. Suppose you fell sick. Suppose—oh, I can look ahead farther than you can, perhaps! I can see a hundred ways in which I can be useful to you. And you don't need to fear that I'll be in your way—I'll see to that. But I'll be within reach when I'm wanted; and I've always had a hankering to see those outside parts of the world. It was my dear James's dream too. He was a great botanist, when he had any time to spare from his logic. He'll be glad to think the chance has come to me at last."

And so when Blair came back next day from an exciting time in the city, Jean solemnly announced—

"You'll only find out by degrees all you've undertaken, young man. You've got to marry Aunt Jannet Harvey as well."

"Polygamy is still practised out there," he said heartily. "As a matter of policy we have to countenance it at times; but we set our faces against it, because it does not work well. If this means that Mrs. Harvey has consented to accompany us—"

"Consented? She proposed it, or rather took it for granted, and won't hear a word against it."

"Then my heart is lightened of one of its cares, and I am truly grateful to Aunt Jannet"—and Aunt Jannet was his from that moment. "God surely put the thought into your kind heart," he said, as he wrung the capable old hand warmly. "You will be more to Jean out there than words can tell. I thank you with all my heart."

"I knew it," said Aunt Jannet, with emphasis. "I wanted to ask you, Mr. Blair—"

"Kenneth, surely, now, Aunt Jannet!"

"Surely!—Kenneth—what the ladies wear out there."

"Well, the native ladies don't wear much, and the ladies of the missions wear much what you would here, if you cared only for use and comfort, and nothing for fashion. They always look very neat and clean"—at which Jean smiled reminiscently.

"I see," said Aunt Jannet. "Jean and I will lay our heads together. I think we can live up to that standard, at all events."

He had a cup of tea with them, and then ran along to the hotel to bring old Mr. and Mrs. MacTavish over to dinner. And after dinner they sat and talked and talked, and he laid some of his ideas and plans before them, and had only just begun when it was time for the old people to go home to bed. For his plans and ideas were blossoming in the golden sunshine like an orchard kept back by a late spring, and flung suddenly into the quickening warmth of coming summer.

He had gone down that morning to see the secretary of the Society which had originally sent him out, and to whom he still felt officially bound, to inform him of the changes in his plans which his marriage would bring about, and to request an extension of leave.

There happened to be a full meeting of the committee in session when his name was brought in, and the secretary at once suggested his introduction to the meeting. And so, when Blair was shown into the board-room, expecting to meet Mr. Secretary alone, he found some fifty ladies and gentlemen eagerly awaiting him.

The great glad light in his face—the light that Jean Arnot had helped to rekindle—drew all their eyes. They whispered among themselves that the Queen's Hall meeting had done him good after all. Some of them had been fearing the effects of such tremendous emotion on a weakened body.

The chairman, the noble head of a house devoted to good deeds, gave him hearty welcome, and said the committee would be delighted to hear any further details he would like to give them of his work or future plans in the Dark Islands.

Blair jumped up as the old man sat down.

"I came, sir," he said, "on a very definite errand—to ask for a slight extension of my stay here."

"It is granted, my dear sir, before you put any limit to it," said the old man cordially. "Every member of this committee feels, I am sure, that the matter may be safely left in your own hands. We know also that you are anxious to get back to your work. I will only express the hope that it is not through any relapse in health that you think it necessary."

It certainly did not look like it, as Blair, with a smile that would not be controlled, said—

"I am glad to say it is not a matter touching my health, though one that very intimately affects my happiness and well-being. Since that somewhat trying meeting in Queen's Hall a piece of very great good-fortune has come to me—"

"Good indeed to set such a light in his face!" thought they, and hung upon his words.

"Miss Arnot has consented to become my wife and to join me in the work out there."

"Miss Arnot!—Jean Arnot!"—a buzz of excitement ran round. For Miss Arnot was a personage of importance, known alike for her beauty, her wealth, and her good deeds. Rumour, indeed, had fixed upon Miss Arnot as the mysterious donor for the last two years of a £1,000 note each year for the special benefit and use of the South Sea Mission.

And he was going to marry Miss Arnot, and she was going out with him! No wonder there was a light in his face!

But he was speaking again.

"You will see, sir, at once that this happy circumstance brings about many changes in my plans and hopes. The vista of usefulness which it opens before me—before us, may I say?—is magnified one hundred-fold. Miss Arnot dedicates her fortune, herself, and her enthusiasms to the work. There is a mighty field out there. It is not white to the harvest—it is black as darkest night. By God's help we hope to lift the fringes and let in some rays of His blessed light. I shall have the opportunity of discussing my ideas in detail with your secretary. But broadly speaking, this is how they point. We contemplate purchasing and fitting out a steamer suitable for mission-work among the Islands, and going out in her ourselves. We would like several assistants, married or unmarried—but big men, please! Big heads are good, and big hearts are better, but best of all if they are contained in big bodies. You have no idea what a vast impression a big man makes on those big Islanders compared with a small man. As to the size of the ladies, I would not venture to offer any suggestions. But the men should be—must be—big men. One further matter, sir, and I have done. Those Islanders must come under the protection of the British flag at once. And I want—you will not misunderstand me if I go the length of saying I must have—the appointment of Commissioner or Deputy Commissioner, or any position that will give me the official right to deal with certain matters which block our way out there.

"The wrongs the people of some of those Outer Islands suffer, from the scum of the earth who prey upon them, to their utter ruin of body, soul, and spirit, are almost incredible.

"I could tell you facts—bald, brutal facts—concerning the labour traffic carried on there which would make you shudder and doubt my veracity. But I have seen these things with my own eyes, and heard them with my own ears, and been powerless to stop them.

"Now, by God's help, and Miss Arnot's, I will wage war on these doings—hot war—yes, red-hot war with Maxim and Lee-Metford, if necessary"—his voice rang out militantly—"on those who do these dreadful deeds. Those hideous wrongs shall cease, and those poor kinsfolk of ours—God's children as much as we, though they know it not yet—shall have their chance. I would of course prefer to act officially in the matter; but, officially or not, act I shall.

"This may seem to you strange talk for a peaceful man. I have a precedent. As long as I tread in the Master's steps I shall not go far wrong."

He sat down, and they cheered him to the echo. They had heard many noble men and women speak in that room; but I doubt if they had ever heard words which gripped their hearts as these had done.

The news of the approaching marriage of the penniless young missionary to the great heiress, Miss Arnot, spread rapidly and evoked much comment, candid, caustic, congratulatory, from Jean's friends and otherwise.

"Clever man, that young sky-pilot!"

"Absolutely thrown herself away, my dear, and actually going to live among naked savages!"

"Trust the missionary to feather his own nest. Why should he lose sight of No. 1 while saving brother man?"

"The missionary man has done himself well. Poor rich Miss Arnot!"

"Oh, well, you know, she's twenty-seven if she's a day, and when a girl gets to twenty-seven—! And they say he's exceedingly good-looking. Still, don't you know—"

These behind her back. And to her face:

"He's simply charming, dear. I envy you—I do indeed!

"He's a splendid fellow, Miss Arnot. You will be very happy together."

"My dear,"—this from a very old lady, bearing a very old title, whose early married life had been a hideous martyrdom—"you have chosen very wisely. He is a noble Christian gentleman, and he would lay down his life for you. Believe me, dear, compared with what you have got, all the wealth of the world and all its titles are nothing but dust and ashes and misery. I know it!"

And everybody else knew that she knew it. And Jean kissed her very tenderly.

And Mr. Punch, when he heard of the matter, in his playful little way quoted:

"Doän't thou marry for munny, but—goä wheer munny is."

CHAPTER VII

SOME ODD FURNISHINGS AND A HONEYMOON

Aunt Jannet Harvey's wardrobe was rapidly approaching completion.

She and Jean had had a busy six weeks. They had neither of them ever been quite so busy in all their lives before, and the curious thing was that it seemed to agree with them mightily, and they, both one and the other, had visibly renewed their youth under the demands made upon them.

Aunt Jannet developed new and surprising traits of character every day; and as for Jean, the days were not half long enough for the joy of life that lay in wait for each one as it came.

She and Kenneth Blair had been quietly married by special licence a month ago, and the sight of their faces, wherever they had been since, had brought new ideals and new possibilities of life to all who looked upon them—all except the cynics and philosophers of Jean's former world, of course.

"Quite so!" said they. "But just wait till the bloom is off the honeymoon, and she finds herself all alone with her little tin god among the savages! Then she'll find out what's what and sigh for the vanished fleshpots and fripperies."

But there were no signs of incipient sighing about Mrs. Kenneth Blair at present, anyway. She had always been sweet and charming, with a wistful eagerness in her face that filled you with a desire to do for her any mortal thing she might require at your hands. There was still something of that about her, but it was almost hidden now beneath the radiant happiness which enveloped her.

She had urged Blair to a speedy wedding—where no urging whatever was needed—for the delight of spending their last weeks at home, in the house where most of her life had been passed. She had had long and peremptory interviews with her lawyers, making wise provision for all possible eventualities, so far as it was possible to foresee them. It was not till she was half-way across to the other side of the world that the aunties in Greenock, and old Mr. and Mrs. MacTavish, and several other old friends, learned what she had been up to, and then she was well out of their reach.

And every day since, she and her husband had been out in the market-place with open purse and very definite ideas as to their requirements, and the things they had bought were very extraordinary and about as different from the usual purchases of newly-married couples as they possibly could be.

Item.—One 300-ton auxiliary schooner, built to Class 17 A.1., by Scott & Sons, Greenock; dimensions 143 O.A.; 23-½ ft. beam; 13 ft. draught; 7 ft. headroom, etc. A handsome, roomy boat, stoutly built for comfort and long voyages to the order of a financial magnate, whose health unfortunately broke down before she was quite ready for him, and forced him to seek more genial climatic, and other conditions, in Argentina.

Mr. and Mrs. Blair ran up to Greenock to inspect her, found her exactly to their liking, settled the matter in five minutes in the office inside the big gates, christened her the Torch with a hastily procured bottle of champagne, gave orders for the duplication of every piece of machinery she contained; walked out of the big gates ship-owners, and dropped in on the astonished aunties in Brisbane Street and announced that they had come for a cup of tea and to stop one night.

They stopped more than one night, however, for after tea Blair walked in to see the Rev. Archibald for a last talk and a pipe of peace. And when the Rev. Archibald recovered wind and wits from the rapid details Blair gave him of the work he was engaged on, he at once offered to find him a crew through some of the members of his church. Blair desired nothing better, and in five minutes the maid of the Manse was skipping through the dripping streets with kilted skirts to summon to instant conference some nearer members who might be able to advise in the matter. He laid his plans before them, told them to a hair the kind of men he required both for officers and crew, and went back to Brisbane Street in due course, comfortably assured in his own mind that within two days the Torch would be fitted with a crew worthy of her and the work for which she was destined.

Next day the ship-owners went out for a walk, and did not return till close on tea-time.

They had been on their honeymoon trip: past the cemetery gates, up the brae between the brown stone houses, past the pond, up the cinder path, and along that glorious walk, with the swift brown water of the Cut swirling past to its appointed work in mills and town, on the one side; and on the other, across the brimming firth, the everlasting hills, grey and green and purple and black, as the sunshine chased the shadows to their hiding-places in the glens; the full sea welling about their feet, now green, now blue; and the sky overhead bluest blue after the rain, with piles of snowy cloud passing along in solemn silence like a procession of the chariots of God.

They did not speak much, hardly a word, but walked hand in hand like a pair of country lovers, till they came to where a flat stone lay alongside the beginnings of a cabin.

And there they stopped; and looking into one another's faces by a common impulse, put their arms round one another's necks and kissed, with brimming hearts, and eyes that saw none of the glories around because of the glory within them, which was too much for either sight or sound.

The happy tears were running down Jean's cheeks, but they were swallowed up in reminiscent smiles as her husband seated her gently on one projecting rock and himself on the other.

"This is my twelfth birthday," he began; and when Miss Inquisitive looked at him out of her sweet brown eyes, still soft from their recent shower, he explained: "To all intents and purposes my life began that day I met you here, though there had been a previous troubled life in which my dear father gave me all he had to give—the desire to learn."

"And I am about two years old," she said, smiling; and when she saw that he did not understand, explained:

"After meeting you again that second time in the church, when you hardly recognised me—"

"I knew you the moment I looked into your eyes."

"I came up here the next day—I did not know why, but something drew me, and I came. And I sat down here on this stone, and saw you sitting on that stone munching oatcake and cheese, and thought what a greedy little pig I was not to have made you take some of my sandwiches—"

"You couldn't have made me. I wouldn't have touched one for—"

"I know. But I ought to have made you, all the same. And then I thought of you as you were now—that is, then, you know—and what a great, big, strong soul and body you had become, and what great things you were going to do, and how you had got your heart's desire. And then I thought of myself, and the little I had done with all my opportunities. And after that you insisted on coming into my thoughts at all times, and I could not get rid of you. And then you sailed, and I knew I should never see you again, and life felt hollow and hopeless. And then I saw in the papers about your being murdered. And then you came home, and—here we are. And oh, Ken! it is almost too good to be true."

"Not a bit of it, my dear; it is only just beginning."

Then he drew out two parcels from his pockets, and hers contained some neat little sandwiches and cookies with jam inside, and his contained oatcakes and cheese.

And, being in a raised mood, she laughed till she cried at his oatcakes and cheese, and then insisted on dividing up equally all round, and vowed that his fare was quite as good as her own.

"Of course it is," he said. "I knew that all the time. A boy on the hillsides who can't enjoy oatcakes and cheese would deserve to go empty."

When they had eaten, they still sat looking out over the water at the hills and lochs opposite. In all likelihood they would never see that fairest of scenes again, and they could not have too much of it.

And after they had sat a long time in silence, Blair, leaning forward with his arms on his knees and his eyes drinking in great draughts of delight, said, suddenly—but slowly, as though the words had to be called, or recalled, from afar, and said them, not to her or for her, but to and for something quite outside them both—said them, in fact, as though he were impelled to say them, and could not help himself—

"The hills of God stand fast and sure."

The words described those hills opposite exactly. Then a pause, and presently—

"His mighty promises endure
For ever and for evermore."

Then he fell silent again, and thoughtful, and presently—

"His Mercy is a boundless sea,
For ever flowing, full and free."

She saw it there before her just as he saw it. And after another pause—

"Through Time into Eternity."

She looked at him quietly and questioningly, but his gaze was fixed absorbedly on the opposite shore. It seemed almost as if he had forgotten her for the moment. She was content to watch him and to listen to him—

"And as the wide blue sky above,
Encircling us where'er we move."

There it was above them. The chariots had passed away. The sky was unflecked blue—

"So is His all-enfolding Love."

Then came a longer pause, and she thought he had ended, but she would not speak. And presently he began again—

"For these, Thy gifts, we thank Thee, Lord!
Hills, sea, and sky, take up the word,
And thank Thee!—thank Thee!—thank Thee, Lord."

He sat still, gazing out intently at the hills and the sea and the sky, and sat so long without a word that at last she spoke.

"Whose is that, Ken? Surely he must have sat just here, and seen just that."

He turned slowly to her, as though he found it difficult to leave those wonders beyond.

"I really do not know, dear.... They seemed to come of their own accord from somewhere. But whether I recalled them from somewhere else, or whether they came hot from the anvil, I do not know. I do not think I ever made a line of poetry in my life. There has been always so much else to be done."

"I think you must have made them," she said.

Then, in turn, she had her own amusing little monologue. For she began suddenly telling off the lochs and hills, just as he had named them to her that other day—"Loch Goil, Loch Long, Ben More, Ben Lomond, The Cobbler, Ben Ihme, Holy Loch!"

"We shall often think of them when the prospect is a very different one," he said quietly. "You never regret all that you are going to leave behind you, Jean?"

"Never for one moment, dear. I am taking with me, and going to, so very much more than I leave behind, that my heart is full of gladness," she said. "There is not room for the smallest shadow of a shadow of regret."

And they joined hands again and went on along the windings of the path, in and out of the curves and dimples of the mountain's breast, till the bold peaks of Arran rose purple in the distance, and they came to the Sheils Farm.

Blair's kinsfolk had long since left the place. He just took a look round the familiar byres and stables, and poked his head into a room whence a fresh-complexioned dairy-maid, in short blue skirts and bare feet, was busily chasing hens. He came out with a reminiscent smile on his face, and they turned down the hill towards Inverkip. He led her by the short cuts his boyish feet had known so well; past the old burying-ground, where the body-snatchers plied their gruesome trade and the village folk sat up night after night to protect their dead; past the gates of Ardgowan to the sea. And so along the shore road, with the waves splashing up among the boulders on one side, and the dark policies on the other, and the great trees meeting overhead; past the sturdy white pillar of the Cloch into Ashton, and so at last home. A honeymoon trip which neither of them ever forgot as long as they lived.

"Well, you two," said Aunt Jannet, when they came in. "We began to think you'd given us the slip and gone across the border without saying goodbye."

"We've been a long round," said Blair, "about—"

"About twelve years," said Jean.

"Then you must be starving. We expected you'd come home ravenous, and provided accordingly."

"We've been living on the fat of the land," laughed Jean; but they both fell to all the same, and proved beyond doubt that high thought and good living were by no means incompatible.

CHAPTER VIII

GOING STRONG

That same evening a burly, middle-aged man came to the house and requested audience of Mr. Blair.

He bore the unmistakable hall-mark, and Kenneth liked the looks of him and the ring of his voice.

The two men eyed one another closely as they shook hands.

"Mr. Duncan told me you were wanting a captain for your schooner, Mr. Blair. I only heard it half an hour ago, and I've come straight."

Blair nodded. "What are your qualifications? It is not everybody's job, you know."

"I know all about it, sir. And I think I'm the man for it. My name is Cathie—John Cathie. I sailed my own ship as master for over fifteen years. Quitted the sea three years ago because I'd made enough to live on and the wife wanted me to stop ashore. She died six months ago. I've neither chick nor child, and I want back to the water. When you've spent thirty-five years with live water under your feet, the land comes strange to you!"

"Ever been in the South Seas?"

"Spent ten years in the Island trade, sir. Know 'em like a book, from the Carolines to the Paumotus; and if you can find a brown man in the whole stretch that has a word against John Cathie I'll—well, you can name your own forfeit."

"And the white men?"

"Ah—there! Most of 'em all right. Some I'd like to see strung higher than Haman. But that kind's mostly yellow, though some are dirty white."

"Know the Dark Islands?"

"At a distance. I never landed there. I was only a trader then."

"And these men you'd like to see strung up like Haman, only more so, Captain Cathie?"

"You know them as well as I do, sir. Kidnappers, black-birders, treacherous devils, scum of the earth. They don't have the times they used to have, but they're not wholly cleared out yet in the outlying groups. I'll be glad to give what time's left me to helping clear them."

"You're up to steam?"

"Had five years of it."

"Any hand with a Long Tom?"

"Was gunner's mate for three years on the Blenheim before I got married, and we always carried guns in the Islands," and the bold blue eyes snapped with a touch of puzzlement. "But—I thought it was a missionary cruise you were bound on, Mr. Blair?"

"I'm a new kind of missionary, Captain Cathie. The faithful shepherd protects his flock. If the wolves try to steal his lambs, the wolves must take the consequences."

"By God, sir, I'm your man!" and the burly one jumped up with a flame in his face, because he could not sit still under the hopes that were in him.

"I'm inclined to think you may be," said Blair. "You will understand, Captain Cathie, that the master of our ship will be one of the most important links in the chain. If you will look in about this time tomorrow, you shall hear what we have decided."

"Right, sir! I'll be here." He turned back when he had reached the door. "If you should find some better man for captain, put me down for chief mate, Mr. Blair; and if I'm not good enough for that, I'll go before the mast sooner than be left out."

Blair had already decided in his own mind, but in a matter of such immense importance he could take no possible risks. His inquiries, however, only confirmed the impression he had formed. When Captain Cathie came hopefully in, the next night, the matter was settled on the spot, and he went away a new man, gripping with feet and hands the rungs of a new ladder.

Blair laid his plans fully before him, and, so far as the schooner was concerned, left him to carry them out.

Then they were back in London, and the busy days sped past, scarce long enough for all that had to be done in them.

It was the necessary business with the Colonial Office that tried him most severely. The Secretary accorded him an interview, received him with gracious warmth, listened with interest to his views, agreed that it would be a good thing for the Dark Islands to be accorded a protectorate until the time was ripe for formal annexation, but— There were many buts, and they would have driven a less patient and less determined seeker after other men's good to despair. There was Australia; there was France; there was Germany; there was the Opposition; there was that loud-voiced party in the land which screamed at any extension of the Empire's shoes.

But upon all and everything Blair quietly brought to bear his unique personal knowledge of the conditions out there, a large common sense, and an inflexible persistence that would admit of no rebuff or turning aside.

The minister smilingly accused him of being one-eyed as regards the Dark Islands.

"Absolutely!" said Blair quietly—"one-eyed, one-hearted, and one-lived! Body, soul, and spirit I am for the Dark Islands, and I want to do all that man can do. Give me the legal right and a reasonably free hand, and, with God's help, I can do a great work out there. I do not think it need cost you a farthing. I have a revenue to start with of over £10,000 a year, and a considerable capital for initial development purposes. Within five years, with reasonable success, the islands will be self-supporting. But—I must have my foundations sure, or I cannot build as I would."

"The matter has already been debated among us, Mr. Blair," said the Secretary. "The Earl of Selsea brought it up and has made it his particular pet project. You seem to have captured his heart, and when he takes a matter of this kind in hand he sticks to it like a bulldog. But you can understand that there are many collateral issues, and we have to consider them all. I understand exactly what you want and why, and I promise you to do my utmost to bring it about. It may be some months before it can be arranged. Meanwhile, no doubt, there is much you can be doing to prepare the ground."

"There is much to be done, sir, and I will set to work on the strength of what you say. But the sooner it is definitely settled the better for us all."

"A very fine young fellow," said the Secretary to himself, before he turned to another quarter of the globe. "The kind of man I could make splendid use of if I had him to myself."

But Kenneth Blair was another Man's man.

CHAPTER IX

ARMS AND THE MAN

The Torch had been brought round from Greenock by Captain Cathie, and was lying in the London Docks close alongside Wapping Basin, an object of interest to all her neighbours.

Captain Cathie's clock had gone back at least ten years since he and Kenneth Blair struck hands in the drawing-room of the Aunties' house in Brisbane Street. He was then a fine old specimen of the very best type of retired mariner. Now he was a jovial young sea-dog, bristling with energy, and overflowing with hearty goodwill to humanity at large. He was Kenneth Blair's man to the backbone, and prepared to follow him to the death.

Jean delighted in him and he in her. She had taken Aunt Jannet Harvey down to inspect her future home, and the ladies' comments had filled Captain Cathie's cup to the brim and won his heart completely.

Jean had asked him endless questions, but not one more than he delighted in answering; and Aunt Jannet Harvey's characteristic summing-up of the whole matter had been, "Child, I feel as if I'd wasted half my life in never having been to sea before. I've always had an idea that I knew something about neatness and comfort and packing, but this"—with a wave of the hand which comprehended the cabin she was standing in, and the Torch generally, and Captain Cathie—"this puts me to shame. I shall never want to live on shore again," and Captain Cathie was repaid for all his labours. With full understanding, and thirty years' experience, and no stinting as regards money, he had laboured to adapt the ladies' rooms to their fullest possible requirements. Their delight in all they saw assured him of his success.

A few days later Blair brought down a party of friends to inspect the little ship, foremost among them the Colonial Secretary and the Earl of Selsea, who had both come straight from a Cabinet Council where the Dark Islands had been the rat in the pit.

"We're getting on by degrees," said the Secretary in the train, as he lit a cigar to counteract the atmosphere.

"It's amazing what an amount of pig-headedness there is in the world," said his friend. "You don't realise it in all its heart-breaking stolidity till you run your own head against it."

"That's so. But what can you expect when men like B— are pitchforked into the positions they occupy? I was at Eton with B— and at Oxford. He always was a fool and he always will be. He ought to have gone into the Church."

"I object! The Church needs the very best men it can get."

"Well, then, into the Army. He couldn't have done much mischief in either, and in the Army, at all events, there'd have been some chance of his getting licked into some kind of shape. As it is, I always want to get up and ask him to come outside into the park with me just for ten minutes or so. It was the one argument that used to prevail with him, and I've an idea it would yet. Anyway, it would do me a heap of good. He was born pig-headed and it's grown on him ever since."

"If we can once get him to see things as—"

"See? B— never could see anything beyond the side on which his bread was buttered. Some men are born dense, and some grow denser as they grow older. B—'s both. He wants trepanning. Here's Mark Lane, and there's your Angel Gabriel on the pounce for us."

Angel Gabriel, in the person of Kenneth Blair, gave them hearty welcome, and piloted them through slums and dockyards till they stood on the deck of the Torch, where Jean, and Aunt Jannet Harvey, and Captain Cathie, were already doing the honours to a goodly company.

"It is a great enterprise you are bound upon, Mrs. Blair," said the Secretary, as Jean expounded Torch to him.

"The grandest work in the world," she said exuberantly. "If you'll only back us up and give us what we want."

"Ah! if only it rested with me. But I'm only one."

"Oh, come! Where am I?" asked Selsea.

"That makes two," acknowledged the Secretary, who would willingly, in the light of Jean's brown eyes, have taken all the credit to himself.

"And we'll soon have the rest. As for B—, if he won't toe the line, we'll worry the life out of him," which was a highly improper remark to fall from the lips of a philanthropic nobleman. But then Jean Blair's hopefully eager face and wistful eyes were upon him, and allowances must be made.

"I do hope you will," she said earnestly.

"What, worry the life out of him?" laughed the Secretary.

"H'm—yes,—if he won't toe the line."

"Hullo!" said the Secretary, as he entered the deck saloon, an exceedingly comfortable room, fitted in bird's-eye maple with fine woven cane cushions and backs to the seats instead of saddlebags or velvet plush.

But it was not at the room itself at which he exclaimed, but at the arm-racks ranged round the walls, empty at present, but full of meaning.

"Yes," said Blair quietly. "Winchesters. They're down below with the Maxim. Let me show you something else," and he led the two gentlemen along the deck to a longboat, keel up, on a stand well forward. The boat stood high and was covered with tarpaulin.

"Do you care to peep under?" he asked. And the Secretary bent and peeped, and straightened up again with raised eyebrows.

"You mean business, evidently, Mr. Blair. That's an odd passenger for a missionary ship."

"She throws a 9-lb. shell a mile and a half," said Blair, "and Captain Cathie is an old naval gunner. Yes, we mean business. But this business"—patting the long gun's cover—"only in case of absolute necessity. You quite understand the situation? I hope you have confidence in me?"

"I quite understand, and I have perfect confidence. Mr. Blair. I believe for once the right man is in the right place. We will do everything we possibly can to further your views. If we can't get all we want, we can no doubt keep our eyes closed."

Their visitors were delighted with all they saw, but all of them did not see everything. Even if one is prepared to tackle one's problems with an iron grip, it is not always highest wisdom to shake one's fist in the face of the world.

Blair showed them also the thousand and one other things he was taking out, seeds and germs of civilisation, from which he hoped a mighty harvest, and named many more which he would procure in Australia. He limned his ideas lightly, and gave them even fuller glimpse than he had ever yet done of his ultimate hopes; and, waxing eloquent, held them spellbound at the magnitude of the far-reaching possibilities. And to all, Jean's eloquent face and sparkling eyes played ready chorus, and Lord Selsea and the Secretary went away deeply impressed with what they had seen, and more with what they had heard, and most of all with what they had been made to think and hope.

"A very fine young fellow!" said the Secretary, as he neutralised the sulphur again.

"Ay!—a man, every inch of him. May he live to see his golden dreams realised!"

"I tell you what, Selsea, it's mighty refreshing to come in contact with enthusiasm such as that running in harness with sound common sense."

"Big heart and level head—a fine combination!"

"I feel as if I'd been a trip on the sea, or up on a mountain top. I wish we could swop B— for him. Half a dozen of him in a Cabinet now—eh?"

"My dear fellow, don't! The contrast is too painful."

CHAPTER X

A BLACK OBJECT-LESSON

"It's a wonderful world!" said Aunt Jannet Harvey, for the four hundred and fourteenth time since, one by one, the Forelands and Dungeness and Beachy Head faded over the quarter as they ran down Channel. "And it gets more and more wonderful the further you go. Jean, my dear, have you ever in your dreams seen anything equal to that?"

"Never!" murmured Jean, wide-eyed and breathless, lest the smallest display of the ordinary functions of living should resolve into its natural elements the ethereal vision before them.

And yet it was only a tiny South Sea atoll, one of the myriad gleaming gems that deck the bosom of the great southern ocean in clusters, and strings, and ropes, and solitaires, from the Pelews to Pitcairn, of visible beauty indescribable, and in some cases possessed of natural latent treacherousness hardly second thereto.

It was still dusky twilight when they three climbed the companion, to taste the sweet of the dawn and watch the perpetual wonder of the coming day. They had learned already to rejoice in the dawnings as the purest and fullest revelations of Nature's exuberant largesse. The sunsets were gorgeous and magnificent beyond compare, but they had in them the elements of dissolution and decay, whereas the pure pearl splendours of the dawn sang full and true of new birth, new hopes, and the deep springs of life and joy.

Anxious as he was to get to his life's work, and grudging every moment and every league that lay between it and him, Blair had still felt it a duty to afford Jean every possible enjoyment of travel which the voyage could offer her. She was giving up much, she was going into outer exile for his sake; the chance might never come again. She should see all that was possible before the fringes fell behind them. And so they had come by way of Suez, and touched at Bombay and Ceylon, and then away to Australia and New Zealand, and then a great stretch round the outer skirts of the Australs and Paumotus, with only such stoppages as were absolutely necessary, and then straight for the work that awaited them.

"The rest of the Islands we can take by degrees," he said. "They will be our holiday grounds in the years to come. But now I am anxious to know what is going on in the Dark Islands. So very much may be happening behind that black curtain."

They were a gay and gallant company on board, not a long face among them. They were going to whatever might await them of strenuous life and heroic endeavour. No single one of them but was ready to lay down his or her life in the cause that lay so close to their hearts, and they found therein reason, not for doubts or fears, but wholly of exaltation. It was a mighty work, and they rejoiced in being chosen for it.

Blair had selected for his fellow-workers, from among a host of applicants, two young fellows whose qualifications satisfied him in every respect, and whose special training supplemented the deficiencies in his own. He is the wisest man who best knows what he knows least. The man who knows everything is generally useless at a pinch.

Well-equipped as he was in most respects—perfect, indeed, in the eyes of his wife, as was only right and proper—no man had a deeper appreciation of his own limitations than Blair himself. He had the fiery heart for the righting of wrongs, and the clear head and strong hand. But there were things beyond his ken—that is, in their very fullest compass—and in choosing his co-workers he kept these steadily in view.

For instance, he had a fair knowledge himself of medicine and rough-and-ready surgery. But he wanted very much more. And so Charles Evans, a Devonshire man, and M.D. and M.S. of London, became his medical right hand.

Then he had himself a certain aptitude for languages and dialects. He had picked up the lingua franca of the islands rapidly. But he wanted very much more. Charles Stuart, M.A., of Edinburgh, had made languages the congenial study of a lifetime which ran to nearly twenty-eight years. If any man could reduce phonetic elisions and hiatuses to written and printed symbols, Stuart was that man.

Then they were both big athletic fellows, runners and swimmers, great at games of all kinds, and handy with their hands, and they were as keen on letting light into the dark places of the earth as Blair himself. And they had both got married, at Blair's suggestion, and to the great satisfaction of the four people most immediately concerned—Evans, the Devonshire man, marrying Alison Carmichael, daughter of Dr. Carmichael of Edinburgh, and herself a medical student of no mean pretensions, and withal a good-looking, hearty girl, full of energy and spirits; and Stuart, the Scot, had married Mary Coventry, an English girl, daughter of a professor in a Lancashire theological college. She had a great natural aptitude for teaching, and was governessing when Stuart fell in love with her. She had promised to marry him when his circumstances should permit, and was cheerfully facing that very indefinite future when Blair's offer of the coveted post swept all the clouds away, and lifted her to a pinnacle of happiness which she was only becoming accustomed to by degrees.

With these four we have not very much to do. They proved most devoted assistants and pleasant and helpful companions throughout. But this is the story of Kenneth and Jean Blair, and if these others receive but slight mention, it is not because their hearts lacked fire or their lives incident, but simply through limitations of space.

So the Torch held three happy couples on their honeymoons, and Aunt Jannet Harvey played mother-in-law to them all, and kept the whole ship in high good-humour by her own energetic enjoyment of every smallest item of the day's doings.

Captain Cathie, by means of diligent search and stringent inquiry, had secured a crew after his own heart, every man a Clydesman, and some of them he had known since they were boys.

They carried a full complement. Besides himself and the mate, there were twenty men all told, stalwarts all, and Blair expected to find use for every man of them. Besides the big white whale-boats at the davits, there were two extra steam-launches in sections in the hold for inter-island work, and there were other reasons why he wanted behind him a thoroughly dependable band of tried white men instead of the usual mixture of Kanakas.

Forecasted shadows of those other reasons might have been found in the way in which he set to work, during the long weeks that lay between New Zealand and the Australs, to make marksmen of his peaceful crew. Bottles, hung from the yards, or set afloat on the sea, were their targets, and they most of them became fair shots. And one day Captain Cathie turned a cask overboard and stuck a white flag in it, and when it had floated almost out of sight he trained the long brown steel gun amidships on it, and bent and squinted carefully, and kept them so long in suspense, that the ladies screamed aloud when the gun did at last go off, and the white water flashed up close alongside the white flag.

"Within three feet, I should say, captain," said Blair, with the captain's glass at his eye. "Your hand and eye have not lost their cunning." And again and again the smiling captain displayed his prowess.

Another day he had the Maxim up and showed the men how to handle it. And cutlass drill became as regular a part of the daily routine as the fifteen-minute service that opened and closed the day.

Strange traffic indeed for a ship dedicated to peace and the spreading of the Light! But they all understood the meaning of these things, and the necessities that might arise, and the advisability of being prepared. For the very first Sunday night out from New Zealand, Blair, in that quiet, masterful fashion of his, which carried conviction once and for all into his hearers' souls and admitted of no shadow of a doubt, had taken occasion to explain the why and the wherefore of these apparent incongruities, and none of them ever forgot it.

It was a windless evening after a blistering day. The sea was like oil, with a long, slow, unbroken swell that set the little ship rolling in solemn rhythmical fashion which Stuart, the man of tongues, had long since dubbed heroic hexameters. And there, to the little company sitting facing him on deck in the gathering darkness, with an occasional sleepy "moo" from the farmyard in the bows, or the shrill squeakings of discontented piglets, and an admonitory grunt from their over-taxed mother, Blair described some of the things he had seen with his own eyes, and others which he had had direct from his dear old friend and leader, John Gerson, whose experience had been so much vaster than his own. Their hearts boiled at the mere recounting of the things he told them, and not a man or woman of them all but was ready to answer his utmost bidding in the effort to put them down.

"Ignorant these islanders are, and degraded, and the victims of horrible superstitions and practices unspeakable," he said, in closing; "but they have common living rights with the rest of us. Until those rights are secured to them, and until they learn that a white face is not necessarily the mask for a black heart, our work is futile. That security, by God's help, we intend to bring to them. If we can do it peacefully, I shall be grateful. If force is necessary, force we shall apply. But remember—we are going, not to punish, but to protect. Christ in righteous anger drove the defilers out of the Temple so that the Temple might be clean. God's Temple is here also. To the extent of our power and opportunity we will cleanse it, and by freeing these simple folk from bodily perils, we will give them the chance to redeem their souls alive."

They had swept along on the steady west wind for weeks. Now and again it dropped and left them rolling idly, with listless sails and jerking masts. But it always blew up again in time, and sent them swinging once more on their way, and at times it blew up so strong, and set up such an awkward sea, that their lives were almost battered out of them.

Blair, Evans, and Stuart apprenticed themselves to carpenter and engineers, and learned many things they did not know before. The men grew intimate with their rifles and cutlasses, the ladies talked much, read much, and they all took regular lessons in Samoan, as a foundation for the Polynesian tongues generally, from a native teacher who had been sent over to Sydney to meet them at Blair's request. His name was Matti, and he was a pleasing specimen of his kind, intelligent, painstaking, and of infinite good temper, but of a most peaceful, not to say lamb-like, disposition.

Among the many other diversions of their long voyage, Evans one day suggested that they should all be vaccinated, and was unmercifully chaffed for the idea.

"Isn't that like a young sawbones?" laughed Captain Cathie. "Just because we've got a clean bill, and he's got nothing to do, he's after making work just to keep his hand in."

But Evans persisted that they were going they knew not where, and no precautions ought to be omitted. And he talked so learnedly, and with so grave a foreboding, that by degrees they came to think he was perhaps right, and that it might be as well to be on the safe side of possibility. So, one after another, they meekly submitted their arms to the needle, and time came when they were glad of his persistence.

"Wonderful!—wonderful!" said Aunt Jannet Harvey once more that morning, in a whisper of concentrated rapture, and the others gazed at the tiny atoll without speaking, lest a breath should destroy it.

They had sighted the island the evening before, just a feathery fringe on the rim of the sea; but Captain Cathie was a devout believer in the enchantment of distance till full light of day should disclose possible pitfalls. For in these Southern Seas Nature sometimes gets ahead of the cartographers, and he had no desire to mark new reefs for the next comers with the stark ribs of his ship.

But now, in the dim of the dawn, they were wafting slowly towards it, with intent to land there for vegetables and fruit and water, and it grew visibly on their sight like a new-created thing.

Until a moment ago it had lain in the shadows. Then the eastern dimness softened, a mere quickening of hidden life, almost imperceptible, felt rather than seen. Then a soft pulsation, a throb from the heart of the coming day. The dimness trembled, a rosy softness diffused itself, and suddenly the background of the sky was filled with colour, palest green and tenderest rose and amber. And these grew and grew and deepened into crimson and gold, with swathes of diaphanous purple as the soft greens strengthened slowly into blue. And as it was above, so it was below, all duplicated in the flawless mirror of the sea. And there, between the upper and the lower glory, lay the enchanted isle gleaming darkly in the broken lights—a ring of feathery coco-palms and bosky undergrowth round an inner lagoon, a placid lake outside it, and outside that, still another protecting ring of reef dotted here and there with tiny feathered islets. A most wonderful and entrancing sight, so fairy-like and fragile that Jean felt it almost dangerous to breathe aloud.

Then the sun soared up above the sea-rim, and the atoll solidified and came out in its natural colours of dazzling white beach, and blue lagoons, and greens of every shade, from the tender tints of the budding palms to the cast-iron crests of the grey-boled giants, and the huddled mixture of the undergrowth. It lost in beauty as it gained in strength, but it looked more like solid land and less like a fairy vision, more like possible fruit and vegetables and less like a dissolving view.

All the company was on deck by this time, and all eyes were fixed on the island, as Captain Cathie in the bows conned the little ship slowly towards a wide opening in the outer reef, with a vigilant eye for hidden perils.

He had told them from the chart that it was the Three-Ringed Island of Atoa, but he had never been there himself and one could not be too cautious.

Then in the clear depths below them, as they crept slowly through the water-gate, they could see the wonderful forestry of the branching coral and the gleam of many-coloured shells, and the place was all alive with fishes of every tint and hue, sailing and darting like fragmentary rainbows.

But Captain Cathie was staring through his glasses at the distant white beach for signs of occupation, and found none. It was still early, however, and the village might be round the bend of the island. He carried the Torch in as far as he deemed safe, and then, at the word, the anchor plunged and the chain ran merrily out, and the little ship rode at rest for the first time in many days.

"Who is for the shore?" cried Blair, in the voice and manner of a jolly schoolboy offering treats.

They were all for the shore. After three weeks of continuous sailing the feel of solid ground under one's feet would be a novelty.

"Though I expect," said Aunt Jannet Harvey, "it'll be as hard to walk straight at first as it was not to walk crooked on the ship. I've got so used to walking on the sides of my feet, and balancing to the rolling, that I've almost forgotten what it feels like to walk any other way."

In ten minutes they were all speeding shorewards in one of the white whale-boats, and when Aunt Jannet Harvey cumbrously made the close acquaintance of the white beach, she found her feet no whit behind those of her younger companions in their eager activity.

They all stamped up the crunching coral with merry talk and laughter. Aunt Jannet Harvey stood at the foot of her first really intimate coco-nut tree, and gazed up the slim spire to the great benignant fronds and hanging fruit, with such intention of longing, that Jean, in a convulsion of laughter, cried—

"Do try it, auntie! I'm sure you could manage it if you tried hard."

"And if at first you don't succeed, try, try again, Aunt Jannet!" laughed Blair.

They left her still gazing, and scattered, Jean and Mary Stuart and Alison Evans diving into the undergrowth after armfuls of greenery and trailing vines, and twittering like escaped birds when, now and again, they came on treasure-trove of scarlet hibiscus blooms glowing on the green like fiery stars—or splashes of blood.

The men pressed on at once up the ridge to get a general view of their surroundings, and Captain Cathie, with a couple of his men, pulled slowly down the lagoon in search of the village.

He heard the merry calls of the explorers, and wondered at the absence of any sign of life on the island. The very sight of an approaching ship used, in his time, to bring the population to the beach. But things had changed of course since then, and byways had become highways.

The white boat jerked slowly along round the bend, and the voices ashore grew less distinct. And suddenly his lips pinched and his brow crumpled, and he gazed ahead with a fixed, angry glare which set his men wondering what they were coming to, and carried their chins to their shoulders unconsciously.

A stretch of white beach, a bristle of black posts jutting out of the cleared ground above—that was all. But Cathie's experience read them like three-feet letters on a city hoarding.

He threw up one hand and jammed the tiller hard down with the other.

"Round with her, boys!" and they were swinging back up the lagoon to get the women aboard again. For there might be sights in the brush along that ridge to shock the souls of men.

Blair, Evans, and Stuart, with Matti, the Samoan, and the rest of the boat's crew, climbed the backbone of the island, whose highest point attained an altitude of perhaps thirty feet.

They were standing looking across the flawless mirror of the central lagoon, when the Samoan broke out suddenly, "Sirs, I presume advice. Return fortwit to ship. This place is not good," and when they all turned on him in surprise, they found his brown face strained and pallid with fear, his eyes starting, and his nose dilated like a startled stag's.

"Why, Matti, what's wrong?" said Blair.

The brown man shook his head.

"I know not, sirs," and his white teeth chattered so that his chin wagged visibly. "There is evil abroad. It is in the air, in the tree-tops."

They looked up for sign of the evil, but saw only the heavy plumes of the coco-palms nodding mournfully in the breeze. Down below the air seemed heavy and somewhat sickly, and so far they had seen no sign of life on the island.

"The place seems deserted," said Evans.

"We will go on along here a bit further," said Blair, "and if there is nothing more to be seen, we'll turn back I'm afraid it's a poor look-out for fruit and vegetables," and they tramped on in silence, Matti well in the rear, reluctant to go, still more reluctant to be left.

And presently the brush thinned, and they came out on the clearing, and Blair stopped abruptly with a face as strained as Matti's, but grimmer and whiter, and Matti, stumbling up to the rear, gave a groan as though to say, "I knew it."

"God help us!" said Blair through his teeth, for they had found what Cathie had feared.

The blackened posts of the houses stuck up starkly through the sand as though in mute and pitiful appeal. Beneath them were heaps of wind-blown ashes barely covering that which they had mercifully hidden. And among the mounds as they drew near was a sound of rustling and stealthy movement, and here and there monstrous crabs, too gorged to move almost, essayed escape into their temporary burrows.

The newcomers stared wide-eyed and horror-stricken. Blair had seen it all before, and the grim white of his face gave place to grim red and black as his heart drummed furiously with righteous indignation.

"This is the horror we have come to fight," he said hoarsely. "This is what I told you of. Now you see it with your own eyes. The place has been swept bare by kidnappers. These died in defence of their homes and wives and children. Let us get back. It is no sight for the women."

He waved them away, but something caught his eye, and he went forward and bent over it with tight-pinched face for a moment, and then turned abruptly and followed the others.

But, even as he turned, a shriek from the lower brush told that it was too late to save the women from some visible knowledge of what had taken place. They turned and ran back along the ridge.

Mary Stuart, reaching for a flower, saw at her feet what she took for a fallen coco-nut, and stooped to pick it up, and then screamed aloud and sat down suddenly with a sick, white face. The others hurried up, Alison Evans and Aunt Jannet Harvey reaching her first.

"What is it, dear?" asked Aunt Jannet, and then she saw, and sat down heavily beside her.

Alison had her nerves under better control. She had seen little dead bodies before, but the sight of a murdered child is a shock to any woman. Her face was white and rigid, but she had her wits about her also.

"Take them all away," she whispered fiercely to Aunt Jannet Harvey, and Aunt Jannet, just needing that spur, scrambled up and gripped Mary Stuart by the shoulder and dragged her away as Jean came running up, asking, "What is it? What's the matter?"

"Come away, child!—come away! It is a little murdered baby. Alison is seeing to it, but it is quite dead. Let us get away. Here is the boat and Captain Cathie."

Everything was changed as the white boat plunged back across the lagoon to the ship. The men's faces were hard and angry, the women's white and pitiful. Alison Evans wept silently now. She had seen more than the others, and that soft little head, crushed in by one murderous blow against the tree, would haunt her dreams for nights to come.

The sun shone as brightly as before, but there was something pitiless in his unwinking glare. The sea was as placid and sparkling as before, but there was a fawning treachery in its very smoothness. The palms behind waved their feathers just as before, but now they were funeral plumes. The very oars no longer chirped merrily in the rowlocks, but croaked in a way that got on the women's nerves. And not one of them spoke till they were safe aboard the ship.

"Yes," nodded Blair to Cathie's look of interrogation, "we will go on at once," and the anchor chain rattled up hoarsely, and they went slowly and silently on their way, and left the beautiful island to its dead.

"I saw it from the water," said Cathie later to Blair, "and turned to get the ladies away, but I was too late. Did you see anything to give you any hint as to who it was, sir?"

"Yes. Peruvians, I should say. There was one yellow man among the dead, and they recruit mostly from these outer islands. Before God, captain, I will put a stop to this kind of work, whatever the cost may be."

"We're with you, sir, every man of us. See those men's faces!"

And grim and determined enough were the men's faces as they went about their work. For those who had seen had told those who had not seen, and the impression was a deep one.

That night Blair called them all together, and spoke of the matter in a way that went home and confirmed the spirit that had been roused in them by that holocaust on the island.

"It is devil's work, men," he wound up, "and, please God, we'll stop it. Are you with me?"

"Ay, ay, sir!" "That we are, sir!" "All the way, sir!" and so on, in tones that left no mistake about it.

"You can understand the effect of that kind of work on these islanders. It is not often so clean a sweep is made as the one we saw this morning. And where part are taken and part are left, can you wonder that those who remain hate and fear the very sight of a white face? Have they not reason? It will be our endeavour to stop these raids, and, by protecting the islanders, gradually win them over to better ways. Once we can make them see that we care for them, and think of their welfare and not our own, half the battle is won. On the one side we may have to fight—not our own countrymen, I am glad to say. These raiders come mostly from the west coast of South America, and they go to lengths which the Queenslanders rarely do. And, on the other hand, in our dealings with the natives, we must remember what they have suffered, what reason they have to mistrust us, and we must be very forbearing and longsuffering. On the one side I want you—and I shall need the whole-hearted assistance of every man of you—I want you to be bold as lions, and on the other side as mild as milk. Only so can our work be done, and it is a mighty work."

CHAPTER XI

TOO LATE

Following instructions, Captain Cathie shook out every stitch of canvas the Torch could carry, and laid her course dead for the Dark Islands. They made good way, but their progress still seemed slow to Kenneth Blair; for his fears outstripped the flight of the little ship, and, anxious as he was to reach the Islands, he still almost dreaded the cry that should tell of their sighting, in fear of what he might find there.

And grounds for fear were not lacking. The Dark Islands lay some five days distant, east by north—on the line, therefore, of the marauders' way home. From the atoll they had already raided, he judged, from the number of dwellings and general appearances, they might have got some fifty or sixty souls, not more. Their holds would still be far from full. If they had invaded the Dark Islands in similar fashion, it was a stormy reception the next comers might expect. At best it would be a negative welcome, and a matter of slow and cautious approach to their few good graces; but if the islands had been raided, the work would be thrown back for years, and all his hopes with them. He could scarce eat or sleep for thinking of it, and the pricking off of their position each day on the chart, and the calculation of the hours that still intervened between them and full knowledge of how matters lay, were matters of supremest interest and absorbing anxiety.

He could settle to none of the ordinary routine, and his evident upsetting, the causes of which they perfectly understood, disturbed them all in like fashion.

He spoke little, even to Jean, and she never once, by word or look, expressed anything but the utmost sympathy and confidence in him.

He tramped the deck day and night almost, with eager outlook over the waste of waters ahead, and never a look behind unless at the seething bubbles of their long, straight wake, which told of the speed and directness of their flight.

Once only, in these days of biting anxiety, he said to her—

"Dearest, I am poor company at present. Can you forgive me? I am on the rack about these poor souls ahead. I cannot help fearing the worst, and it means so very much to us."

"I am with you, Ken, heart and soul. We can only pray for the best. If what you fear has happened, all we can do is to do our best to right it."

He shook his head unhopefully. The idea had taken possession of him that they would arrive only to find death and desolation and the wild fury of revenge.

"Even if it is so," said his comforter, "I can see possibility of good coming out of the evil."

"It will throw us back years," he said gloomily.

"If your people have been carried off, we will follow them and release them and restore them to their homes"—there were new sparks in his eyes as she spoke like one inspired—"and that will give us the footing it might take years to obtain."

He kissed her hand.

"You give me new hopes, whatever may have happened. That is what we will attempt if the worst has taken place," and thereafter he brightened up considerably, but relaxed no whit of his anxiety to reach the islands.

They swept gallantly along on the northern fringe of the westerly wind, which maintained a propitious amplitude, and just before sunset on the fourth day, the lucent rim where sea met sky was dented with a filmy tooth which the sinking sun drew momentarily into view from the farther distance, and Captain Cathie and Blair pronounced it Kapaa'a, the highest peak in the Dark Islands.

There was not much sleep on board that night, the morrow would be so big with events. General opinion among the men ran somehow to a fight. That was, perhaps, the natural tendency of the pent-up feelings of the last few days. An outlet would be grateful, a violent outlet from choice. When a man's feelings suffer maltreatment, the natural man within him develops a violent desire to find relief in kicking, in which last word is comprehended the whole known range of methods of assault, with the exception, of course, of the circumscribed and properly debarred use of the feet.

They travelled warily that night, and the first of the dawn showed them the peaks of Kapaa'a, bold and beautiful, dead ahead, and growing bolder and still more beautiful with every graceful roll of the ship.

They hung over the sides, every man and woman of them, and eyed their future home with an eagerness which its outward aspect at once amply satisfied and further quickened.

For what they could see was grand in its opulence of crag, and cliff, and gorge, and greenery. And the clouds which wreathed the higher summits, and the gauzy films of mist, which floated along the hillsides and hung reluctantly in the tree-tops, gave promise of still daintier beauties in that which they held half hidden.

They drew in cautiously to within a mile of the outer reef, and then, not venturing the ship nearer till they should learn how matters stood inside, Blair and Evans, with a crew of ten, eight to pull and two in case of need, and Matti to interpret, shot through one of the openings in the reef on the back of a long blue roller and made straight for the white beach. They carried no visible arms, but each man of the crew had his Winchester between his feet.

The lagoon ran up into a spearhead of white sand, between two tall cliffs opposite the widest opening in the reef, as though the constant impact of the outer waves, tempered as it was by the compression of the opening and the subsequent run across the lagoon, had forced the beach inland at that spot. It was helped, however, by a river, which came down between the hills and divided the white sandspear into two equal parts.

Here, according to usage and natural proclivity, a village should have stood, but in this case did not. John Gerson had told Blair that other morning, when they came racing up the lagoon in similar brave case, that it lay up the valley near the taro fields.

His heart beat painfully as, one by one, he picked up the points which had charted themselves for ever in his memory.

There, to the left of the stream, was where they landed.

There was the rough scarp of rock round which they had followed the bristling crowd to the death.

There his former life had ended in turmoil and darkness, and the new life had begun in twilight dimness and the painful groping after broken threads.

And yet, how mercifully he had been guided! The shadowed valley had led, after all, to the fuller life and the mountain-top, and he bowed his head gratefully.

The white boat slid gently up the white beach, and so far their keen outlook had seen no sign of hostile life. But experience had taught him that appearances are deceptive, and that sometimes when least is seen most is to be feared.

They disembarked cautiously, and stood looking round. The palms about the mouth of the valley waved sombre welcome, or it might be warning. The thick brush below lay still and silent, but bright black eyes by the hundred might be watching them from it.

The very lack even of opposition was a menace, and suggestive of trickery and ambush.

"We will go round the point," said Blair at last. "And—yes, you must take your guns, men. I would have preferred not, but we don't know how matters stand."

So, leaving two in the boat, the rest shouldered their guns, and the little party went forward round the point where Kenneth Blair had been once before in his life, and almost in his death.

But no bristling mob confronted them this time. They went on step by step, with eyes for every rock and bush, and ears alert, and every nerve tight strung for the faintest hint of treachery, and Blair's face crumpled somewhat at the menace of the silence and the solitude.

Step by step they left the white beach and the friendly sea, and drew in to the blank hostility of the woods. He would a thousand times sooner have been confronted by the visible hostility of the natives. For that which is visible and tangible one may hope to cope with and subdue, but the invisible and intangible contain possibilities beyond the compassing, and the elements of unreasoning fear.

On one member of the party these were already having their effect. Perhaps on others also, but not so perceptibly. The knowledge of better things had not, in Matti, effectually eradicated the superstitions of a lifetime. Terrors of which the white men had no conception beat like bats about his soul, the indefinable terrors of bygone ages of horrors and darkness. His face was green. He sweated fears at every faltering step. His eyes bulged crablike in quest of that which he dreaded to find.

"Sirs, sirs!" he gasped, in an agonised whisper, "it is not good. I counsel—"

"Be quiet," said Blair. "We must see," and they went on warily, expecting the sudden outleap of death at every step.

But they saw nothing, heard nothing. That dreadful menacing silence brooded over the place just as it had brooded over the atoll. A flock of gay little paraquets whirred suddenly from the hillside and dived into the bush ahead, and the silence and the spell of it were broken. The paraquets started chattering and quarrelling like a school of sparrows, and Blair's danger-pointed wits suggested to him that they would not behave so if the brush was otherwise tenanted.

With a last careful inspection of the hillsides he moved forward, and the rest followed. There was a track through the brush, and the trampled ground showed signs of much traffic.

Five minutes more and they had found all they feared.

The thicket thinned and widened towards the valley and they were standing once more amid blackened ribs of houses, and heaps of ashes from which thin wisps of smoke still curled lazily. They had arrived too late!

CHAPTER XII

THE FLAMING SWORD

Blair's face was tighter and grimmer than ever as he took it all in, and the faces of the rest were sympathetically hard.

But this was no time to stand glooming. The wrong was done. Now to see if it could be righted.

He turned and led the way back to the boat, thinking too hard for speech. He knew what had to be done, but there were disquieting items in the programme for which he had been unable to make provision, and which he would gladly have escaped.

They would follow the marauders and rescue the victims—that he took as settled.

The settlement could hardly be a mild one, and he would fain have spared the women the sight of it; but there was nothing else for it—they could not possibly be left behind.

The raiders had doubtless filled their holds here to the last man. But there must be many left. They would be in hiding yet, but presently they would come out of their retreats, full of grief and anger, and it would go hard with the first white faces they encountered. The women must go with them—that was one of his troubles. And the next, supposing they caught these blood-thirsty and body-hungry rascals— and catch them they would, if it took a month's circling round—what were they to do with them when they had them?

There would probably be fighting, though the results did not trouble him. What he wanted was to put an end once and for all to this horrible traffic. The only way that suggested itself as adequate and final was to string them up to the yard-arm, every man-jago of them, and whether that might be done with impunity was more than doubtful. The only impunity he desired was for his future work. Morally, he would feel justified. And whether or no, the spirit that was in him would have borne lightly the burden of such a deed, even though its outward results to himself were personally painful and disastrous.

It took no more than two minutes after they had scrambled on board to set things in motion.

"We are too late," said Blair to the anxious waiters. "We follow at once, captain. They will have filled up here, and will make straight for home. Lay her straight for the Chincha Islands, please, and make all speed possible."

Captain Cathie had foreseen the possibility. He set their course due east for the present, and spread his wings again to the last stitch, and they swept away past the other islands, with no more than fleeting glimpses of them in the mellow distance.

Then Blair begged them to confer with him in the saloon, and laid his difficulties before them.

"I take it for granted we shall catch them," he said.

"Certainly," said the captain.

"I am distressed at thought of bringing you ladies into contact with bloodshed and violence. But there is no help for it; it would not be safe to leave you behind."

"Certainly not," said Aunt Jannet Harvey emphatically.

"We would not have been left in any case," said Jean. "Our places are by your sides," and the others quietly endorsed her.

"The next thing is this: we shall catch this ship, we shall rescue these islanders, by force if necessary. What are we to do with the crew and the ship?"

"Hang them and scuttle her," said Captain Cathie, with decision.

"That is one's natural first feeling, and possibly it would be the wisest thing in the end. And yet—"

"It is a question if we are justified in going that length," said Charles Evans gravely.

Stuart, too, shook his head doubtfully.

"Fighting in so good a cause is one thing," he said slowly, "but hanging in cold blood is another."

"Exactly," said Blair. "And that is the point of my dilemma."

"Do you know what will happen if you let 'em go?" said Cathie brusquely.

"I'm afraid I do, captain. And yet—even then— You mean, of course, that they'll come back in larger force, and with a double incentive—plunder plus revenge."

"That's it to a T, sir, and you know it. There'll be no peace and security till they're wiped out. Wipe 'em out at once and completely, and you're all right till a new lot comes along, knowing nothing of these others, except that they never came back. And when the new lot comes we'll tackle them same way. I'm not by nature a bloodthirsty man, but if there's one thing can set me afire, it's this kind of work. I've seen so much of it. They're not men. They're scum of hell—asking your pardon, ladies!"

"Speak your mind, captain," said Aunt Jannet Harvey. "No good being mealy-mouthed when it's a question of life and death. I think they should be scuttled."

"I've no doubt we all agree as to what we would like to have done, but whether, in our position, we are justified in pronouncing and executing judgment to the extent of death—it is a difficult matter to decide."

"If you let one single man of them go, Mr. Blair, you're only breeding future trouble."

"I know it, captain. And yet—at times—I have seen the attempt to clear the future of trouble lead only to greater. Is there no alternative?"

"There's alternatives," said Cathie gloomily; "but they're only makeshifts—playing with nettles to get stung: you could fling all their arms overboard, and threaten 'em with worse if they come back. And they'll come. You could scuttle the ship and maroon 'em somewhere. You could bring 'em all back here and make 'em work. But there's trouble in it whatever you do, unless you hang 'em out of hand."

"I'm afraid there is, and I would dearly like to rid the earth of them; but—"

And Evans and Stuart felt as he did. They lacked nothing in courage, but to their minds this matter of essential right went deeper than any mere question of courage or future trouble.

Jean, and Alison Evans, and Mary Stuart listened with grave, troubled faces, but ventured no opinion. These were deeper waters than any they had ever sailed on, and they felt rather out of their depths.

"Well, we have some little time to think it over," said Blair, at last. "If any illumination comes to any of us, let the rest have the benefit of it. You will get all ready for what we may need to do, captain?"

"All's ready, sir. Long Tom's loaded, and the men are keen to square things with these rascals if we can come up with them."

"I suppose even these terrible men may have wives and children waiting for them at home," said Jean thoughtfully, as they rose.

"Like enough, ma'am," said Cathie—"and so have the brown men."

"Men like that have no right to have wives and children," said Aunt Jannet Harvey, with vehemence past grammar. "If they have they'll be better without them. They ought to be scuttled."

Nevertheless, Jean's suggestion remained in all their minds.

Never was such a bright look-out as the Torchmen kept for the Blackbirder, as they dubbed the chase. The rigging was never free from anxious gazers. It looked as though a flight of great birds had lighted on the ship.

Jean remarked on it to Aunt Jannet Harvey.

"They're fine fellows and all of one mind. See how eager they are to catch her."

"Ay, ay!" said Aunt Jannet. "They'll find her if she's to be found," and did not think it necessary to add that, through Captain Cathie, she had offered five pounds to the man who first sighted the other ship.

Blair walked the deck strenuously, mostly alone, occasionally with one of the others. And the more he walked and the more he thought, the more averse he became to the idea of hanging.

"We're doing right for right's sake in freeing these islanders," he said to Evans and Stuart one time. "If we hang those men I can't help feeling we're doing wrong for right's sake, and there we come to the old Jesuitical practice which we all condemn. We do a wrong in the belief that it will save future trouble. I don't believe we're justified. We've got to do what seems to us right now. The future is in God's hands. If trouble comes, He will show us how to meet it."

"That, I think, is highest wisdom," said Stuart. "If the trouble comes, we shall meet it with clear consciences, and clear consciences make stout hearts."

"I'm with you," said Evans. "I'd like to see them wiped out as much as Captain Cathie would, but I think we're on a higher plane in doing as you suggest. You feel sure of catching them?"

"Hopeful—and determined to do it, if it can be done. They've got at most two days' start. Less, perhaps, for the village was still smoking. They're heavily laden, and we are making good way. We cut into a belt of calms and variables soon, and there we can take to steam. And then—they don't know they're being chased. We do."

There was, however, this one element of doubt in the chase: would the raiders carry on due east, in order to get all possible out of the fairly steady westerly winds,—thereby lengthening the distance they had to cover, and having, after all, in the end, to encounter the possibly adverse winds of the coast,—or would they take their chance across the doubtful calm belt and make straight for the Peruvian coast?

It was an even question, and the board on which the game had to be played was several thousand miles square.

Blair and Cathie discussed the matter in all its bearings.

"What would I do if I was them?" summed up the captain. "Well, that would depend too. If I had two or three hundred passengers aboard, and each one worth so much alive and nothing dead, I'd want to get 'em home alive as quick as possible. If I was well stocked with provisions I might carry on with this wind for the coast. If I was anyways short I'd probably try a beat straight for home. If we don't sight them in two days we'll edge up north-east a bit; but I'm pretty sure they'll keep this wind as long as they can, and chances are we'll sight them within twenty-four hours. They're probably not hurrying, and we're making every inch we can."

But it was the morning of the third day before the welcome hail from aloft brought every soul on board into the bows, to search for the tiny mote on the horizon on which all their hopes were concentrated.

It was a very early bird who had discovered the worm. He had gone up aloft before the dawn, and, as the sun shot up, the rim of the sea was lucent like the edge of a glass plate brimming with water. An almost invisible flaw, a mere film against the light, was enough for the practised eye, and his joyful "Sail ho!" turned the ship upside-down.

Captain Cathie swung up alongside the look-out with his glasses, and was presently on deck again beaming contentedly.

"That's her right enough," he said. "A brig, and we're raising her fast. You'll see her from below here inside an hour."

"When shall we catch her up?" asked Blair anxiously.

"Perhaps by three o'clock or so," said Cathie, after a moment's consideration, but added cautiously, "if the wind holds," and, as if resenting his doubt, the sails gave an ominous warning flap.

"Right," said the captain, with a determined nod, and set the engineers to work at once to get up steam. "We'd be as well to have it on anyhow, to keep the weather gauge of him when we come up," and presently the screw was churning the merry bubbles up astern, and the chase was rising slowly on the horizon.

The brig, however, had held the wind longer than they had. It was mid-afternoon before they got within range of her, and she was still drawing slowly along with sails that bulged and flapped in desultory catspaws.

"Shall I send a shot over her, just to show we mean business?" brimmed Cathie.

"No shots unless they're absolutely necessary, captain," said Blair. "We'll hail her first. And I think you ladies had better go below. Their answer may be lead."

Aunt Jannet was for resisting.

"I want to see," said she.

"There may be things not for your seeing, Aunt Jannet," said Blair quietly, "and other things besides. Please go with the others and keep them from feeling nervous if you can."

So the ladies went below, and we may imagine to what helpful furtherance of patient waiting they betook themselves.

CHAPTER XIII

THE MAN'S MAN'S MAN

The sides of the Blackbirder were lined with sallow, scowling faces, as villainous a crew as ever gathered aboard one disreputable ship since time began.

They took in all the points of the trim little craft that nosed quietly up within speaking distance; the British flag, to which they were by nature antipathetic; the long brown gun forward, with its black mouth pointing plumb for every shifty eye of them; the glancing barrels of the Winchesters, and the steady determination of the men who carried them; the covert menace of the whole silent display. Muttered blasphemies rolled along the line of yellow faces, and the rumble of them was heard aboard the Torch.

"What you want?" shouted a burly figure, standing aft behind the deckhouse.

"Your cargo," replied Captain Cathie, patting the breach of his big gun affectionately, and the objurgations aboard the enemy broke out afresh.

"What you mean?"

"You'd better come aboard here and we'll explain."

"You better fetch me."

"Very well," said Cathie, with joy in his face.

He stooped behind his long gun for a moment, trained it carefully, and instantly its angry bellow filled sea and sky, and sent the women below to their knees. They heard a crash, aloft and below, aboard the Blackbirder, and the yells of the men as they scattered to avoid the falling spars. The smoke, drifting lazily away, showed the brig's maintopmast nipped neatly at the crosstrees, and hanging with its yards in a fantastic tangle of ropes to the deck.

"That's the first time of asking," shouted Cathie. "Are you coming?" and he bent behind his gun again.

"I kom," and they saw the black-a-vised crew set to launching a boat, with vicious side-glances at their oppressor.

Presently the dirty boat and its dirty crew lay alongside, and the burly one climbed slowly up the ladder they dropped for him.

His small eyes glared viciously out of his bloated cheeks, "like a hunted boar's," said Cathie afterwards.

"Now then! You are pirate?"

"Not at all—we're missionaries," said Cathie.

"Missi—!" and the fat one came within measurable distance of apoplexy.

"You've stolen our people. We want them back. Do you understand?"

But the Blackbirder's English was limited, and the shock of meeting missionaries of so strange a texture had bemused his wits.

Blair begged Stuart to speak to him in Spanish, and the wandering wits came back at sound of it.

"Tell him," said Blair, "that the islanders he has kidnapped are our people, and we intend to take them home again."

And Stuart put it to him so.

"If he makes any resistance we shall overcome it. What does he say?"

"He asks how you're going to take them back."

"We will see to all that presently. First, he will bring aboard here all the arms they have over yonder," said Blair, and as that sank through Stuart into the other's understanding, the little boar-eyes gleamed more viciously than ever, and the fat body rumbled with volcanic fires.

"We will give him half an hour to deliver up the arms. If they are not here then, his other mast will go. He will bring them over himself."

The little eyes glared furiously round, but found nothing but grimmest determination in the faces that hemmed him in. Possibly they did not fail to note all the other points bearing on the question. He shambled to the side with a growl in his throat, and got heavily into his boat, and was pulled across to his ship, and immediately they heard the simmering of a hot discussion tipped with sharp flakes of invective.

"They don't like it," said Captain Cathie.

The minutes passed. Now and again a scowling face turned their way, and shot a venomous white-eyed glance at them, but there were no signs of the arms coming over.

"Five minutes more," shouted Cathie at last, bubbling with excitement, and clapping the breech of his gun. "And, my goodness, I hope you'll run it out! I want that other mast," he added softly.

"Five minutes more," shouted Stuart in Spanish, so that there should be no misunderstanding.

Cathie stood watch in one hand, lanyard in the other, one foot tapping restlessly. He hungered for that other mast, and the lesson its fall would teach the yellow dogs.

At last he closed his watch with a snap, stooped to the gun, and with a roar and a rattling crash, and a blasphemous scatteration below, the foretopmast shared the devastation of the mainmast.

"Now we have them right as a trivet," said Cathie, "and they'll begin to understand where they are."

They understood, and five minutes later the boat shoved off again, bringing the spoils of war, such part of them, at all events, as they chose to surrender—some thirty muskets, as many cutlasses, and half a dozen revolvers.

"Now," said Blair, to the downcast captain of the Blackbirder, through Stuart, "you will stop here. We shall tow you back to the islands. When your cargo is discharged, you will be at liberty to go. If you ever return on this errand, you will find us waiting for you. Now, captain," to Cathie and, at a sign from the captain, one of the white whale-boats dropped to the water, and half a dozen men jumped into her, carrying the coil of a stout hawser, which ran out over the stern of the Torch and was secured amidships.

The Torch herself swung into line ahead of the other, and the big steel gun swung slowly round till her muzzle grinned threateningly round each side of the mainmast.

"Tell those men to get back, Stuart, and say the captain waits with us," and the brig's boat pushed sulkily off. "Now, Stuart, you come with me, and Matti. We will take revolvers, though we shall not need them."

Matti shivered into the boat, and Stuart and Blair followed with four Torches carrying Winchesters, and pulled to the brig and climbed up among the truculent crew, every man of which had his knife at his back and hands that itched to get using it.

Blair called for the mate and told him curtly what he had already told the captain, and added some special instructions for his own benefit.

"First, make fast that hawser!"

They did it to the satisfaction of the Torches, and at a call from Blair the Torch started slowly ahead, the hawser tightened, and every solid thrust of the blades in the blue water cut an upward step in the life of the Dark Islands.

"Now, understand! There will be a hand on that rope night and day. If there is any tampering with it you will hear from us. This mess"—pointing to the dismantled masts—"you will not touch till we reach the islands. Now I am going to inspect your cargo. How often do you feed them?"

"Twice a day."

"Some of us will come across each time and see it done. I hold you responsible. If they suffer, you will suffer. Understand? Now lead the way! You"—to Stuart and the four Torches—"please keep your eyes about you while I go below. Matti, you come with me."

A grating, through which came a most horrible smell, was hauled up, and the three went down into the inferno, and felt sick before their feet quitted the ladder. For the mate was sick at this unexpected turn of fortune, and Blair and Matti came near to physical sickness with the stench.

Blair clung to the side of the ladder and gazed mistily round. There was little light, but the dimness seemed to come not so much from lack of light as from superfluity of nastiness of every possible description and human misery indescribable. The feel of the place was like a hot breath from the pit. It closed silently upon one like the hand of a crawling death. It dimmed the eyes, and choked the throat, and lay like a weight on the heart.

To breathe it seemed death, yet three hundred miserables breathed it and lived, and by degrees his eyes discerned them and never lost the sight.

A great confused tangle of brown limbs and bodies, many entirely naked, a forest of shock heads, a hypnotising multitude of dark eyes all focussed on him, and all pitted with sparks of light from the opened hatch—mostly men, a few women, no children—short panting breaths, sighs, groans, the dull rattle of chains.

"Have they been fed to-day?" gasped Blair, and pointed to his mouth.

The mate nodded.

Blair went two steps up the ladder and called to Stuart.

"Tell them to feed and water these poor things instantly. Now, Matti, ask them in all the tongues you know if there is any headman or chief among them. And say we mean them well."

Matti tried them without success in two or three dialects, but at last hit upon one that evoked responsive movements in some of those nearest the light. He felt his way, and at last got a word in answer, the meaning of which he understood.

Here a couple of men came down the ladder carrying baskets of what looked like dog-biscuits, which they commenced handing round, one to each prisoner, and the latter sprang to the limits of their tethers for them, and snatched and worried them like dogs that had not been fed for a week. Blair looked at the mate, but the mate looked elsewhere.

It took a long time and many renewals to supply them all; but Blair would not move till it was done, nor until every one had had a drink of water. Then the interrupted conversation was resumed.

Yes, there was a chief there, and Blair ordered the mate to release the man and bring him forward. He came without eagerness, a tall, brown, well-built man of middle age, with a gloomy, but not absolutely forbidding face, pinched just now, perhaps with hunger, perhaps with despair. Experience had taught him to expect nothing but evil at the hands of white men.

But even his dull misery could not but perceive a difference between this clean, white-clad white man and those he had become accustomed to, and he gazed at Blair with a note of sullen inquiry.

"You are a chief?" asked Blair, through Matti.

"I am a king," he said, answering Blair, and bestowing no look on Matti, who, he perceived, was only a voice. And there was that in his tone and manner which carried conviction in spite of the misery of his condition.

"We have come to set you free and to take you back to the island."

And when the words beat through Matti's attempt at his dialect and got into his brain, it was as though an electric shock had galvanised him suddenly into new life.

"Free?—the island?" he stammered, and stared, still doubting. "All?" he asked.

"Yes, all," and he turned and told the news to the rest in quick, clipping words, and after a moment's amazed silence a shout went up, and the fetid hole was filled with a deafening buzz of talk.

It was only after anxious consideration of the point that Blair had decided to tell them the good news. He grudged every lost soul there. He would not lose one. There might be some given over to utter despair, and there is no tonic like hope.

"You will come with us," said Blair, to the discrowned king.

The man looked back into the gloom, and then again at Blair, and spoke eagerly.

"He says one of his wives is there," said Matti. "She shall come also."

The man pointed her out, the mate released her, and they climbed to the blessed upper air, all a-tremble with eagerness.

"Now, understand!" said Blair to the mate, through Stuart, so that all could hear him: "when your cargo is discharged, you will be at liberty to go where you will. If you attempt any treachery, we will blow you to pieces. If you ever return to the Dark Islands, you do so at your own peril," and he saw his guests into the boat and followed them.

The woman was young and not uncomely, but subdued and apparently somewhat dazed still at these sudden reverses of fortune. Neither spoke a word as the Torch slowed down for them to come aboard, but the man's eyes roved to and fro in ceaseless questioning, and he seemed to arrive at an intelligent understanding of matters. The long steel gun claimed his attention the moment he reached the deck, and from his instant glance across at the shattered hamper of the brig he evidently associated the two things.

Their only visible clothing was a native mat wrapped round the waist and falling nearly to the feet, and the very first thing to do was to cleanse them of the visible results of their 'tween-decks imprisonment.

Blair led the man down to the men's bathroom, and turned on the taps and filled the bath before his astonished eyes. He showed him also the use of soap, by washing his own hands, and left him to complete his toilet. He could not, however, forbear listening outside to hear how he got on, and was rewarded at first by a long silence, then by several tentative turnings on and off of the wonderful taps. Then a slight splashing suggested an experiment with the soap; and finally grunts of satisfaction and much wallowing told of savage man's enjoyment of the amenities of civilisation, and the return to his natural cleanliness. When he had had time to wash himself several times over, Blair knocked on the door and went in, and found his guest lying full length under water, with only his brown nose showing, and evidently feeling very much better.

He sat up and gurgled some words expressive of his feelings, and was mightily astonished at the sudden disappearance of the water when the plug was pulled up. He wanted to fill the bath again at once to see it run out again, and Blair let him engineer a final sluice for himself.

He was a much pleasanter companion after his wash. His fine brown skin shone under the unusual treatment of a towel, and his hair stuck out from his head like a twirling mop. He was about to assume his dirty mat again, but Blair hauled out some clean towels, tied one round him like a loin-cloth, draped another from his hips as he had worn his mat, and threw another over his shoulders, and the man was dressed as he had never been dressed in his life before. The towels happened to have broad red bands along the edges, and moreover had fringes, and their wearer was as proud of them as any Piccadilly dandy of his newest thing in spring suits.

Somewhat similar doings had been in course in the ladies' quarters, but, thanks to Aunt Jannet Harvey's very determined, but equally mistaken, good intentions, the results were less happy.

Aunt Jannet believed firmly that decency as well as cleanliness were first steps towards godliness, and she was too recent an arrival in the equatorials, and perhaps also too conservative in her own ideas, to understand that decency of attire is after all purely matter of custom. To her, a girl dressed, or undressed, only in a ridi fringe which clung precariously to her hips and fell half-way to her knee, was practically unclothed. She did not know that it was death for a man to touch that scant, precarious garment. Strange anomaly of the cannibal isles—a dangling fringe of smoked coco-nut fibre a more stringent safeguard than the multitudinous garments of civilisation! When Aunt Jannet did learn that fact she thought considerably, and thereafter took a somewhat wider view of things.

Meanwhile, in the mistaken goodness of her heart, she had insisted on arraying the newcomer in garments of her own, the most visible of which was a light print dress, in which the poor creature looked almost as uncomfortable as she felt.

At sight of her transformation the brown man stared hard, and then grinned vigorously, and the girl hotched and wriggled in disgustful discomfort. She came up to the man and fingered his soft towels wistfully. She spoke to him, and he instantly handed her the one he had over his shoulder. She tore at the neck of her dress with evident intention, and Blair begged Jean to take her away and provide her with what towels she wished.

"Well, I never!" began Aunt Jannet remonstratively.

"That is a mistake that has wrought infinite mischief, dear Aunt Jannet," he said. "Our work must begin inside, not outside. Meddle as little as possible with manners and customs or you do more harm than good."

"My goodness me! It's absolutely indecent for a woman to go about with nothing on but a towel. Don't tell me you allow them to eat one another, Kenneth!"

"Well, we break them off that as soon as we can. But in all these matters we have learned that it is highest wisdom to hasten slowly."

"Well, I—"

But here the brown girl came back, all smiles and modest grace, clad in red-fringed towels like the man, and even Aunt Jannet, in her heart, could find no fault with her appearance.

Then Blair called Matti, and, sitting on the deck by the new arrivals, he quietly commenced his approaches towards the conquest of the Dark Islands.

Briefly—in the telling, though very much otherwise in the extracting—this was what they learned. The man's name was Ha'o—which he pronounced Hacho, the ch as in loch—and the woman's Nai or Na-ee.

He was, he asserted, chief of that one of the Dark Islands which had been raided by the brig. A number of the islanders had been enticed on board with soft words and presents and then suddenly made prisoners. The ship had then apparently sailed, but that same night the village was burnt and he and the rest carried off.

It was not easy to make him understand what had induced these other white men to follow and bring them back. If they did really land him on his own island again—of which he was by no means sure—he would be their friend and brother. As for those others—looking venomously at the captain of the brig, who was sitting amidships in gloomy contemplation of the scurviness of fortune—he would ask nothing better than to eat them if the chance offered.

"You eat men, then?" asked Blair, through Matti.

"Of course. Why not? Properly cooked they are excellent eating"—or words to that effect.

And Aunt Jannet Harvey and the other ladies shuddered and wondered, for he did not by any means look the monster his words implied.

Blair tried hard to convey to him the idea that they had come from the other side of the world for the sole purpose of helping him and his people; but that was too much for him—he could not comprehend it.

He got tired of being questioned out of his depth, and strolled about the ship, examining everything attentively. The long brown steel gun, the revolving screw, the engines, and the smoke pouring out of the funnel claimed his chief attention. During the next few days he hung over the stern watching the revolving blades and the bubbling wake by the hour, with absorbed and puzzled face, and every now and then would lick his hand and hold it up to feel the air. There was little wind, for Captain Cathie had purposely run up into the calm belt to lessen the strain of the towage, but such as there was it was dead against them, and the brown man could not understand it. As to the gliding pistons and smooth-running wheels in the engine-room, they were white men's magic of the most virulent description, and Matti himself understood the business too little to be able to convey any clear idea of the connection between them and the never-resting screw astern.

For the rest, both the brown man and the girl found ample grounds for wonder in the farm-yard in the bows—the contemplative cow, the sullen-eyed young bull, the stolid goats, and the rooting piglets and their mother, and the cocks and hens in their coops, and the men's pet cat, which occupied their various bunks in turn, and accepted all their attentions with the utmost complacence and gave nothing in return. But of all the things that set sparks in the girl's wondering eyes, the crowning delight was the piano in the saloon and the little harmonium which was lashed alongside it.

She would sit with her ear pressed tight to the frame and her eyes like saucers as long as any one would play for her; and when her own slim brown finger touched one of the white keys and elicited due response she jumped with delight, and would have practised one-finger exercises of her own composition all day and all night. There were other wonders in reserve, but she had enough for the present, and more than enough.

"She has an ear for music," said Jean to her husband one night. "She was crouching by me during the singing, and I heard her humming the tune quite nicely."

"They are famous singers, some of them," said Blair. "I count a good deal on working up to the citadel through Eargate."

The Blackbirder captain was lodged in an empty cabin, and had his meals there. He had ample time for introspective musing, for none cared to associate with him.

In the middle of the first night Blair jumped up in a sweat of terror. The idea had suddenly occurred to him that the hostage might make a break for liberty or revenge by setting the ship on fire. He went hastily to the spare cabin and found him snoring comfortably. Nevertheless he sat there all night, and after that the man was never left alone, day or night, till they finally got rid of him.

Twice each day some of them, with Matti as interpreter, dropped down to the brig and saw the islanders duly fed and watered, and said a word or two of cheer to them. And day after day the sallow crew scowled across at the quiet ordered life on board the schooner—the pleasant, friendly relations, the morning and evening services on deck—and cursed sparks into its vicious eyes; but ventured no more because of the ever-present Winchesters and the black mouth of Long Tom which gaped hungrily at them whenever they looked that way.

Their weighted progress was slow. It was the evening of the sixth day before the distant peaks of the Dark Islands bit up through the setting sun, and on the morning of the seventh day they were steaming slowly for the entrance to the lagoon.

Ha'o and Nai had refused to lie down all night. All night long they had hung over the bows, peering into the darkness in a fever of anticipation which left them no words. When the flaming east lit up the giant peak they knew so well, they could scarce contain themselves. Cannibals they were and benighted heathen, but this was home, and there was hope in them and for them.

Captain Cathie, with admirable skill, and a couple of his whale-boats, humoured the brig in, stern foremost, since she had no steerage-way on her. He dropped her down the lagoon as close to the white sand spear as he deemed advisable, then bade them drop their anchor and loose the tow-rope, and heaved a sigh of content as his gallant little ship shook herself free of that most undesirable partnership.

He took up a position to seaward of the brig, and Blair, and Evans, and Ha'o, with Matti and the usual guard in attendance, went on board of her to discharge cargo.

It was a thing to remember, one of the high times of life that stand out in the past when other things have faded.

A great shout went up from the chaotic mass of brown men as the white-clad figures came down the ladder and Ha'o shouted the good news to them. He had been across each day with whoever was going, and Blair, watching carefully this corner-stone of his enterprise, had come to think well of him.

A thing to remember, indeed, as the brown figures came tumbling up the ladder in batches. They fairly scrambled over one another in their haste, and, after one wild glance round to make sure, flung themselves headlong into the familiar waters, and made straight for the shore, shouting breathlessly as they went, eager only to set foot on that white beach once more.

Blair had reckoned on carrying them ashore in the boats, but who would wait for boats when the sparkling water called?

That long string of urgently bobbing black heads from brig to shore—first-fruits of victory—spolia opima in very truth—was a sight none of them ever forgot. The Torches laughed aloud with enjoyment. Even the sullen-eyed Blackbirders watched with interest.

Ha'o stood among the white men with wonderful self-control. Instinct drew him to the water with the rest, but he would not. Even these few short days on the higher plane had not been without their effect. He had watched ceaselessly. He had seen much that was beyond him. For the first time in his life, he had come across a force greater than his own, which made for good and not for evil. There were stirrings within him which he did not understand, but the first expression of them made for restraint.

When the stream of brown bodies ceased pouring out of the hatch, and the last batch had leaped overboard with joyful shouts, Blair and the others climbed down into the empty dimness to make sure that all had gone. They found three lying with starting eyes, too weak to move and fearful that they had been forgotten. These they wrapped in abandoned mats and passed up on deck and lowered into one of the whale-boats. Then a flying visit to the Torch for Nai, and they sped to the shore.

It was only when they all stood on the white beach that Ha'o, shaking with excitement barely to be restrained, turned to Blair and, grasping his hand in his own two trembling ones, carried it to his forehead and said some words in a low voice.

Blair glanced at Matti for enlightenment.

"He says he is your man from this day, and will be to you as a brother," said Matti, and the white hand and the brown gripped firmly on the compact. Then Ha'o turned and walked rapidly towards the village, and they went with him.

So Ha'o of Kapaa'a became the Man's man's man. And the first sparks of light for the Dark Islands leaped from the match that set fire to the village thatch ten days before.

So good comes out of evil, and no man may safely say this is good and that is ill. For no man knows, save Him Who knows all things; and His ways are so very different from man's ways that wisdom and experience drive one only to the doing with one's might the thing that is in hand, in the faithful hope that He will round the corners and shape the work to its appointed end.

CHAPTER XIV

CLIPPING A BLACKBIRD

Before we proceed to other matters, let us get rid of the Blackbirder.

She lay like a black blot on the smooth swell of the lagoon, and till we are quit of her the place will not feel clean. Civilisation, as represented by the dismantled brig, was as foul a thing as any the Dark Islands could show—not excepting even the terrors of the feasting-places. For what the dark men did they did in their darkness, and what the yellow men did they did in their light, and condemnation goes with knowledge.

And as it was here, so it was elsewhere. Vicious civilisation gashed Nature with a broad red wound and trampled her to earth. Fortunately, in this case there was healing and reparation. But it was not always so.

Blair and Cathie had had ample time during the return voyage to arrange their plans, Blair's part in the discussions consisting chiefly of acting as brake to the captain's whirring wheels. For Captain Cathie, honest man, foresaw such certain trouble from letting the raiders go that he would have strained many points to put it out of their power ever to return.

But Blair would have none of it.

"I haven't a doubt that you are right, captain," he said, "but even these men have got to have their chance. If they do come back, they must take the consequences. We will deal with them then as may seem best."

So while Blair and Evans followed Ha'o towards the village, Captain Cathie was busy in his own way. With his long brown gun menacing the brig, he sent his other two boats over in charge of his mate and Stuart, with instructions to deport the yellow men to a tiny crown of rock where the wall of the reef had crept up a few feet higher than elsewhere. It was a precarious lodging at best and uncomfortably damp, for the great ocean rollers broke on the seaward side in ceaseless thunder, and their spray lashed up to heaven, and came crashing over into the lagoon, and the rock was always wet. Captain Cathie jocularly expressed the opinion that the yellow men would be none the worse for a bit washing, for not one of them looked as if he had known soap since he was a kiddie.

He sent by Stuart, on his own responsibility, the information that he was going to disinfect their ship, and that if they were not all out of it in ten minutes he would sink it with a shot between wind and water. The yellow men turned green with apprehension, grabbed their meagre belongings under the certain belief that they were leaving their ship for good and all, and did as they were bidden. Then, leaving the captain of the Blackbirder in strict custody, Cathie pulled over to the brig and proceeded to overhaul it with all the enjoyment of a humanitarian highwayman going through his victim's pockets.

Every bond and shackle they found was promptly tossed overboard. Every ounce of trade they could find—cloth, beads, knives, and so on, which might still be used for the enticement of unwary natives and the replenishment of a depleted exchequer—was annexed as salve for native wounds. Several rifles and revolvers, which the haste of the previous surrender, or malice prepense, had overlooked, were now included. Every keg of rum they could lay hands on was stove in and emptied into the lagoon, and when the captain was fairly satisfied that he had clipped the Blackbirder's wings, for this voyage at any rate, and, as he jocularly said, had given the yellow men a chance of practising teetotal principles for a spell, though he feared the effect would only be temporary, he returned to the Torch and sent his boats to bring back the prisoners from their damp roosting-place.

He explained to the gloomy-faced captain of the Blackbirder what he had done, and why, and sent him back to his ship with instructions to refit as quickly as possible, to take in what water he needed, and to get away without delay, lest the natives should take it into their heads to pay him in their own way for his maltreatment of them.

"And tell him, sir," he said to Stuart, "that if I'd had my way I'd have strung every man of them up to the yardarm, and if they ever come back that's what they may expect, and I'll be delighted to have a hand in it."

When Blair and the rest came on board, they reported the village still in ruins. No attempt had been made to rebuild it yet, and they had seen no other natives than those who had come ashore from the brig.

The atoll men and women had camped in a bunch among the ruined houses, by starting a fire with a borrowed match and proceeding to cook some taro from the adjoining fields. The Dark Island men had scattered among the hills to find their friends and relatives, and to tell them of their wonderful deliverance.

Under the compulsion of the grinning long gun the Blackbirders worked hard at their rigging, and the party on the Torch sat and watched them till the shadows chased the red glow of the sunset rapidly up the hills, and work was over for the day.

"It is very wonderful," was Blair's summing-up of the whole matter: "good once more comes out of evil. If the arranging of matters had been in our own hands, they could not have fallen more fortunately for us. In the ordinary course of things we might have been years in arriving at the position this catastrophe and its remedying have put us into. Ha'o and Nai will, I think, prove staunch friends. They know we desire nothing but their good. Through them we shall get all the rest by degrees."

"All I wish is that we'd hung those yellow blackguards, sir," said Cathie, with lingering regret. "It would only have been right common sense, after all."

"Hear, hear!" said Aunt Jannet Harvey.

"Well, well," said Blair. "It's generally easier to undo than to do. But our aim is life, not death. We shall have all we can do to put new life into our brown friends, without spending our energies and bruising our consciences by choking the old life out of our yellow enemies."

"All the same, sir, we'd have been safer for the future if those rascals were rolling at the bottom of the sea than floating quietly on top of it. If they don't come back here, they'll go somewhere else and play the same game."

"I'm afraid they will, captain; but all the same I don't see my way to hanging them. If they come back here, as they quite possibly may—"

"Will, sure," said the captain.

"Well, if they do it will be our duty to protect the sheep from the wolves."

"I'm half hoping they'll try it on," said Cathie. "Yon long gun would make fine play with 'em."

In the morning Blair and the other men went ashore again. The ladies begged to go too, but he thought it wiser to wait till they learned the minds of the rest of the islanders.

They found the atoll men busily at work running up shelters, and quite content with their new surroundings. This was a place of infinitely wider scope than their own circumscribed island, and they had no desire whatever to go back to it. Knowing how intense the racial hatreds were among the islands, Blair could only hope that Ha'o's influence might suffice for their protection.

He was wondering when any of the original inhabitants would turn up again, when he saw a straggling company descending the hill, and at the head of it Ha'o, easily recognisable by his costume of white towels.

He waved his hand at sight of them, and quickened his pace. As he drew near they saw that his face was very grim, and he began to speak so rapidly and energetically that Matti could only wait and absorb the sense of it without any attempt at translation.

"There is trouble," said Matti, turning to Blair as the other paused for breath. "In his absence, and thinking he was gone for good, his brother has become chief, and he will not give up his place."

"And what do the people say?" asked Blair, and Matti put the question.

"They are divided. There were some who were never contented, and there are some who always want change, and there are some who stand on one side to see which party is strongest. Those who were with me on the ship stay with me, and there are many others, but Ra'a"—Racha or Raka, his brother— "has also many. It will lead to trouble."

This was a quite unexpected development and obstacle. From his slight knowledge of island ways, Blair foresaw that it was a matter that might lead to constant strife. For there is no quarrel so bitter as a family quarrel, and the tribe is but the family on a larger scale.

"Come to the ship, Ha'o," he said, "and let us talk it over. Where is Nai?"

"She is with her people. She will come when I send for her. My other wives my brother has taken, but I do not want them."

"Is he likely to do anything unpleasant at once?"

"No; at present everything is—." And with his hands he indicated chaos.

The situation was a grave one in some respects, though still far better than it would have been had they landed entire strangers with all their footing to win.

It might even contain advantages, for Ha'o and his party would be driven by stress of circumstances still closer to them, and there was material enough to occupy them there for a long time to come.

Captain Cathie was for grasping this nettle again in such a way as to neutralise its sting.

"If we tackle them at once, Mr. Blair, we can knock the brother out and make things safe, and it'll maybe be the shortest cut in the end, and cost fewest lives. You know what these brown fellows are when they get to loggerheads among themselves. It's just Stewarts and Campbells over again, and no peace till one side or the other goes under."

Blair nodded.

"I know, captain; but, all the same, we can't begin by killing the men we want to convert. Gentle handling and patience may bring us to the appointed end. It may take longer, but the end, I think, will be the larger."

But Captain Cathie shook his head, and Aunt Jannet Harvey shook hers in unison.

"Some things are best nipped in the bud," said she, "and it seems to me that Mr. Ha'o has been very badly treated all round."

"Well, we've done our best for him, and we'll go on doing it, but we must do it in the way we think wisest."

Ha'o himself now struck in through Matti, and his question was the very natural one as to whether the white men, who had done so much for him, would continue to do so, and help him to recover his rights.

It took time and patience to explain to him that they would do everything they could without fighting, unless the other side attacked him, in which case they would help him and his people to defend themselves. Ha'o saw no use for the other side except to be killed—and possibly eaten. It was not possible as yet to make clear to him their object in coming to the islands. The root idea was beyond him. He had hoped with their help to smash the opposition out of hand, and was inclined to resent this, as it seemed to him, very lukewarm offer of defensive assistance. Blair, however, was at pains to explain, as far as was possible, that they had come not to fight—at which the brown man's eyes rested appreciatively on the long brown gun—but to teach him and his people better things than fighting, and that they would help him in every possible way—except, as Ha'o's face plainly showed, in this one way, for which he would willingly have foregone all the rest.

Blair showed him the tribute exacted from the Blackbirder, and told him the things were for himself and those who had been carried off with him, and the black eyes sparkled greedily.

Then Blair suggested that the first thing to do was to rebuild the village, and asked him to allot them land where they could build their own houses. At which Ha'o waved his hand regally over Kapaa'a and said, "Choose!"

They chose a spot at the head of the white sand spear, with the brush curving round behind, and the little river gurgling alongside. A dozen tall palms swung their crests above, in front lay the placid stretch of the lagoon, and beyond it the reef, and the white jets of foam, and the never-ending thunder of the breaking rollers.

By way of setting a good example to the islanders, and no less to impress upon the Blackbirders that they had come to stop, Captain Cathie got out and sent ashore the frames of the houses they had brought with them. One of the little steam-launches was got into working order, and before nightfall was chuffing merrily back and forth with load after load of necessaries, planks and beams and fittings; and what with the work on board the Blackbirder, and the traffic between the Torch and the shore, and the doings on the beach, the lagoon of Kapaa'a was livelier than ever it had been since time began. Deadlier it had often been, but this was the beginning of the new life, and the dawn came to the Dark Islands in such commonplace guise as doors and windows, and chairs and tables and bedsteads.

By Cathie's advice they built their houses on piles, with roomy platforms under which the fresh sea breezes could blow at will.

Every man who could be spared from the ship helped in the building, and the work went on apace. Blair and Evans and Stuart, stripped to shirts and trousers, carried and sawed and hammered with the rest, and spared themselves not at all. The ladies would have come too, but reluctantly obeyed orders, and stopped on board till the political horizon should become somewhat more determined.

Ha'o and his people, after watching the small beginnings of a work that was far beyond their understanding, turned to their own business. Blair had a quantity of spades and axes brought ashore, and gave them to Ha'o for his building operations, and the effect on their spirits, as their hands closed on the handles, was magical. They rushed to the woods to try them, and when the white men went along presently to see how they were going on, they found the village already getting into shape.

There had evidently been some argument with the atoll men, who had thought to establish themselves on the old site, but they had now drawn off, and were stolidly building shelters a short distance away, and regarding with envious eyes the new tools of the island men.

That was soon put right, and a supply of axes for themselves transformed them into an excited, chattering crew, without a grievance in the world. Food was plentiful, the taro swamp was there to their hand, coco-nuts abounded, they had fire and water: what more could any man want, unless it was a slice of brother man to add zest to the feast? And at present both they and brother man were much too busy to give the matter the necessary consideration.

It took the Blackbirder three days' hard work to clear away her damaged spars and refit sufficiently for the voyage. Her sulky master suggested a trip ashore to procure some new topmasts. Captain Cathie urged him to go, but expressed doubts as to the probability of his return; and on the morning of the fourth day, the launch having filled their water barrels for them, the Torch got up steam and towed her enemy through the opening in the reef and out to a fair offing, and then cast her off and lay watching till she was hull-down on the eastward horizon. And the very last thing the scowling crew saw—for that time, at all events—was the menacing black mouth of the long gun, and Captain Cathie standing patting its big brown breech affectionately, but in a most unpleasantly meaning way.

"Well, thank God we're rid of them at last!" said

Aunt Jannet Harvey with fervour, as the brig caught the breeze and drew slowly away.

"We shall see them again, ma'am," said Captain Cathie.

"I wish we'd scuttled them," said Aunt Jannet.

CHAPTER XV

WHERE THOU GOEST

The building operations were progressing apace, and so far they had caught no more than distant glimpses of the malcontents, as they crept cautiously about the hillsides to oversee what was going on below. The proximity of the white men in such force kept them from any expression of what might be in them, and Blair was not without hope that, if he could only get time to develop his plans and demonstrate clearly the advantages of the white alliance, they might still think better of it and come in.

Time, however, is what no man can count on. Cautious Captain Cathie, as soon as he had seen the Blackbirder fairly off, proceeded to "bolt the front door," as he said, by running a stout hawser with a kedge at each end across the opening in the lagoon. As this was buried by each incoming roller, it would inevitably overturn any boat running in on the swell, and he felt comparatively safe.

Nevertheless, he paced the deck for several nights to make safer still. For the Torch was still the greatest factor in the enterprise, and any accident to her would spell disaster to them all.

That first night he was not without his fears of a possible attempt from without.

"You never know where you are with rascals like yon, until you've seen 'em hanging for an hour at the end of a rope," said he. "It would be a mighty fine thing for them, and a mighty bad look-out for us, if they crept in and caught us napping." And more than once he stood for minutes at a time listening intently, under the impression that he heard the cries of drowning men above the rhythmic roar of the outer surges, and in the morning he looked eagerly about, but found nothing.

He was also somewhat surprised at the complete absence of native canoes, and had visions of such also creeping up in the darkness and carrying his ship by assault. But the canoes had mostly been smashed by the raiders, as a matter of precaution, when they enticed the natives on board, and the rest they had destroyed when they came ashore in the night, and the captain's fears were groundless.

The ladies were allowed ashore for a time each day to inspect the progress of their future homes, but they still slept on the schooner.

Aunt Jannet Harvey demanded of Blair how long that kind of thing was to go on, as they were all anxious to get to housekeeping again as soon as possible, and Blair could only tell her that they could not hasten developments, but that he hoped each day passed in peace might make for healing.

But the peace was suddenly broken. That which had befallen the head of the community had equally struck its tail. Just as Ha'o, supposed to be as good as dead, had been supplanted by Ra'a, so on a smaller scale had most of his companions in misfortune. It was a matter only of degree. The hurt was the same.

Yams and taro do not come to maturity in a day. The rescued ones were rebuilding the village on its old site, close to the taro fields. The rebels on the hills and the perchers on the fence wanted their share of the common goods. They ventured down by night, warily and in mortal fear of more than Ha'o and his men, to procure them, and the fat was in the fire.

At first it spluttered in hot words.

"We want our proper share of taro," said the hillmen, not without reason. "You went away"—which was a provocative way of putting it—"and left us to tend the fields, and now you come back and sit on them."

"The fields belong to the community. We are the community. Come back into it and you will share with us. Where are our wives?" was the answer.

Some few, such as cared little who ruled so long as their stomachs were filled, did come back, and Nai brought down a number of the women and children, her towel costume and her descriptions of the white men's wonders forming strong inducements to the others. But many stood out, and the arguments developed from words to blows. Ra'a's men came down in force by night to replenish their larders. Ha'o's men resisted. One of the former got his head smashed in by an axe, and the feud was complete.

Blair did his best to prevent the rupture, but it was beyond him. Ha'o was, not unnaturally, hot against the usurper and his followers, and it was all the white men could do to persuade him from attempting a coup-de-force for the full rehabilitation of his fortunes. Under Blair's forcible arguments, and a grievous shortage of weapons, he agreed to postpone any active movement till his village was rebuilt. Then, when time lay on his hands, Blair knew that it would be next to impossible to restrain him. He hoped, however, that opportunity might arise which would afford a chance of intervention with some hopes of success.

Meanwhile skirmishes went on almost nightly, and there came a time at last when two of Ha'o's men, in repelling an attempt on the taro fields, were speared and their bodies carried off.

In the morning Ha'o came up, wearing his grimmest face.

"They have killed my men," he said, through Matti. "Now I go to kill them."

Blair had been considering the matter ever since the report reached him, and he had made up his mind what to do.

To understand Kenneth Blair fully you must bear in mind all that he had gone through, and the effect it could not fail to have upon him.

Once in his life, in the face of imminent death, he had flinched and he had never forgiven himself. To all the world outside he could be tender and forbearing. To himself he was harder than iron.

He would condone in another what he would never permit in himself. In the intensity of his feeling on this matter even his strong common sense was liable to be thrown somewhat off its centre. His only fear was of himself, and in that fear he was liable to choose the hardest and most dangerous path, lest a smoother one should prove but a pitfall to his duty.

In his somewhat morbid dread of doing too little he was constantly in danger of doing too much. He was quite aware of it, and he held himself tightly. But where two ways offered, it was almost inevitable that he should choose the more dangerous and difficult. It was a weakness, perhaps, but, after all, he was only human, and no man is perfect.

Just as the soldier on whom has rested an imputation of lack of nerve will, when the chance offers, rush to seemingly certain death in order to wipe off the reproach, so Kenneth Blair. It was the spirit of the Six Hundred at Balaclava over again, save that, indeed, in their case their courage had never been called in question, but only their utility.

And so, when Ha'o came up, thirsting for his brother's life, Blair said quietly—

"This matter must be settled without shedding of blood. I will go and see Ra'a, and will do my best to persuade him either to come in or to leave us in peace."

"He will kill you," said Ha'o briefly.

"I hope not. We shall see."

"He hates the white men. The hardest thing he has against me is that I ever had any dealings with those others."

"Those men were yellow, I will show him what white men are."

"He will kill you," said Ha'o once more.

"I hope not," was all the reply he got.

When the rest heard of his undertaking they also tried hard to dissuade him from it—all except Jean, who sat silent and thoughtful.

"It's risky," said Captain Cathie, with a gloomy shake of the head.

"Few good things come without risk, captain—besides, I don't believe it's as risky as you imagine."

"It's simply suicidal," said Aunt Jannet Harvey. "It's just throwing yourself away, Kenneth, and spoiling all your great plans, to say nothing of Jean's life."

"I shall go too," said Jean quietly.

"You, Jean?" said Blair, with a catch in the throat and a sudden weight at the heart.

"Yes, dear. If you go, I go. If it is death for you it is death for me in any case, and I would sooner it was together."

A terrible temptation this to choose the easier path—on her account. What right had he to drag her life into so great a danger? For imminent danger there was, though he had made light of it.

He halted, and she saw it, and understood much of what was in him.

"Don't hesitate one moment on my account, Ken. I must go. It is possible my being with you may help. It will show them, at all events, that we mean them no ill."

"We are in God's hands," he said quietly, but was visibly disturbed at her insistence.

Stuart and Evans also strove with him, but with no better effect.

"The peace must be kept, if it is possible," he said. "And this seems to me a possible way to it. I would sooner my wife had stopped behind, but I quite understand her point of view. And—we are as safe there as here."

"You've no objection to my firing a blank round or two, Mr. Blair?" asked Captain Cathie.

"What's the idea, captain?"

"Just to impress them with the fact that we're here behind you, sir. A bang or two from the big gun will maybe have as big an effect as anything you can say to them."

"Well, I see no objection. All we want is to keep the peace. The big gun may impress them, as you say."

"You wouldn't take a dozen of the men with you, would you sir?" asked the captain insinuatingly.

But Blair shook his head at that.

"That, I fear, would hardly carry the impression that I want to make. I look on all these people as my parishioners. Sooner or later, please God, they will be. But we must win them, captain; we can't force them."

He walked the deck alone that night, long after all but the watch had retired, and thought and thought.

And at thought of Jean going into the peril of the morrow the temptation was strong at times to find some other and less dangerous way—for her sake. For himself he would not think twice. For her—ah! for her he would think many times. And, after all, had he the right to persist in his own way, even though he believed it to be the right way, since it meant undoubted danger to her?

But he found in such thoughts the visible cloven hoof of avoidance, compounding, cowardice, and resolutely shut down upon them. For her sake he could have wished that she had been content to stay quietly on board, and let him face the danger alone. But duty called him with a clear voice, and go he must, whatever came of it.

And so it came that, very early the next morning, Kenneth Blair and his wife Jean set out on a somewhat perilous journey. And with them went Matti, the Samoan. And Matti by no means relished the undertaking, yet compassed a fairly stout face, since it was a matter of duty and a tangible business, with nothing ghostly about it, as yet at all events, though as to what it might presently develop into he had his own very grave doubts.

They were surely as peaceful-looking an embassage as ever sought a distrustful enemy. They were all in spotless white, and their only visible weapons, beyond Jean's green-lined white sunshade, were some small bundles containing presents, and a new axe and spade carried by Matti. Blair, indeed, had a revolver in his hip pocket, but it was only there because Jean was there. Had he been alone it would have stayed behind. It was, no doubt, somewhat of an anomaly after his confident "We are as safe there as here" of the previous night. But he was very human, and, as I have said, no more perfect than you or I, though an infinitely finer specimen than either of us.

As they quitted the ship, the long gun thundered out over their heads, and the noise of it bellowed up into the hills, and clanged to and fro in the valleys. And when they touched the shore it bellowed again, and went on bellowing at intervals like the threatening little monster it was.

Ha'o met them at the landing with some of his people, and shook his head gloomily at their prospects. He offered to accompany them as far as possible; but, as he bitterly said, they had not a spear among them, nothing but the axes Blair had given them, and axes are of little use against spears and poisoned arrows.

But Blair would not hear of it. He begged him to keep his people at their work as usual, and went on quietly through the disputed taro fields, up through the yam plantations and banana groves, and stood for a moment to look back over the lagoon, with the shapely little ship at her anchorage, and the bursts of white foam along the reef behind. A puff ball of white smoke fluffed out from her deck as they looked, and the roar of it went past them into the hills. It was not by any means impossible that they looked on it all for the last time. And Kenneth Blair's heart was not light as he took Jean's arm through his own and pressed it close to his side, and felt the trustful pressure of her arm in reply.

They understood one another fully. They had said all that needed to be said. In this and in all they were one; and if this meant death, they had no other wish than that it should be together.

"You are very brave, Jean."

"I am where I would be, and as I would be, Ken. We are in God's hands."

"Amen!" he said, and lifted his hat and led her round the shoulder of the hill.

They did not know where they might come across Ra'a.

"You will find him," Ha'o had said meaningly.

So they climbed on and up, through tangled thickets of hibiscus and branching matpandanus, under grey-boled palms, along bare patches of rock, certain that scores of dark eyes were watching them, wondering when and how their journey would end.

The hills had echoed many times to the voice of the long gun, when, from a clump of brush in front, a couple of bristling warriors rose suddenly and barred their way. They carried long, thin, venomous spears and heavy bows, and each had a bundle of arrows at his thigh.

"Aoha!" said Blair quietly, and they stared grimly, first at him, and then, and longer, at Jean. She sat down on a rock and opened her fan and began to use it with an equanimity which covered a jumping heart.

The climb had been somewhat exhausting, her face was radiant with colour and a great wistful expectancy, and her eyes shone like southern stars. She was a goodly sight to any man. To these brown men, who had never in their lives seen anything like her, she must have seemed almost more than human. After an appreciative glance at Matti's axe and spade, they stared at her with stolid insistence.

"Tell them we have come to speak with Ra'a. We bring him presents," said Blair to Matti, and a conversation of clips and jerks ensued, and in the result the brown men turned and led the way into the bush.

They came at last to a number of houses which had a hasty and temporary look about them, and were surrounded instantly by a buzzing crowd of men, women, and children, Jean again the centre of attraction, and bearing it, as before, with surprising equanimity.

They almost mobbed her, and shouted their comments aloud from one to another. Her sunshade, her fan, her dress, her face, her hair, her hands, every bit of her was a new sensation, and they made the most of it.

Then sudden silence fell, as a tall man strode through the lane they made before him, and stood in front of the strangers.

"You are Ra'a?" asked Blair of him direct.

"I am Ra-ch-ch-ch-a!" and his raucous name sounded worse in his own throat than it had ever sounded to them before; and as he said it, so it seemed to fit him.

He was tall and well made, evidently younger by some years than Ha'o, but his face was truculent and his eyes quick-glancing and shifty.

They rested, however, on Jean, and under other circumstances, and from a civilised man, Blair would have resented the look.

"What do you want?" asked Ra'a harshly.

And, through Matti, Blair answered him—

"We want peace between you and Ha'o"—and at the very mention of his brother the other scowled— "and between your people and his."

"It is you who have made the trouble. Why did you bring him back?"

"If it had been you we would have brought you back just the same."

"Ha'o is a fool to have dealings with white men."

"Those others were not white men, they were yellow. They are not of our tribe. We, too, hate the things they do, and we have come to stop them."

"You are all the same. If you hate them, why did you not kill them?"

"We do not kill if we can help it. If they come again, we may have to kill them."

"Why is that noise?" as the voice of Long Tom bellowed in the hills once more.

"It is the voice of my big canoe."

"It is only a voice. It does no harm."

"When I choose. You saw the other big canoe's masts? It did that with twice speaking."

"What do you want?" asked Ra'a once more.

"We have come from the other end of the world, where the people are all white, to try and be of use to you."

"We do not want you. We do quite well."

"There are many things you do not know, many things you have not got. Axes, spades," and he laid them down at the brown man's feet, "and cloth, and beads, and fish-hooks, and knives"; and he opened the bundles and gave them to him, and the black eyes round about snapped greedily. "Very many things we have, and we would share them with you. But we must have peace. If you will make things as they were before, we will share all these among you, and many more. It is far better than killing one another."

There was a visible inclination in the crowd towards a share in the good things, and Ra'a saw it and countered quickly. The man was a savage and brutalised, but he did not lack brain.

"We do not need your gifts. We can take them—all you have."

"You cannot take them. My big canoe could blow you all to pieces. But it has come to fight for you, not against you, and when it has done fighting it will go back and bring many more things for you. But it must be in peace."

Ra'a, whatever else he was, was a diplomat. Truculent he was without doubt, treacherous if it served him, and his word was probably of small account; but such things are not unknown in even more accomplished diplomatic circles.

He saw the inclination of his people, and that he must go with the tide.

"Give us our share of the things and we will be satisfied."

"You shall have your share if it is peace. There must be no more killing."

"The taro and the yams belong to us also?"

"Certainly. We will divide equally. If you will draw a line, we will draw a line, and you and your people will keep to your side, and Ha'o and his people will keep to his side."

"We will draw the line and tapu it. When will you send the things?"

"When the line is drawn. Will you come and draw it now?"

"You will go—and you," he pointed to two of his men. "You will put in tapu sticks and bring back what the white man gives you. Who is the woman?" staring hard at Jean, who had managed to keep an unruffled face in spite of the inquisition to which the women were subjecting her—touching her hands, her face, her hair, and the puzzling appointments of her dainty toilet. She had even induced one mother to let her pat the head of one brown mite, who was mumbling its fingers after reluctant teeth and stared at her with big round eyes.

"She is my wife."

"What is she wanting?"—a question evidently inspired by Jean's Miss Inquisitive look, which showed strongly at times and was much to the fore under the strain of the present interview.

"She is wanting everything," said Blair, with a smile. "It is probably that brown baby at present."

"She can have it. Is she hungry?"

"I don't think she is hungry, and she would not take the baby from its mother."

"Is she white all through?"

"White all through," said Blair.

"Have you any more in the big canoe?"

"They are all married—except one."

"I will marry her. How many coco-nuts will you take for her?" and he stared appreciatively at Jean.

"We do not sell our women. You would have to ask her yourself."

And at last they got away without further compromising Aunt Jannet, and very gratefully they went back by the way they had come, with full, yet lightened hearts. For the way, though it had opened before them, and now, to look back upon, seemed neither very difficult nor very dangerous, had been a perilous one, and one where death might have opened at their feet at any moment.

They went in silence with over-full hearts. Blair did not in the slightest delude himself with the idea that he had settled the matter at one stroke. He was quite prepared to find the agreement turn out but a temporary one, but it was a step towards the light to have arrived at any understanding whatever.

He was not surprised, also, to find Ha'o anything but satisfied with the arrangement. He would have preferred wiping out Ra'a and the malcontents, and settling the business at once on a sound and final basis.

With infinite difficulty Blair succeeded in showing him that those others had rights as well as himself, even though they had wronged him, and tried hard to inspire him with his own hope that matters would eventually work out for the best.

Ha'o, however, knew better.

"Their hearts are like this," he said, laying his hand on a length of twisted creeper dangling from an adjacent tree. "They are as grasping as a convolvulus for the water. They will take all you will give them, and they will keep the tapu just as long as it suits them." And he said to himself, "But by that time we shall perhaps be ready for them"; while Blair was thinking, "Every approach they allow us to make is a point gained."

The taro fields and yam plantations and banana groves were soon roughly divided off in a fair equality, and sticks with plaited palm leaves set up to warn off trespassers from either side. Then, with the idea of impressing them to the utmost, Blair invited the two plenipotentiaries to accompany him on board the big canoe to get the things he was to give them.

To this they demurred at first, though obviously desirous, and it was only after much argument among themselves that they at last agreed, and then only on condition that the white woman stopped on shore till they were brought safely back.

They stepped gingerly into the steam-launch at last, and eyed her bustling, unaided progress with obvious but well-concealed amazement. They were shown over the ship, the big gun was fired for them at close quarters, they inspected the farmyard and the cat, and they finally went home laden with gifts, and with new impressions enough to set their brains spinning and their tongues wagging for a month to come. And it is not likely that their stories lost anything in the retailing.

CHAPTER XVI

SAWDUST AND SHAVINGS

"Aunt Jannet," said Blair, as they sat in great relief and content discussing the day, when their visitors had left, "we had an offer for you this morning."

"An offer?—for me, Kenneth? Whatever do you mean?"

"A brown gentleman desires to correspond with a white lady with a view to matrimony. He wanted to know what we would take for you in coco-nuts."

"In coco-nuts indeed!" and Aunt Jannet bridled red. "And who was the impudent fellow?"

"Our enemy, our host, Mr. Ra'a. Jean made such an impression on him that I fear the brown ladies' noses will be permanently out of joint."

"H'mph!" with a snort of disgust. "He'd better keep out of my reach."

"I told him he'd have to ask you himself."

"I'd like to see him."

"A hint to that effect will bring him along hotfoot, I've no doubt. The matter is worth consideration," he said, with an assumption of weightiness. "Royal alliance—union of opposing factions—peace secured—a very good solution of our difficulties. Say, Aunt Jannet! will you sacrifice yourself for the good of the community?"

"Get along with you," said Aunt Jannet. "No naked brown cannibals for me."

The ice being broken with the factious ones, Blair and Stuart and Evans, with Matti still necessary as interpreter, though they were all rapidly picking up words and phrases of the island tongue, paid Ra'a several visits and did their utmost to strengthen the slim foundations of peace.

Ha'o and his people, however, declined any active intercourse with the rebels, and never ceased to warn the white men to be on their guard, asserting that their present amenableness was only assumed and would be thrown off as soon as no more was to be got by it. Blair judged that likely enough, but gave no sign of it, and treated the others as though he believed them in every way worthy of confidence. And Ha'o and his people meanwhile went on steadily replenishing their houses, and constructing the weapons without which they felt but half men and wholly insecure.

The mission-houses were completed and furnished. The farmyard was transferred from the bows of the Torch to suitable premises ashore, and what with the discontented bellowings of John Bull—who was always wanting something he hadn't got, though what it was neither he nor any one else could make out—and the mellower remonstrances of his more thoughtful consort, and the satisfied gruntings and squeakings of the delighted piglets and their mother, and the bleating of the goats, and the crowings and cluckings of cocks and hens, and the gabbling of geese in the river pools, the little settlement began to assume a most home-like appearance.

The ladies rejoiced in the feel of solid earth once more, and discovered endless delights in the nearer woods and along the beach. Limits, however, had to be placed on their wanderings, till assurance of good intent on the part of the outsiders was made doubly sure or proved entirely worthless.

Their nearest neighbours were the atoll community. These, not unnaturally, felt somewhat doubtful as to the permanence of their security among the discordant elements around them, and looked anxiously to the white men for protection. Left alone they would undoubtedly have been slaughtered and eaten out of hand, for human flesh was still the choicest dish where the only other variations from a vegetarian diet were occasional wood-pigeons, paraquets, and an unreliable choice of fish.

So far as Ha'o and his people were concerned, the atoll men were safe enough for the present and until cause might arise. They had been bed-fellows in misfortune and had shared a common deliverance, and so they were allowed to work beside the others in the taro swamp and to take their allowance of the fruits of the earth.

But there was a spirit of fear and distrust abroad—the fear that walks by night and makes light sleepers in palm-thatched houses, and no man went abroad after dark if he could help it.

With no little difficulty Blair succeeded in getting into communication also with the fourth community in the neighbourhood—the sitters on the fence, who were naturally at odds with all the others and would have fared badly but for their numbers, and for the hope each side had of eventually drawing them into their own folds.

They were perhaps more dangerous to approach even than Ra'a. For Ra'a was one, and his men obeyed his words. But these outlanders were many, and each man did what seemed right in his own eyes, and kept on terms with his neighbour and the community simply from motives of safety. In going among them, therefore, the risks were multiplied. They took all that was offered, however, and promised anything that was required of them in hopes of more.

But, obviously, four more or less distinct communities in one district were at least three too many. It was like having four savage dogs at large in one small back yard, and the proper thing to do was to get some of them to move.

Captain Cathie, coasting down the lagoon in the launch, had reported several fine wide valleys opening up into the hills, and Blair determined to try to induce some of the others to move farther down the coast and start fresh settlements there.

So far as Cathie had seen—and he was much too cautious to land until he knew more about what he might meet ashore—these valleys seemed unoccupied and capable of profitable occupation.

But Ha'o, when the idea was mooted, only shook his head mysteriously, and said they would never go there. No one lived there. No one ever had lived there. Farther down there were scattered communities, but the men rarely came up this way because they had made a practice of eating them whenever they got the chance. Over the mountains also there were villages, exclusive for the same reason.

And when Blair suggested the idea to Ra'a and the others, and offered to assist them in laying out taro fields and yam plantations, he was met in the same way. He could get nothing more out of them. The subject was so evidently distasteful that he determined to go and find out for himself, if possible, what the objectionable features were.

And so, very early one morning, he set off in one of the whale-boats, with Matti and Stuart and four men, and they pulled quietly along round the great frontlet of the hills till they came to the first opening into the hinterland, some five miles from the settlement.

Keeping a sharp look-out, they ran in on a fine white shell beach, and took cautious way up a wide valley from which the hills rolled back in long sweeping slopes, well bushed, and thick with palms. Gay flights of paraquets flashed in and out of the bushes, and the soft crooning of multitudinous wood-pigeons was like the humming of bees in a summer garden. A broad stream flowed through the valley, widening into silvery pools and glittering over broken shallows.

"It's an ideal place," said Blair. "What on earth has kept them out of it?"

They passed cautiously on through the tangled undergrowth. In front was the sound of falling waters, an intermittent drenching splash, now heard, now lost, as though a raincloud burst and passed and came again; otherwise a wide and perfect silence, which the droning of the doves seemed but to accentuate.

Through dense tangles of lemon hibiscus, and crowding paw-paws, and stilted pandanus, and the gleaming boles of the palms, they saw the valley widen into a great arc, and caught glimpses of mighty walls of rock which marked the end of it. And presently they were standing below, and gazing up in awed amazement.

In the shadow of the cliff, with their backs to it and their faces to the sea, sat a row of gigantic stone figures, gazing out In solemn silence through the slow-waving tops of the palms, the ephemeral palms which had grown and died in countless generations, and had crept gradually nearer and nearer, since those grim figures first sat down there, with their backs to the cliff and their faces to the sea.

So huge were they that the gazers felt themselves pigmies in comparison. Each grave head bent slightly forward as though listening intently for something that should come up from the sea, and the great stone hands were crossed reverently on the massive stone breasts.

From the sheer edge of the cliff above leaped streams of sparkling water, which broke in mid-air, and swung to and fro in the breeze like veils of gauze, and swept constantly over the seated figures, and wrapped them in fragmentary rainbows.

In their grim everlasting expectancy the great stone gods were very terrible to look upon, even with the eyes of understanding. More than once the gazers found themselves glancing fearfully over their shoulders towards the sea, lest perchance the long-delayed answer to that unspoken questioning might be coming. The sudden confrontation with these mighty relics of a long-vanished civilisation conjured up thoughts which bated their words to whispers.

"This accounts for it," said Blair softly. "What an amazing sight in a cannibal island! What do you make of it, Stuart?"

Stuart had been eyeing the monster nearest him with keenly critical eyes.

"Peruvian, I should say. Of the time of the Incas—or perhaps earlier still. Yes, earlier probably. I see no suns. This is mighty curious, you know. The present natives cannot be descended from them. They are pure Polynesians. And yet"—following out his own train of thought—"I'm not so sure. Ha'o and Nai and some of the others show traces of something more. I have often wondered about it. This may explain. These"—nodding at the silent figures—"or their makers, fled their country, or perhaps got blown across, and founded a new civilisation here. Then the old race ran to seed and got lost among the dark men, and ages afterwards their cousins from the mainland come across to kidnap them."

"Odd enough to think of," said Blair, "and likely enough to be true. What were these figures for, do you suppose? Worship?"

"Worship, sacrifice. Down in the brush there we shall probably find the remains of their houses."

And they did, all overgrown and barely discernible, but ruins without a doubt, and of a city of great buildings. By dint of peeling off the superincumbent growths of the ages they even laid bare a piece of wall, huge squared blocks from which the creeping mosses and lichens had long since eaten out the mortar.

"We shall never get them to live here, that's certain," said Blair. "The place is alive with ghosts for them. It would be an uncommonly safe place for a mission-station, if safety were the only thing. But it's too far from the parish. I think we can use it, however," he nodded thoughtfully, with some of his far-reaching schemes in view. "How those little pigs would enjoy those big paw-paws!"

They rambled about the valley, charmed with its wealth of fruit and flower, gathered quantities of each as evidences of their visit, and pulled back home.

Every one was on fire at once to go and view the wonders of the valley.

"To-morrow we will carry over a pair of goats and half a dozen piglets and some geese. They will have rare times there. If they don't burst themselves, they will multiply rapidly. By the time we have educated our friends here to better taste in the matter of eating, the larder will be stocked. It is better for them to hunt pigs and goats than men. And the wilder the pigs and goats the better. They will carry their own sauce with them," said Blair.

"It's the very place I've dreamed of since I was six years old," said Aunt Jannet, shedding her years. "Girls! we'll go over to-morrow, with the geese and the goats and the piglets, and have a scramble and a rummage."

Which they did, and found even more than the men. For Jean, at cost of a wetting, discovered a narrow entrance behind one of the figures, and inside it a winding stone staircase which led up into its head, and found that through the eyes of the god she could see all that went on below.

And one of the things she saw was Aunt Jannet Harvey wandering amazedly in front of the great stone figures; and then in a moment the earth opened and swallowed her up. For the good lady had stepped on a carpet of beautiful green moss, and the carpet gave way beneath her and precipitated her into a chamber of horrors full of skulls and dead men's bones, whence she was extricated with difficulty and in a state of extreme nervous tension by the men from the boat. Aunt Jannet's taste for exploration was dulled somewhat by the incident, and they went back home promising to return another day.

The goats, pigs, and geese entered into their new possession with delighted gabblings, bleatings, squeakings, and proved forthwith that they could look after themselves without any outside assistance.

Meanwhile, the two nearer-home communities had been taking their first timid steps towards the light, in the very practical shape of elementary lessons in carpentry. The white men's tools, in the skilled hands of the ship's carpenter, appealed strongly to them. Their various uses were speedily grasped—the tools also, unless he kept his eyes about him, as John MacNeil very soon found out. He was inclined to wrath and the bestowal of hard names, but it was simply human nature in its most natural form, and he learned to circumvent them by using only one tool at a time and never letting it out of his hand till he put it back into safety with the others. The driving of nails, especially when they were allowed to do it themselves, marked epochs in their lives and on their thumbs. Screws and hinges were revelations to them, the saw and the plane perpetual wonders, the grindstone an endless delight.

Blair watched them quietly, showed them the uses of the various things, let them experiment for themselves, and was satisfied that his sawdust and shavings would blossom into fruit. Their interest was excited, they were taking in new ideas, more in a day than hitherto in a generation; the rest would follow.

CHAPTER XVII

FIRST FRUITS

Aunt Jannet Harvey's ideas of missionary work and methods differed essentially from Kenneth Blair's.

She wanted to be up and doing all the time. She was anxious for visible fruit before the seed was fairly into the ground. In spite of the practical common-sense which she brought as a rule to the ordinary affairs of life, she was, in this matter, like a child with its first garden, in danger of retarding by her very anxiety for progress. She was inclined to be for ever hauling up the tiny shoots to see how the roots were getting on. Or, to be more exact still, she was like a child placed suddenly in charge of an overgrown patch with instructions to reduce it to order. And Aunt Jannet's ideas ran to such strenuous loppings and bindings and weedings, that the timid brown women and round-faced, pot-bellied youngsters fled, white-eyed and panting, whenever they caught sight of her.

This greatly distressed the good lady, and served only to confirm her views as to the urgent necessity for prompt and radical measures, just as flight from a school-board officer but serves to accentuate the chase.

She wanted the women and children clothed and taught and transformed into the outward semblance of civilised beings at once. She wanted a church built, and a school. She wanted to teach the women sewing and decency, and the children their letters and manners.

And Blair, with his wider knowledge and experience, had to put his foot down on every suggestion she made, and, gently and good-humouredly as he tried to do it since he knew the warm heart that was at the bottom of it all, found himself in constant collision with her.

"Example first, Aunt Jannet," was his constant text, "then precept. It's not the slightest use thinking of a church or a school yet. They'll come all right when we're ready for them. And, really, you must not try to dress any of those women and children again. You'll kill them."

"But they are so—so terribly naked, Kenneth."

"Of course they are, and so they have been for thousands of years, their forbears at all events, and you might just as well begin giving them poison as insist on clothing them. If you want to kill them, clothe them. If you want them to live, just let them go as they are."

"But the men—"

"Now you just leave the men to us. If you good ladies will just keep on at your own proper work, and let these big brown children watch you and see the pleasant results, you will be doing the very best thing possible for them. Make friends with them, pick up all the words you can lay hold of, and, in fact, get in touch with them all round as quickly as possible. But we must lead them; we can't drive them."

His own example was an inspiration to them all. Evans and Stuart seconded him loyally, and by degrees the ladies, who one and all, Jean included, sympathised considerably with Aunt Jannet in her not unnatural discrimination in favour of clothing, desisted from their well-meant efforts and grew accustomed to the scant attire of their brown friends.

They had no lack of personal cleanliness to combat, for which "Thank goodness!" said Aunt Jannet more than once. "If they let you see plenty of skin, it is at all events clean skin. If they'd stop rubbing themselves all over with that nasty rotten coco-nut oil and wear some decent clothes, I wouldn't have a fault to find with them—except in their eating and a few other things."

The mission-settlement lay on the left bank of the little river which ran through the spear of white sand at the head of the bay. On the other side of the river the mountains where Ra'a lived rolled up, shoulder on shoulder, till the farther ones were lost to sight. Behind the mission the ground lay level for a space, where the valley came down to the sea, and here were masses of coco-palms and a great tangle of undergrowth, and farther up, past the village, were the disputed taro fields, and the yam and banana plantations.

On the mission side of the river, behind the level lands, another great hill flung one rough protecting arm into the sea a quarter of a mile beyond the houses. The great ridge, full of cracks and cavities, as though it had broken in its fall, shot right into the lagoon, and the barrier reef started from its outermost point. On the other side the great waves roared everlastingly up a white shell beach, but landing there was impossible, as no boat built by man could survive the tumult of the surf.

This was the island bathing-place, and here, all day long, men, women, and children were slipping and tumbling like seals in the creaming rollers. They shot deftly through the combers before they broke, and away out to sea, then came skimming back stretched flat on their swimming-boards, sitting on them, standing on them, marvels of grace and beauty, with shouts and laughter and life's tide at its fullest.

It was their most rational enjoyment, and the finest possible outlet for their activities. It kept them healthy and it kept them clean.

It also led to friction between the various factions, just as the taro fields had done. This was the only place available for surf-swimming for many miles on either side. Until the late troubles it had been common to all. Now the nearest dwellers, Ha'o's people and the atoll men, monopolised it, and when the others desired to join the sport they were received with taunts and jibes which came quickly to blows, and Blair had to adopt the rôle of peacemaker once more.

Ha'o and his men would have kept the others from the surf, just as they would have kept them from the taro swamps. But Blair would not have it. He reasoned with them, talked to them and at them, in a voluble mixture of Samoan, Kapaa'an, and English, and made them understand what he meant if many of his words were beyond them.

In a pow-wow of this kind, when his feelings ran far in advance of his tongue, he could not wait for Matti's plodding interpretation, but dashed at it himself, and surprised and tickled his hearers with his white-hot vehemence.

They were mighty arguers and had the advantage of the language, but he brought them to his will by sheer force of insistence. He had right on his side, and he would have them to it also. They grumblingly yielded the shore on certain days of the week, and Blair rejoiced in this further sign of growth and progress.

Meanwhile, however, he knew that they were busily at work on the preparation of arguments of a more forceful description, and he had little hope of reaching his ultimate goal without these coming into use. So small a spark might set them all aflame that it was useless attempting to forecast it or to stifle it in advance. All he could do was to endeavour, by every means in his power, to build up among them the new influences which he and his friends represented, so that when the time came they should count as factors in the case.

The houses in the village were all more or less laughable imitations of the mission-house, for they were as imitative as monkeys, so long as imitation imposed no restrictions, and at sight of the white men's houses they pulled down their own and began again with these as models. And when they got to boat-building, the canoes of their fathers were no longer good enough for them. Their new boats must follow the lines of the white men's boats also, to Blair's great satisfaction, since it entailed mighty labours, and while they were busy they were safe from outbreaks on side issues.

At the mission-station all worked alike; the men breaking up the ground for plants and vegetables, and attending to the live stock, the women doing the housework and cooking. All day long the house was surrounded by an inquisitive throng, which watched keenly and commented fully and frankly on everything it saw, and with whom the busy workers carried on disjointed conversations, and picked up native words in exchange for English ones, amid shouts of laughter at the multitudinous mistakes on either side.

Morning and evening the white men held a short service, and the brown men and women caught up the hymn tunes and hummed them lustily, with no slightest idea of what they meant, but with none the less enjoyment.

The small harmonium had been brought ashore and was a huge delight, and for a time a mighty mystery to them. Jean played it, and they could not understand why it should sing when she touched the keys and remain mute when they did the same. Then one cunning fellow, by dint of persistent watching, caught sight of her feet moving beneath her dress, and with an excited "Hi!" laid himself flat on his stomach with his nose at her heels, and the mystery was solved.

The novel tunes ran in their heads, some even of the incomprehensible words, and it was strange indeed to hear a naked brown man chopping away at a slab of timber and singing lustily, "Kown 'im! kown 'im! kown 'im! kown 'im law-daw-faw!" Later on they heard that tune amid still stranger surroundings, for the lilt and swing of it captured their fancy, and they were at it morning, noon, and night—building their boats, working in the taro fields, sweeping along on the tops of the rolling combers, sitting outside their houses when the day's work was done.

There was a hopeful, homely sound in it, and those who sang with understanding hoped fervently that in time the others might do so too.

They were very children, these brown men and women, in their light-heartedness, quarrelsomeness, and lack of restraint. Whatsoever seemed good in their eyes at the moment, that they did, regardless of consequences. Only at times, the innate savagery showed through, and then they were to be feared. Like hot-headed children who had never known restraint, there was no knowing what they would do, except that it would certainly be something unpleasant to the offending one and possibly to the bystanders.

They were very magpies, too, in the snapping up of treasure-trove.

"We won't call it stealing," said Blair soothingly to John MacNeil, the carpenter, who was complaining for the twentieth time of missing tools. "They don't look on it in that light, you see, John."

"Thievin' blayguards!" said John dourly, minus another tool.

"We'll teach them better soon. Meanwhile, leave nothing lying about if you can help it, and give them no opportunities. They are so in the habit of picking up anything they want that it's become part of their nature."

"Juist thievin' blayguards! I'd clour their heads if I could catch 'em at it, but it'd need eyes all round to be upsides with 'em."

And when, now and again, John did catch them at it, and proceeded to clour their heads, they took it quite good-humouredly, and surrendered their prize with a grin, and bore no malice.

It was a strange right-about-face in the lives of the ladies, and many a laugh they had over it.

"Jean, my dear," said Aunt Jannet one day, when all four of them were busily washing and wringing out clothes at the mouth of the river, "this is a change from Hyde Park, isn't it?" At which, and the incongruity of associations which sprang up in them at her words, they all broke into laughter.

Straight in front lay the placid stretch of the lagoon, pulsing softly to the broken influx through the gap in the reef; beyond it, the crisp, white leaping hedge of foam along the reef itself; beyond that, the infinite expanse of sea and sky, and the far-away white line where upper and lower blue met and kissed: on the one side, the bold green shoulders of the mountain, feathered with slow-swinging palms, solemn, mysterious, just a trifle threatening, since Ra'a lived there; on the beach beyond, a mixed company of brown men and white, busy at boat-building, with spasmodic outbreaks of "Kown 'im! kown 'im! kown 'im!" to the tapping of the hammers: on the other side, the tumbled rocks of the ridge and the ceaseless growl of the surf; behind them the white houses of the mission, the bosky valley, peeps of native houses, sounds of women's voices and children's laughter.

"It is certainly a wider outlook," said Jean cheerfully.

Then a slim brown and white figure stole up beside them, and became immediately all brown, as Nai loosed her towel vestments and began to wash them in the same way as the white women were doing.

"And here is first-fruits," said Jean. "Good morning, Nai."

"Mawin," smiled Nai, proud of her accomplishments, and spread her towels to dry in the sun alongside the more complicated garments of civilisation.

The Torch was away with Blair and Stuart on a tour of exploration round the island, and possibly to one or two of the neighbouring ones.

Blair had been waiting for the opportunity for some time past. Ha'o had told him of communities on the other side of the island, and he was desirous of getting in touch with them as soon as possible.

The ladies had wished to go too, but he thought them better at home till he had spied out the land himself. He intended to land at the different villages, and the enterprise might not be without its dangers. Of these he made light, however, and it was with tranquil minds that those ashore waved their farewells in the early dawn, as the Torch slipped from her anchorage and wafted lightly down the lagoon.

The times seemed in all ways propitious. Ha'o, indeed, would have preferred that the white men's favours should have been kept all for himself, but Blair was at pains to explain to him that nothing less than the whole island, and if possible all the islands, would satisfy him. In view of what he knew would follow sooner or later, he tried to explain to the brown man that if it were possible to unite the various communities on Kapaa'a under one paramount chief it would be for the great benefit of all.

To which Ha'o replied succinctly—

"Then we must kill Ra'a," and rose to the prospect.

Ra'a had been quiescent for some time now. There was occasional friction between members of the various factions, but nothing more than was to be expected under the circumstances. They were simply squabbles, resulting in no general disquiet, though symptomatic of the underlying feeling that was abroad.

Ha'o, however, never ceased his warnings. Ra'a he said feelingly, was not to be trusted, and the only right and proper thing for the white men to do was to join him in wiping him out, and the sooner the better. And, simply from a political point of view, Blair could not but confess to himself that the weight of evidence was in Ha'o's favour. For Ra'a remained in truculent retirement, and doggedly rejected all efforts at conciliation. Blair had gone up the mountain more than once since that first time, and had done his utmost to win him over. Ra'a accepted all his presents as his rightful due, but gave absolutely nothing in return, not even worthless promises. He was the black cloud on the horizon, and they could only hope that he would remain a cloud and not develop into a storm.

Each week that passed strengthened Ha'o's hands. Not only did it give him time to arm and consolidate his own little community, but his numbers were constantly increased by ones and twos, as the dwellers in the hills took note of the advantages enjoyed by those on the shore through their intercourse with the white men, and desired to share in them. Ha'o permitted the return of these prodigals, since it was better to have them under his hand than beyond his reach. He put little faith in them, but had the wisdom to keep his feelings to himself. Blair welcomed them as straws indicative of the current, but Ha'o, better versed in the ways of his race, pushed on his preparations for the conflict which he foresaw these very secessions would sooner or later precipitate.

When Blair told him of his impending trip of exploration, and tried to induce him to come with them, Ha'o stated bluntly that he preferred to remain at home. It was not impossible that he had it in his mind that if anything happened in Blair's absence, he would have the freer hand to act as he pleased. For the white men were ever on the side of magnanimity, and magnanimity, where Ra'a was concerned, was to Ha'o simple foolishness.

CHAPTER XVIII

SETBACKS

So the Torch slipped down the lagoon like a picture, and Nai and the other ladies completed their laundry operations, and in due course the red sun dropped into the sea, without the explosive hiss which seemed inevitable, and night fell on the little community as peacefully as usual.

Evans conducted their evening service, and the attentive ring of brown men and women round the platform of the house hummed the tunes gaily, echoed the white "Amen" with the gusto of children after a long sermon, and dispersed like big bumble-bees to their homes.

Jean could not sleep that night. It was the first time she and Kenneth had been separated, since their marriage, and she felt as lonely as the circumstances demanded. She got up at last and slipped on a dressing-gown, and went out and sat on the platform.

The soft lip-lap of the water on the beach, and the distant growl of the surf, were soothing, and she sat looking at the great new stars, with which she was becoming friendly by degrees, and thinking of her husband, and wondering how far he had got, and of the vast change her marriage had made in her life.

She had never for one moment regretted it. All her heaven on earth was centred in Kenneth. So long as he remained to her, all the rest was nothing. And before long they would begin to see the fruit of their quiet sowing, the Dark Islands would be dark no longer, and they would be living a quiet, happy life among a new and contented people. It was a grand and glorious work. No, she had no regrets—since she had Kenneth.

On her right across the river, as she sat facing the sea, the mountain loomed sombre and menacing—the hill Difficulty. Her thoughts ran back to that trying morning when she and Kenneth faced the hill, and what it held, all alone, not knowing whether they would ever come back alive. Like many another hill on life's highway, its menace had been chiefly in their own fears, and had disappeared on closer acquaintance. How she wished that uncomfortable man Ra'a would go away, or be reconciled to his brother, or do anything that would allow the community to settle down in peace to its new life's work.

She knew much of Blair's great hopes and large ideas, and how essential he considered it that the islands should as soon as possible attain to some kind of central government, so that they might unite in opposing an inflexible front to any attempt at interference from the outside. The Dark Islands for the Dark Islanders was his aim and object in life at present, and this truculent savage on the hill there was keeping everything back. She almost had it in her heart to wish Ra'a's speedy and sudden death.

Blair had often spoken of the evils that had followed the admission of traders in others of the South Sea Islands—drink, disease, dispossession—and how the communities were ruined before ever they had a chance of better things. Yes, surely, she thought, if Ra'a could meet with some happy accident, which would end him, it would be for the good of the community at large. That was not a thought that would commend itself to Kenneth, she knew, but she could not help thinking it. What a mighty relief it would be if Ha'o walked in some morning, and said, "Ra'a is dead." She felt as if she could almost forgive him if he had done the deed himself.

Then she thought she heard, a sound in the gloom of the hillside. She strained into the darkness and listened intently. She heard nothing, but still felt a sense of discomfort. After all, it might quite likely be one of the natives prowling about, though, as a rule, their fear of ghosts and evil spirits kept them indoors after nightfall, and it needed very strong inducement to take them abroad.

She was still peering towards the hill with puckered brow, when a curdling, short-cut yell ripped the silence behind, in the direction of the village, and in a moment pandemonium seemed loosed, and the night was alive with horrors—screams and yells and all the turmoil of warfare.

That first deadly cry sent Jean flying inside for Aunt Jannet. The good lady met her at the door of her own room with an anxious—

"What in the name of goodness—?" and then Alison Evans and Mary Stuart came tumbling in upon them, and Evans called to them from the ground outside to stop where they were, and they would be all right.

It was not in human nature, however, to stand huddled in the dark, asking one another questions which none of them could answer, when the answer was shrieking outside, and they all crept, trembling, to the verandah, and stood silently facing the danger, whatever it might be.

They heard Evans quietly ordering his men, and felt safer. And beyond, the shouts and yells waxed and waned and wavered to and fro. Once they thought they were coming in their direction, and their hearts thumped painfully. Then the tumult drifted away again, and at last passed furiously towards the taro fields, and died away on the mountain-side.

Then new sounds arose, cries of victory, little less blood-curdling than the shouts of battle, and the ladies crept back into the dark room, assured of their own safety, but with horrible premonitions of what these might portend.

Presently the shadowy darkness over by the river resolved itself into a mob of black figures which came towards the mission-houses, leaping and brandishing its newly-fleshed weapons, and shouting at the top of its voice, in horrible incongruity, and the more horrible in that the tune was perfectly correct, "Kown 'im! kown 'im! kown 'im! kown 'im! Law-daw-faw!"

They circled the fence, leaping and shouting and singing, and the men of the yacht inside grasped their weapons to repel an onslaught. But the brown men had had their fill of fighting for that night, and were only there to advertise their victory.

Evans said a word or two to them, but learned only that Ra'a had come down from the hill and attacked the village, but that they had been ready for him. They were too excited to be able to give any details yet, and presently they drew off and went shouting and singing home.

Jean, with something of a shock, remembered her ill-wishes for Ra'a, and wondered with discomfort, now that the bald possibility faced her so closely, if they had been realised. If they had, she would feel almost as if she had had a hand in his death.

Then a native drum began beating in the village, and the ceaseless monotony of its deep, dolorous boom fretted their ears, and set their hearts jumping, and jangled their nerves to the point of agony. They covered their ears with their hands, they stuffed their fingers into them, but the drum beat in through their temples. They clasped their heads tightly to keep them from splitting, but the drum beat in all the same. When it ceased abruptly at last, and they ventured to lift their heads, they saw one another's pale faces in a faint gleam that stole in through the windows. The darkness over the village was pulsing with the glow of great fires, and as they glanced fearfully at one another they knew that the same horrible thought was in all their minds.

It was dawn before the noises died away, and Evans came in to them with a grim, grey face. He said nothing, but nodded silently—and their horror was confirmed.

Yes, truly, it was a decided change from Kensington and Hyde Park.

No soul from the village came near them that day, nor did any of them venture out except Evans, who went along twice during the day to see what was going on, but returned each time with pinched lips and a despondent shake of the head.

The following day the brown men were about again, but sluggishly, as though the fight had used up all their energies, or something else had clogged them. It was another two days before they settled down to work, and even then they were not quite as they had been.

Ha'o had kept away from them. When Evans came across him at last, he endeavoured to get some particulars of the fight, and gathered that Ra'a had probably watched the departure of the Torch, and thought it an opportunity not to be missed. He had crept down in the dark, hoping to surprise the village, and then make easy prey of the mission-houses and their contents. Ha'o had foreseen the possibility of such an attempt. Evans understood him to say that in Ra'a's place it was just what he would have done himself. So he had men on the watch, and the rest slept armed, and instead of a surprise, the hill-men walked into an ambush—and paid. Ra'a himself had escaped, leaving a dozen or so of his men behind. They had eaten them, said Ha'o, in a matter-of-course way. Ra'a had gone farther into the hills, and to follow him would be dangerous. And so to the boat-building once more, and much singing of "Kown 'im! kown 'im! kown 'im!" which sounded more than ever out of place under the circumstances.

Nai also put in an appearance that day, and to such an extent does the mind prejudice the eye, that it seemed to Jean and the rest that even she was changed from what she had been. In a word, it was difficult to look upon any of these sleek brown men and women without thinking with disgust of the horrible orgies in which they had been indulging. Their humanity seemed but skin deep, and just below it the wild beast lurked and peeped through the glancing black eyes.

Nor was it easy to conceal their feelings entirely, and perhaps Nai's womanly intuition perceived a touch of frost in the atmosphere. She stayed but a short time, and then went quietly away.

"I'm sorry," said Jean, with a sense of discomfort; "but really I could not feel towards her quite as usual."

"Of course you couldn't—nobody could," said Aunt Jannet briskly. "If I knew how to talk to them, I'd tell them what I think of the whole business. I'd make their ears tingle, I warrant you."

"I wish Kenneth was here. He would know just what to do."

"He'll tell you, my dear, that it's no good talking to them. You must just go slow, and break them off it by degrees. All the same, it would be a relief to one's mind to give them a right good scolding."

"They've been used to it all their lives, you see."

"All the worse for them. They ought to be ashamed of themselves."

"But that's just what they don't understand. Suppose a brown man came over to England and remonstrated with us for killing and eating beautiful little lambs and graceful cows—"

"Fudge, child! Lambs and cows aren't human beings," grunted Aunt Jannet. "They haven't souls."

"I don't know that the fact of men having souls makes much difference when it's only a question of their dead bodies being eaten. But I do hope Kenneth can break them off it! It is too horrible! And one can't help thinking of it every time one looks at them. Though I suppose it was just the same before we came."

"What they did before we came was not our fault. What they do now is, and the sooner Kenneth puts a stop to it the better," was Aunt Jannet's final word.

Matters went on quietly—Evans and the men of the yacht clearing and breaking up ground for trial plantings of various seeds, the brown men busy on their boats to the tune of "Kown 'im!" the women, brown and white, busy on their household duties, the children laughing and screaming—till, on the seventh day, a brown runner came, fresh from the surf behind the ridge, to tell them that the Torch was in sight. And instantly they dropped what they were at, to scramble up the shoulder of the hill and wave their joyful welcome. Not a white man or woman there but felt a new sense of security and hopefulness at sight of her, and it was chiefly because on board of her was the wise head and great heart to which they had all come to look for guidance and inspiration in their work.

It was a very joyful meeting when the anchor rattled down, and Blair and Stuart and Captain Cathie jumped ashore from the whale-boat, and the brown men welcomed them, outwardly at all events, with as much gusto as the whites.

And great stories Blair and the others had to tell of their doings out beyond. The brown men and women crowded round the platform till late into the night, laughing and chattering with appreciation of the white men's volubility, though they could not understand a word of it all.

It had been a most satisfactory trip. They had visited all the six islands of the group, and had landed at various places on each of them. They had found the natives suspicious at first, but amenable to presents and open to their advances when they found nothing ulterior in them. In fact, in several places, when the brown men found them actually going away, without any attempts at kidnapping or otherwise molesting them, they followed in their canoes for long distances begging them to return.

"It's a glorious field," said Blair, stretching out his arms energetically as though to gather it all in at once, "if we can only occupy it and fence it round before the degraders come. And we must, for one of those islands given over to the devil would be like a plague spot infecting all the rest."

Then they told him of the happenings at home. He was startled at Ra'a's outbreak and at thought of the consequences if it had proved successful.

"I hate the thought of coercing him or any one," he said thoughtfully; "but until he either comes in, which I fear is hopeless, or is got rid of in some way, he is going to be a terrible hindrance to our work."

"Deport him to yon outer island, Mr. Blair, with such of his people as stick to him," suggested Cathie; "then the rest will have peace."

"Easily said, captain, and a good idea; but how?"

"It would mean fighting, I suppose," said Cathie briskly, "unless common-sense led him to give in quietly. Sometimes it pays best in the long run to grip your nettle at once and grip it hard."

"He'll never give in till he is forced to," said Blair. "Yet I can't see my way to use our force against him. How can we preach peace to these people if we begin by using the sword ourselves?"

"If you give the rest peace, it may be better than preaching it," said Aunt Jannet. "I agree with Captain Cathie. There'll be no peace till that man is got rid of. And, for goodness' sake, do stop them eating one another, Kenneth. I haven't enjoyed a meal since, and I can't look at one of them without thinking that a day or two ago he was munching one of his fellows."

"We shall break them off it by degrees."

"By degrees!—by degrees!" cried Aunt Jannet. "It is too horrible. You ought to go straight to Ha'o and tell him we won't have any more of it."

"And suppose he said, as would be very natural, that he'd do as he pleased? What would you do then, Aunt Jannet?"

"I'd tell him if he didn't stop it I'd make him, or else we'd all go away and leave him."

"Ay, well, you see, we can't make him and we're not going away, so it's no good telling him that. We must use our common sense. These people have eaten human flesh all their lives. It is the greatest treat they can have. If you argued the point with Ha'o, he would probably say that, as between man and pig, man is the cleaner feeder of the two, and therefore must be the better eating. When we have pigs enough, we'll work them on to pork. Until we can get them on to something they like as much, or, better still, get them to feel that man was not meant to be eaten by man, I fear words won't go for much."

"And do you mean to say that you'll pass the matter over without a word, Kenneth?" asked Aunt Jannet.

"I don't say that, and I don't intend to. But if you imagine, Aunt Jannet, that a cannibal is going to give up his daintiest dish simply for being spoken to, I'm afraid you'll be disappointed."

He made his first attempt against cannibalism the next day, and returned from it with a humorous twinkle in his eye.

"Well?" asked Aunt Jannet.

"Well," said Blair, "Ha'o holds that it can't be wrong for him to eat men when we do the same."

"If he'll wait till he sees us doing it, I'll find no fault with him."

"I assured him that white people never ate human flesh. And what do you think was his proof that we did? He pointed to some of those corned-beef tins with George Washington's head on the label, and said, 'There!' and nothing I could say would convince him that George Washington did not represent the contents. He is under the impression that we can our people at home for convenience, and carry them about with us in that way. I assured him it was cow, but it was no use. He could not believe anyone would kill such a beautiful animal as a cow simply for food. He said he would give ten men for one cow any day. So there we are, you see. It will be a matter of time. Meanwhile, I suggest peeling George Washington off the rest of those meat tins!"

"Well, I never!" said Aunt Jannet. "And Ra'a?"

"He is as anxious as you and Captain Cathie to make an end of him; but he acknowledges that it would be dangerous to follow him into the hills, and would certainly mean considerable loss of life, so for the present I have dissuaded him from it."

CHAPTER XIX

FORWARD

This is not a missionary chronicle, but simply a brief record of some of the doings of Jean and Kenneth Blair. It is impossible, therefore, to enter into anything like a detailed account of their work among their chosen people, interesting as that would be. Only the more salient points can be touched upon, such as stood out from the level of hard, plodding, often dry and dreary work, as God's mountain masterpieces stand out in our travel-memories, and remain with us when the long level plains are forgotten. And just as the mountain's grandeur is the record of Nature's strife and endurance, so these salient points in a man's life as a rule mark battle-grounds and commemorate strife—and sometimes victory.

Kenneth Blair always found a vast and quite unique enjoyment in the first beginnings of things. I myself have heard him express a whimsically-veiled, but none the less profound, regret that it had not been possible for him to be present at the very first beginning of all, when "in the dim grey dawn of things, earth drew from out the void and rounded to its shape."

It was very characteristic of the man, and explains to some extent the whole-hearted delight he found in his work in the Dark Islands.

Here, if not a new-created world, was one sunk in nether gloom, to which no glimmer of the light had yet penetrated. As regards things spiritual, it was virgin soil—worse, it was a veritable swamp of heathenism, a quagmire overlaid with the strangling growths and festering remains of ages of superstition, cruelty, and thick darkness. And this in one of the fairest spots on earth.

You anti-missioners, who sit at home and mumble platitudes on the needless waste of life and time and money, spent in the effort to lift these outer fringes of the night, how very little you know!

They are quite happy as they are, those outer ones, you say. Life comes—and goes—easily with them. They have all they want. Why disturb them? Why introduce upsetting notions? Why open their minds to wants only to fill them at so heavy a cost?

The answer is so simple. Would you see any child of yours condemned, for no fault of its own, to sit in outer darkness, if at any cost to yourself you could open the door to the light and warmth you yourself enjoy? Would you refrain from opening the door to a neighbour's child, to a stranger's child, to any child whatsoever, if your hand was on the handle?

These others are children also. In spite of their blue skies and crystal seas and waving palms, they are buried in a darkness like unto death. It is for us who rejoice in the light to help them towards it. Our own great inheritance carries with it an inevitable and inalienable obligation. Shirk it we may and do, cancel it we cannot.

It was the recognition of this paramount duty, in perhaps somewhat abnormal measure, that made Kenneth Blair what he was. He brought to the work the white fire of a mighty enthusiasm which nothing could damp, and which did one good to look upon. The spur of what he deemed a former lapse urged him at times, perhaps, to extremes in the matter of personal risk; but if any man ever carried the courage of his convictions to their fullest limit, without a thought for himself, that did Kenneth Blair. With it all a simplicity of manner which was never at fault, because it assumed nothing; a natural gaiety and high-heartedness which carried him bravely through many a difficult place, and drew even the brown men to him; and a width of view, with a long forward reach, which might have made a statesman of him, had he not chosen this higher path.

To see him at football on the beach with a shrieking crowd of brown boys, himself as much a boy as the nakedest of the lot, was one thing. And to see him pondering, or hear him unfolding to the others, his plans for the Dark Islands, was quite another.

He had seen the strange, and in some cases awful, developments of civilisation in some of the other islands. He had pondered them for years, and had studied cause and effect from germ to ultimate issue. They were as warning lights to him. The wonderful chance which placed in his hands the financial lever had awakened mighty hopes in him. In his mind's eye he saw the Dark Islands enlightened, self-governing, self-possessing, self-supporting—a prospect worth any man's life's work.

Of the preliminary clearing work, then, we will say little. It was dry and dull and dreary enough at times to provoke Aunt Jannet Harvey to active remonstrance at the apparent inactivity of the propaganda. But the quiet work, confined as it was almost entirely to the presentation of better ways of life by force of example, and the very occasional dropping here and there of a seed of precept, began to show some small signs of fruit at last.

Within a very short time Nai's advanced notions in the matter of dress had caught on, and instead of the precarious ridi fringe, towels, or, in default of them, a strip of striped calico, had become the fashionable female attire. Within six months the brown men were going about fully clothed—in a loin cloth.

"It's better than nothing," said Aunt Jannet. "It keeps them from looking absolutely indecent anyway, and as for the children it doesn't matter," for the children all flatly refused any attempt to clothe them. Time after time she had made furtive experiments on them, but they all proved abortive. They took her gifts of cloth and so on willingly, but turned them to unexpected and unintended uses.

Within six months the children were coming to school—some of them, and irregularly—and were actually, in some cases, beginning to have vague ideas as to why they came. It was not much, but it was in the right direction.

Within six months the white men had learned enough of the language to be able, with their additional slight knowledge of Samoan, to understand and make themselves understood—to some extent. And the brown men, in exchange, had acquired a number of English words and had added considerably to their repertoire of hymns—the tunes they picked up marvellously, and the words they chattered like parrots.

They had also learned to handle white men's tools with facility, and they still stole them when opportunity offered, though not quite so freely as at first. They had also seen marvellous things come up out of the earth from the white men's plantings, and had learned to what uses they could be put. They had seen wonders of the white men's ingenuity, chief among which was the diversion of a rapid little stream, which from time immemorial had flowed to the sea on the other side of the ridge. By a very simple damming operation, to which the cracks and cavities of the ridge readily lent themselves, the torrent now came down the nearer side, and by means of a water-wheel, of John MacNeil's construction operated a circular saw and various other labour-saving appliances, and then flowed in a sparkling stream through the middle of the mission settlement. The water-wheel and the circular saw were endless enjoyments to the brown men, women, and children, and they would sit watching them by the hour when they could have been more profitably employed about their other affairs.

Matters politic had also advanced somewhat. In place of three parties in the close neighbourhood of the station, there were now only two. Ra'a was still at large in the hills, but the leaderless faction had gradually disintegrated, some few joining him, but the larger portion returning by degrees to their allegiance to Ha'o, drawn thereto by the manifest advantages of the white men's friendliness.

And Ha'o himself had behaved well. Constant intercourse, even through the misty medium of scarce understood tongues, with men like Blair and Stuart and Evans, could not but have its effect on any man, and on this clear-headed, sharp-witted savage the effects had been very marked.

He was naturally intelligent, and, according to his lights, of a most gentlemanly disposition. His understanding developed still more through his observation of the white men and their ways. He recognised their superiority in most things and, as headman of his tribe, was emulous of their accomplishment. He lapsed at lengthening intervals into his natural savageries, but, beyond this, never swerved by a hair's breadth from his loyalty to the men who had restored him to his home.

Nai was rejoicing mightily in the possession of a sleek, plump, black-eyed baby, the first son born to Ha'o. His other wives had given him daughters, but since his return to the island, and their tardy return to him, he had declined to have anything to do with any of them beyond seeing that they were fed. Nai's community in his dangers and sufferings had concentrated all his savage affections upon her, and now she had justified him by giving him a son.

Blair reposed great faith in these three, and counted on them as corner-stones in the mighty future.

The valley of the gods had proved a famous breeding-place. Goats and pigs and ducks abounded there. The brown men had been introduced to roast pig and goat flesh, and found it equal almost to man flesh. But nothing would induce them to go there for it.

So, with mighty labours, for the animals were become perfectly wild in their freedom, a number of them were given the run of the island, and the novel excitements of the chase bade fair to afford the brown men full vent for the energies that had hitherto run in the direction of battle and murder and sudden death. Certainly the newcomers played havoc for a time with the taro fields and plantain and banana groves. But this also made for good, since it involved fencing operations on an extensive scale, and steady work tended to keep the devil of idle hands at bay.

"The curse of savagery is the lack of employment," was one of Blair's maxims. "They get to fighting simply from having nothing else to do. Get them to work, and it is a mighty step upwards."

So, but for Ra'a, the recalcitrant, the reunion of the tribe on this side of the island would have been complete. And this was so essential to Blair's far-reaching plans for its safety and redemption that he spared no pains to bring it about.

At risk which could not be estimated, he went up alone into the hills more than once to endeavour to reconcile the insubordinates to the facts of the case. He guaranteed them life, liberty, and equal advantages with the rest if they would return to their allegiance. Failing that, he offered them safe conduct to one of the smaller, thinly-populated islands, with supplies of tools, seeds, and animals, and the assistance of one of his colleagues in turning these to account.

But Ra'a would have none of it, and his dominant will so far was strong enough to keep his turbulent crew from breaking away towards the fleshpots. The loosing of the pigs and goats had provided them also with food and sport, and, since collisions between the various hunting parties were not infrequent, life was eminently tolerable, though it lived on the point of death.

On these embassies Blair had emphatically declined to take Jean with him, on account of the indefiniteness of the journeying. Ra'a was constantly shifting camp, and each time he had to be sought afresh, with the imminent chance of the seeker meeting death in the quest. Jean dreaded these lonely journeys terribly, but she acquiesced sensibly, and each time bade him farewell in the full knowledge that it might be for the last time.

She was, indeed, becoming reconciled to partings as incidental to the missionary life. The Torch was constantly coming and going among the islands now, and sometimes the ladies were allowed to go and sometimes not. Relations with the outlying tribes were progressing satisfactorily. In most cases, after two or three calls with no exhibition of cloven hoofs or ulterior designs on the part of their visitors, the natives welcomed them in the most friendly fashion. In some cases they still held back, and regarded them with suspicion and distrust, but on the whole the tendency was towards confidence and friendship.

CHAPTER XX

MANY FORMS OF GRACE

We have glanced at the higher phases of Kenneth Blair's character, the more homely ones were no less strenuous and striking.

Anything less like a saint in daily life one could hardly imagine. In his love of fun and frolic he was a big, clean-hearted schoolboy, full of jokes, and with a laugh that did one good to listen to and was as infectious as the mumps. Out of harness, on the sands or in the sea, with the brown men and boys and his own, or up the hills after pigs and goats, he let himself go with an abandon which only helped to brace the straps when he geared again.

He set them to football, cricket, boxing, and fencing, for all of which his foresight had made provision, kite-flying on a scale so gigantic as to set the natives gaping, rowing, swimming—anything and everything that might harmlessly take the place of the excitements their savage natures craved, and which served at the same time to strengthen the bonds between white and brown, he pressed into the service.

The boxing-gloves and basket-hilted fencing-sticks became absolute means of grace to the islanders. Here was scope for fighting to any extent, with no ill results. They took to them amazingly, and what was lacking in science was more than made up in zeal. And if these fighting bouts filled specific wants of their own, they also provided no less excellent entertainment for the onlookers.

At first they put both gloves and sticks to the primitive service of belabouring their opponents to the utmost capacity of their muscles, and the sight of two stalwart brown men, clad only in boxing-gloves or basket-hilt, pounding away at one another with every ounce that was in them, and with never an attempt at defence, kept the white men in paroxysms of laughter. But punishment even of so comparatively mild a character as that soon led to more advanced ideas, and before long the browns were a match for the whites, and were never tired of the sport.

Captain Cathie, when he was not ranging the seas in the Torch, put his men through their cutlass drill on the beach as regularly as if the houses behind had been a coastguard instead of a mission-station, and to the brown men this was a sight never to be missed. The measured sweep and clash of the glancing steel fascinated them. Presently they were asking for cutlass drill also, and it was not denied them. Such things might to some seem roundabout steps on the road to salvation—to Kenneth Blair they were very direct and important ones.

With these brown men and women he was forbearing and long-suffering to a degree which, in the opinion of some of his friends, passed reasonable bounds. That, perhaps, only went to prove the breadth and depth of his nature. He could flame, however, with the best when occasion called, yet there was a righteousness in his anger which lifted it above the common anger of smaller men.

From whatever distant strain they drew, the girls of Kapaa'a were undoubtedly good looking. Physically they were models of sinuous beauty, wild, dark-eyed nymphs, with manes of flower-decked hair and natural graces of action that came of ages of unfettered life and limbs. Their pretty faces and kittenish ways might well play havoc with the hearts—or say the fancies—of hot-blooded young sailormen, and these coquettes of the ridi-fringe were no whit behind their kind in the full appreciation of their powers.

Blair saw the danger as soon as he saw the girls. He had a way of looking facts square in the face without any blinking. He talked very straight to his boys, pointing out the cons of the case with the utmost frankness, and exhorting them to caution and restraint in their dealing with the island women. That so few casualties occurred spoke volumes for his moral grip over his men.

The danger was very real, for the brown girls' estimation of the attentions of the white men was open and unblushing, and tended to irritation on the part of discarded brown lovers.

Captain Cathie, in one of his bluffer moments, bluntly suggested wholesale marriage as a preventive of irregularities, and the starting of a new race on that basis, instancing the Pitcairners as typical resultants. But Blair bade him postpone any such notions until the islanders had at all events attained to some degree of civilisation.

"Trained and educated, there is no reason why our island girls should not make excellent wives," said he; "but the time is not ripe yet. Nothing but bitterness and disillusion can come of the mingling of natures so opposite. Meanwhile, if our lads can stand the test they will be all the better for it."

Nothing serious happened—outwardly at any rate, though it is not impossible that a good deal went on of which the authorities were not aware—until, one day, one of the men was missing, and no one knew—or at all events would say—what had become of him.

Captain Cathie discovered the lapsus when he had his men out for drill on the beach.

"Where's Sandy Lean?" he asked.

No answer, but covert grins from the rest, and flashes of laughter from the girls who were watching—laughter which evoked a growl from the brown men.

"Very well! We'll deal with Sandy afterwards. Fall in, men! 'Tention!" and the drill proceeded.

When it was over, the captain questioned two or three of them as to Sandy's probable whereabouts, but got nothing out of them. So he marched over to Blair's quarters, where the four heads of the community were hammering away at the language, Ha'o giving and receiving, and Matti straightening out kinks.

"Sandy Lean's away, Mr. Blair, and I can't get track of him," announced the captain.

"Ah!" and Blair drummed quietly on the table till the hot anger cooled. "So that's come at last," he said presently. "I'm sorry. The man's a fool, but as he has chosen, so he must lie."

He explained the matter to Ha'o, who showed no surprise and still less annoyance. His manner even implied that he looked upon the alliance as an honour to Kapaa'a, and that any other view of it might be popularly resented.

"Can you find the man for us?" asked Blair.

"What do you want with him?" asked Ha'o.

"He must marry the girl."

"I will find him," and next day he brought word that the fugitives were camped lightly in the hills, in one of the houses vacated by the dissolved third faction.

Blair, Cathie, and Ha'o accordingly set off at once to straighten the matter out, and a couple of hours' climbing brought them to the place.

Sandy Lean's old mother in Greenock Vennel would surely not have known him in his present estate. With the bonds and trammels of civilisation he had lightly discarded also its outward and visible tokens. His only clothing was a kilt of white cotton, whereby he was already paying tribute to folly in the clouds of flies and mosquitoes which levied toll on his white skin. In the hope of circumventing them, or with a loverly idea of assimilation to his brown bride, he had smeared himself with mud from the taro fields, and was now a motley pastel in black and red and white.

The sound of his voice, droning a comic song, drew them to the house, where he lay flat on his back on a mat. By his side sat the brown girl, doing her best to keep off the flies with a bunch of leaves.

"Hoots, lassie, scat 'em!—scat 'em!" he broke out. "They nip like the de'il himsel'. It's the kiss of a cold Scotch mist I'm wantin'."

The dusky bride greeted the newcomers with a smile broad enough to typify her happiness and victory. She had proved herself stronger than the white men, and was satisfied with her prize. She had woven a garland of crimson hibiscus into her dark hair and another round her neck, and with her lustrous eyes and gleaming smile she made a very pretty picture. In a playful mood she had also inserted a crimson flower behind each ear of her captive, and when, at her warning word, he sat up suddenly, he looked supremely silly and was aware of it.

"So you've made your choice, Lean?" said Blair quietly.

And Sandy glowered back at him with defiant confusion, while the flies settled on his shoulders.

"You're the first to fall away from us," said Blair, "and it would have been better, I think, if you had waited. However, as you have decided, so it must be. You have no wife at home?"

"No, sir."

"Very well. Stand up before me with the girl and take her hand."

They stood up in their surprise, and he read the marriage service over them, insisting on Sandy's responses and taking the girl's for granted, since there was no possible doubt about her wishes.

"Now," he said, when it was over, "she is your wife, and you are at liberty to return to the village. Ha'o will see you married again there according to the island custom, so that the people may understand that you really are married. You have taken yourself off the ship's books, of course, and you will have to support yourself and your wife. I hope you will treat her well. No doubt her relatives will see to it if you do not. It would, I think, be as well for you to keep in touch with the mission, and we will do what we can to help you. You can have tools and seeds. If you get into any trouble, come to me. Now goodbye—and—see you treat that girl well." And they left the newly-married couple to their honeymooning.

It was some days before Mr. and Mrs. Sandy descended from the clouds to the humdrum cares of life. Ha'o punctiliously performed over them all the rites and ceremonies observable in marriage on Kapaa'a, and before they were ended the bridegroom began to weary of all the fuss and to long for the easier accommodations of civilised life.

But Sandy's troubles were only beginning. With much labour he built for himself and his wife a house of parts, and his wife's relatives expressed themselves highly pleased with it, and immediately quartered themselves there, not simply in very great contentment, but fairly uplifted with their lot. They began to put on airs on the strength of the lofty alliance, and at the same time to put off even such trifling habits of labour and thrift as had hitherto supplied their daily wants without any undue exertion. Sandy remonstrated verbally, and at times otherwise, but custom was against him, and there was no shirking the burden. The other men visited him pretty regularly, and gave him a hand with his planting in their spare time; but in spite of his pretty wife, with her odd, outlandish ways, the sight of his full house offered them no inducements to follow his example. He was a standing warning to the rest, and so was not without his uses.

CHAPTER XXI

MIGHT OF RIGHT

Matters were progressing thus, surely if slowly, when a sudden sharp stroke fell upon them—sudden, but not altogether unlooked for.

With the individual as with the nation, peaceful times are growing times; and yet, to both individual and nation, there come times of stress and strife, when the slow upbuilding of the years is put sharply to the test, and, surviving, is the stronger for the strain. Winter's storms provoke the oak to deepest rooting.

At times, indeed, too long a period of peaceful growth may lead to over-fatness and deterioration. The nation and the man that waxes over-fat grows lean of soul. But that is a side issue at the moment. The little community on Kapaa'a was too near to its swaddling bands to be in any danger of fatty degeneration. And yet the stressful time that came to it made for good in every way. It had been striking roots and feelers. Well for it that time had been given them to grip the soil before the storm burst. As it was, they only gripped the tighter, and the breaking of the storm cleared the air, and made for more prosperous weather.

Captain Cathie, in his capacity of watch-dog, had never for a single moment relaxed his precautions at home, or his keen-eyed vigilance abroad. When he was touring the islands, his glasses swept the horizon continually, with a special eye to the east, which was the threatening quarter.

"Those yellow deevils will come back, as sure as we're here," was his constant word.

And so the beach was never bare of stacks of neatly-cut wood from away up the valley, and the bunkers of the Torch were always full, and the men were regularly drilled, and Long Tom was ready to speak at a moment's notice.

Each day, when the Torch lay at anchor in the lagoon, he took the steam-launch, or, occasionally, one of the whale-boats, by way of exercise for muscles, through the reef, to an offing whence he could obtain wide views of the approaches to the islands.

"In there," he would say, "I feel like a man with his back to the wall. It's safe enough, but there's no telling what's behind it."

And the wall was quite too high to climb, for the only eastward view from the summit of the hill was of the higher ridge, which ran right across the island, with only one possible passage, and that but a narrow one.

They used to mildly chaff the old man about his fears, but he took it all with characteristic good humour.

"Ay, ay, all right!" he would say. "Just you wait, and we'll see who laughs last. When they come, it'll be no laughing matter, I'm thinking."

"They've probably forgotten all about us by this time, and have found easier pickings elsewhere," said Blair.

"That kind doesn't forget in a hurry, and they know they've only got to break us up to get all the pickings here they want," said Cathie stubbornly.

And it was thanks to these ceaseless precautions that, when the time came, they were not taken unawares.

Cathie had run out in the launch one morning as usual, and presently came plunging back through the passage with a haste that betokened the unusual.

"They're coming," he said quietly, as the others met him on the beach.

"What, the nightmares?" said Blair, with a keen glance, for the captain was not above a joke.

"Ay, the nightmares, sure enough. A brig and two tops'l schooners working up steady from the south-east. They'll carry a heap of men, I'm thinking, and we'll have our hands full."

"Right? How soon can they be here, captain?"

"Wind's light—a couple of hours, I should say, at soonest."

"Our old plans stand?"

They had long since discussed the possible campaign, though not very lately.

"If they have as many men as I expect, we'll have to change 'em a bit. Unless they're absolute fools, which it's as well not to reckon on, they'll split and strike us more than one side at once. There's easy landing the other side the island."

"But a difficult way across."

"They don't know that, and they'll trust to luck to get across once they're ashore."

"You can keep this side all safe with the Torch, I suppose, captain?"

"Any quarter this time?" asked Cathie anxiously.

"Make quite sure of their intentions first. Then, if they are what we have reason to suspect, hit hard and end it."

"I'll keep this side all safe," said Cathie briskly, "and when I've cleared them here, I'll take a run round to the back and wipe 'em up there too."

"How many men can you spare us, captain?"

"I can do with six besides those below," said Cathie, after a moment's consideration. "Under steam we'll have the weather gauge all the time, and we'll give 'em no chance to board."

"That leaves us ten. Give us your ten best, captain, and see that each man has a revolver in addition to his Winchester and cutlass. Better beat up your men at once with the drum, Ha'o. What about Ra'a? Will he rest quiet, or will he take advantage of the matter to attack us, or will he help us?"

"He won't help. He may attack. If we are beaten, he is chief," said Ha'o, with a look which implied that the proper thing to do under the circumstances was to wipe out Ra'a forthwith.

"Run the ladies across to the Happy Valley at once then, captain, and take Lean and his wife to look after them, if she'll go. Will you send your women and children there too, Ha'o? They would be safe from Ra'a, at all events."

But Ha'o, knowing his people, shook his head.

"They will not go."

And so it proved. Fighting, the women understood, though they did not like it, but spirits they neither understood nor liked, and they would take no risks in such matters. They chose in preference to go up the southern hill, where they could keep a look-out for Ra'a and could scatter if he showed head.

The ladies understood the necessities of the case. Their preparations were quickly made, and within the hour they were landed in the Happy Valley, with Sandy Lean, armed to the teeth, to guard them from any stray yellow skins who might get in, an eventuality which was not at all likely. Sandy's wife chose to go with her man, which was a gratifying sign of moral improvement through marriage, and they tried their best to get Nai and her baby boy to go too, but she would not.

Captain Cathie saw to the armament of the land contingent, and gave them a strenuous word or two of his own. Then he carried the Torch through the passage in the reef and lay waiting for his prey.

Close upon a hundred men answered the call of the drum. They were armed only with fire-hardened wooden spears and clubs, and the axes they had used in more peaceful pursuits. But they had had no fighting for some time past, they were defending their hearths and homes, and with the yellow men keen in their memories, they were aching to be at them. And the little band of heavily-armed whites gave both edge and backbone to their courage and made them formidable.

Blair, Stuart, and Evans carried Winchesters and revolvers.

"Our cause is a just one," said Blair. "We will defend it by every means in our power. These men's blood is on their own heads." And there was that in all their faces which boded ill for the invaders.

The only communication between the east and west sides of the island was over a dip in the central ridge which, from its most prominent feature, they had named One-Tree Pass. On the farther side the slope was gradual and easy. On the mission side the ground was so broken, and the ascent so precipitous, that for all ordinary usage the pass was impracticable. No one ever dreamed of using it unless under most urgent necessity. No more urgent necessity had ever arisen than this present, and One-Tree Pass for once in its life became the active centre of the island.

The defending force scrambled up the broken way, and before it reached the pass Long Tom was bellowing angrily behind them, and was answered by another gun which sounded equally loud and defiant. The hill shoulders, however, hid what was going on, and they could only hope that Captain Cathie would be able to hold his own and something more.

Blair placed his men among the boulders overlooking the pass, and crept on along the ridge with Ha'o and Evans and Stuart, until they could look out over the long, easy sweep of the hill to the farther sea.

Opposite the landing-place lay the two schooners, with boats plying rapidly between them and the shore. The landing had evidently been disputed. The village was in flames and brown figures were creeping cautiously up the hill. The beach was filling rapidly with men from the ships.

"It will be a couple of hours before they get here," said Blair, and with instinctive foresight, in view of his greater work, "I wish we could get hold of those brown fellows. If they know that we're fighting their battle, it will pave our way with them later on."

He put it to Ha'o, and eventually the latter slipped away down the hillside, none too eagerly, to endeavour to intercept the fugitives and bring them in, if it were possible.

There was no difficulty in intercepting them. They were flying for their lives. Bringing them in, however, was quite another matter.

They recognised Ha'o, by his speech, as from the other side of the island—hostile therefore, and not to be trusted; and it took all his diplomacy, through the veil of a different dialect, to persuade the first half-dozen to the venture.

The sight of Blair, however, reassured them. They recognised him from his calls in the Torch, and presently they were off along the hills to bring in their fellows.

Altogether about thirty terrified men and women came in. The women were sent on down the valley. The men lay down among the rocks with the defending party.

Meanwhile the marauders had completed their landing and had begun their march, like the shadow of a black cloud creeping slowly up the hillside. Before them, urged on by blows from behind, crept two reluctant brown guides with ropes round their necks. There was no fear of the yellow men missing the pass. They toiled upward with stubborn determination, and wasted breath in voluble commination of the length of the way, when they could have employed it more usefully in compassing it.

And there was no possible doubt of their intentions. Slaughter and plunder were written all over them, as plain to see as the nature of a hyæna in the cut of its slinking face.

Nevertheless, Blair would permit no attack unchallenged. As the bristling crest of the black wave foamed cursing into the level of the pass, he drew cautiously back under cover till the whole should be there. When he struck, he would strike with all his might. This was a nettle to be gripped hard, to be squeezed to pulp and trampled out of sight.

The yellow men flung themselves flat and cursed their wind back. And the pass lay blank and bare and open under the glare of the sun. Not a stone rattled, not a shadow moved. The one lone palm seemed cast in brown.

In due course, and with the aid of many curses, the marauders got to their feet at last, and came pressing loosely along behind their unwilling guides. They passed unchallenged the place where Blair knelt behind a big rock. Below and on each side, pinched brown faces craned anxiously over restless brown shoulders at him, eager for the word. It was not till the motley crew had passed that he stepped out suddenly from his cover, and stood, a tall white figure, in the sun-glare.

"Hola!" he cried. "What are you after?" And instantly such a villainous array of vicious yellow faces was turned on him as he had never before in his life set eyes on.

A babble broke out among them.

"Dios! It is he!"

"It is the fighting padre!"

"It is the devil himself!"

"Down with him!"

"Our turn now, señor missionary!"

And one answer to his question which needed no knowledge of bastard Spanish for its translation. A sharp report, and a bullet buzzed past his head.

Other guns were rising to correct the insufficiency of the first.

"Give it them, boys!" shouted Blair, and before the words were out of his mouth, rocks and fire-pointed spears were raining on them, back and front, and as they tried in vain to face both sides at once, there came the quick crackle of the Winchesters and a ringing cheer from the Torch men at the end of the pass.

The yellow men reeled under their flailing. The ground was cumbered with bodies and the air with curses. The momentary panic drove them in upon themselves and bunched them together.

But the weak point about the thrown spear as a weapon of offence is the fact that, once hurled, it is gone. The yellow men were an undisciplined mob, Ishmaelites all, accustomed every man to fight for himself and ready to fight at any moment, but their death dealers remained in their hands, and they outnumbered the Torch men by seven to one. The Torches poured in volley after volley. The yellow men tightened their defence and replied in kind; while the brown men danced wildly among the rocks, and hurled stones and clubs, and were shot down like rabbits.

Blair's men were falling all round him. The sight was too much for him. He snatched a club from the ground and sprang down the hillside. In a moment the sides of the pass vomited brown men frenzied for the fight.

"Kown 'im!—kown 'im!—kown 'im!" they yelled, and hurled themselves on the enemy.

The Torch men, reduced in number, fired one more round and came racing in with their cutlasses. The yellow men replied, and then clubbed their guns and thrashed wildly at the advancing tide.

Under such conditions, and with the might of right as well as numbers against them, the yellow men gave way and drifted back towards the mouth of the pass, fighting stubbornly all the way.

And Kenneth Blair forgot that he was a man of peace. He saw his brown men falling all round him, ripped and bashed and broken, and he dashed into that fight as he had dashed into many a more peaceful one on the football field at home. He saw nothing at the moment but the vicious yellow faces and shaggy heads of the despoilers. He knew nothing but the necessity of demolishing them, and with his unaccustomed club he smote with all his might at every head he could reach, as his forbears long ago struck down the Northmen when they came wading ashore from their beaked ships on the coast of Caledonia.

The brown men eyed him with amazement, and yelled with unholy joy at sight of his Berserk fury. The teacher was a man like themselves, and could let himself loose like the rest of them. And Blair thought neither of them nor himself, or of anything whatsoever, save the necessity of ridding the island of the vermin that would pollute it.

For once in his life he tasted the wild, mad joy of battle.

His red club whirled and fell, and wherever it fell there fell a gap, and in him raged a red fury which nothing could appease or oppose.

He would surely have been a terrible sight to himself—his white face set to slaughter, and smeared with blood from a bullet graze on the temple, his white clothes spattered red, his eyes ablaze, and that murderous red club whirling and smashing to the tune that plunged in his veins.

At the end of the pass, where it dipped towards the sea, the yellow men broke, and it was over, so far as danger to the island was concerned. But not by any means over as concerned the yellow men. Never yet did enemy break and flee but prudence and restraint fled with him. Cast-iron discipline may leash it in the bulk, but in the individual the lust of death will out and have its way. The wild beast that lurks in every man once roused is ill to curb, and hardest, maybe, in the man not easily provoked. And here was no pretence of discipline. The furies were afoot that day, and death and destruction were rampant.

Blair found himself plunging down the hill path after a scattered mob of yellow men. They were too breathless to curse. Their only hope was the sea.

The prey was escaping. Terror lent it wings stronger than the fury behind. He hurled his dripping club among them, and one man fell.

At one side, among the boulders, he caught a glimpse of Ha'o, all aflame with battle, doing dreadful things with a dripping red axe. So horrible did he look, so utterly inhuman and wholly possessed of the devil, that Blair gasped at the sight. Then he stumbled to a rock and dropped his bursting head into his hands—and came to himself.

The pursuit sped on down the hillside. The yells and shouts died away towards the sea.

He raised his head at last, and his bloodshot eyes looked heavily after them.

"God forgive me!" he gasped. "I have been in hell."

He jumped up with the idea of stopping the work he had started. But that was impossible. As well try to stop the mountain snow in its death gallop. The red fury had gone down the hill like an avalanche. Until its force was spent it must run its course.

Now that the fire had died out of him he found his legs trembling so that he could hardly walk. He sank down again on his boulder and drew his hand dazedly across his brow, streaking it horribly with fresh smears of blood.

He looked round him, at the blue sea, the white surge, the quiet ships. He heard the shouts below. He saw a boat put off from the shore and labour heavily towards one of the ships.

"God forgive me!" he groaned once more. "I have been killing men."

But the only man he was actually conscious of killing was the one at whom he had hurled his club in his last spasm. And when he got up heavily, and went down to him where he lay in the glare of the sun, he found the man was not dead, and he was glad. He carried him carefully to the partial shelter of a rock, and propped him up, and gave him water from a runlet close by. He drank deeply himself, and washed his hands and face and plunged his head under water. He noticed now for the first time that his white jacket was spattered all over with blood. He tore it off and flung it from him.

The reaction which followed his temporary possession left him limp and exhausted, and burdened with a heavy mental load which as yet he made no attempt at lightening.

Then he went slowly down the hill, and saw one of the schooners loosing her sails in a hurried and shifty fashion. From that he gathered that some of the invaders had escaped, and he was too unaccustomed a warrior to regret it.

The rest, who had followed the pursuit to the shore, were held back by no such considerations however. To them the yellow men were enemies to be smitten hip and thigh, to be destroyed root and branch. When they reached the beach and saw the broken boat-load lumbering towards the schooner, the Torch men and a number of natives flung themselves into one of the other boats and set off after them with the most final intentions.

The schooner caught the breeze and began to make way. The Torch men played on her with their Winchesters, a chance shot dropped the helmsman, her head fell off, and she was theirs. Some of the yellow men jumped overboard. For the rest—well, the Torches knew Captain Cathie's views, and the islanders were of a like mind.

Blair passed several dead men as he went down the hill, but saw no wounded ones. As he neared the remains of the village he came upon the bodies of the first victims of the invasion, brown men and women and children.

He had seen nothing of Evans and Stuart since the fight began. Evans he had placed in command of the Torches; Stuart had been in charge of the opposite side of the pass.

The brown men were leaping about the beach inflated with their victory. The Torch men had anchored the one schooner and were now securing the other.

A sudden shout along the beach showed him a yellow man fleeing for his life with half a dozen islanders after him. He had been hidden in the bushes till they stumbled upon him. The sight of his twitching face and agonised eyes remained with Blair for many a day. There had been many such eyes and faces up there on the hillside, but he had had no eyes to see them. Now he was himself, and would stop the dreadful work.

He ran towards the man to succour him. But succour was the last thing the other looked for in him. His long knife was in his hand. Escape was hopeless, but here was a chance for a blow in return. He flew at Blair like a wild cat, and drove the knife at his neck. Blair swerved instinctively, and it went through his shoulder. The wild cat was on him with gnashing teeth and flaming eyes, snarling, grappling, biting him.

They rolled over and over in the sand. Then sinewy brown fingers gripped the other and tore him away, with a mouthful of Blair's shirt between his teeth, and in a moment he lay still.

Blair lay still also. The last things he remembered were the horror of that animalised snarling grip, and a dreadful agony in the shoulder as he rolled over in the sand with the knife still sticking in him.

When he came to, he found himself the centre of a group of the island men who were looking down on him with troubled faces. They gave a shout when he opened his eyes, and presently he was sitting up showing them how to bind up the wound with strips of his torn shirt. The knife had been pulled out while he lay unconscious—for the sake of the knife.

The Torch men came leisurely ashore after securing the schooner and found him so. He had lost blood freely both from head and shoulder, and felt sick and dizzy. They made a stretcher out of a couple of oars and a native mat, and at his request carried him at once up the hill to the pass.

He was anxious about the others; he had no recollection of seeing them since the fight began. It seemed to him that since he picked up that club and leaped down into the pass he had seen nothing but vicious yellow faces and evil eyes, and broken heads, and bodies that suddenly crumbled and fell.

His mind was relieved by the sight of Evans as soon as they topped the pass. And at distant sight of the stretcher Evans came running up with an anxious face.

"Serious?" he asked.

"Don't think so. A jag through the arm and a scratch on the face, but I felt sick and couldn't climb the hill. Where's Stuart?"

"Back here. Got a bullet through the leg. No bones broken, but he won't walk for a week or two."

"Many others wounded?"

"Two Torches, half a dozen natives, and a dozen of the yellow men. Frightful blackguards they are too. Makes me wish they'd been killed outright just to look at them."

Blair nodded. He could not plead wholly guiltless in that respect.

A dozen yellow men on their hands would be an anxiety and a burden. A light affliction, however, compared with what might have been if the invaders had caught them napping. And so they must make the best of it, and be thankful for things as they were.

"Now see here, boys," he said, sitting up on the stretcher. "We've had our fight and by God's mercy we've won. I'm afraid we all lost our heads a bit while it was on"—at which, and their recollection of him in the fight, the sailors grinned—"and I think we cannot blame ourselves for that. But these men who are left on our hands are tabu. The islanders will kill them if they get the chance, and we must prevent it. What is done in the hot blood of battle is done. But killing in cold blood is murder. You have all fought valiantly. Don't spoil it by any such doings. And, by the way, Evans, there's another of them lying under a rock to the left of the path over there. You might see to him. I flung my club after a bunch of them and this fellow went down, but he was only stunned."

"I'll go and bring him up at once, before the brown fellows come."

"No news of Cathie, I suppose. When did his big gun stop?"

"Over an hour ago. We've no news. I hope it's all right. I'd have sent down but I'd no one to send."

"Which of you boys will go for news?" asked Blair. "I doubt if we can all get down to-night."

"That you can't," said Evans. "It'll be a case of go easy for some days for all you hipped ones."

All the men volunteered at once. Every one of them was keen to know what had been going on on the other side of the island.

"You seem fairly fresh, Irvine. Tell Captain Cathie how we've gone on here, and that casualties are not serious. If he can spare us some more help we can do with it to get the wounded down. Ask him to send word to the ladies also. They will be anxious about us all. And if he can send us something to eat we'll be glad of it. I'm feeling empty after it all."

"I'll go after your half-deader," said Evans. "One of you come with me in case he can't walk."

But he was back empty-handed in a quarter of an hour.

"Gone?" asked Blair, with a pinched face.

"He's dead, but you didn't kill him. Some one came after you and split his head with an axe."

"Ah!" said Blair gloomily, "these others will fare the same unless we see to it. We'll go to them, Evans, in case any of our brown friends come prowling round."

But the brown men were much too busy, and we may drop more of a veil over their proceedings than the night did. Big fires were glowing along the beach before it was dark, and no brown man came up the hill that night.

They went along to the temporary hospital Evans had made among the rocks. The beds consisted of the softest patches of ground he could find, and the only furnishings were the patients. He had hastily bandaged their wounds, however, and all, except the yellow men, were fairly cheerful.

Stuart, indeed, became almost hilarious at sight of Blair as an invalid also.

"I was thinking ill of myself for getting hit," he said; "but since you're in the same boat I feel better."

"Glad to be of use," said Blair, "and very thankful things are no worse. They might have been. There were more of them than I expected, and they fought harder than their cause justified."

"Even rats will fight in a corner," said Evans.

Just before dark Captain Cathie came panting in on them, in the best of spirits and with many rough words for the road. He had half a dozen of his men with him, and they brought an ample supply of food.

"Well, captain, how have things gone with you?"

"We mustn't complain, sir. He'd brought a gun along as heavy as ours and we had a fine set-to. But with our steam we had the weather hand all the time and just waltzed round him. He did his best to board, but we thought differently."

"And how did it end? Where is he now?"

Captain Cathie jabbed his finger downwards two or three times in eloquent silence.

"Sunk?"

"Sunk with all aboard, big gun and all. No more trouble from that quarter. We plugged him more than once below the water-line and we saw he was settling down. But it came sudden at the end."

"And you were not able to save any of them?"

"We were not"—said Cathie emphatically, and after a moment's pause added—"and what on earth would we have done with 'em if we had?"

"We have about a dozen on our hands here—all wounded."

"Humph!" grunted Cathie.

"We couldn't very well kill them in cold blood, you see."

"And what'll you do with 'em, Mr. Blair?"

"I don't know yet. We'll have to think that over. Did you send word to the ladies how things had gone all round?"

"I went over myself with young Irvine and told 'em all about it. They were all very thankful it was over and no more harm done."

"And how is the Torch?"

"Ah!" said the old man, with an aggrieved shake of the head, "she got it pretty hot; that's why I couldn't get round to wipe out those schooners. Both her masts are down, and she got a shot into the machinery. The men are seeing what they can do to it. The masts we can fit ourselves."

"And you've no casualties?"

"Some splinter wounds and some bit bruises from the spars. Nothing of consequence, sir."

"Well, we're very well through a nasty job, captain, and we've reason to be thankful for it. Now suppose we have something to eat—I'm starving."

CHAPTER XXII

PAX

It took some days to get matters shipshape after the general upheaval of the invasion.

For one thing, the brown men were much too busy on the other side of the island to settle down to ordinary work. Most of the women and children had joined them there, the villages were deserted, and there was an intangible something in the mental and moral atmosphere which made for depression.

Blair sent Evans over to see Ha'o, and endeavour to bring him back to his right mind. Evans returned downcast, and described what he had seen only to Blair and Stuart. Aunt Jannet, if she had heard, would have had a fit.

The ladies were back in their own homes, and the crippled Blackbirds were bottled up in the Happy Valley, under the wardership of Sandy Lean and his wife and a small guard of Torch men. It seemed like desecration of the beautiful spot to use it as a prison, but it was the only place in the island where the yellow men would be reasonably safe from the brown ones.

The stars in their courses fought for Joshua. In like manner the strange, stern facts of life fought now for Kenneth Blair. The cloud which had threatened his work with destruction broke in unexpected blessing. The fight in One-Tree Pass was an epoch in the history of Kapaa'a.

In the first place it had brought into line—fighting line indeed, but none the less permanent on that account—the various factions in the island, and developed among them a hitherto undreamed-of community of interests. Not by any means for the first time in history, a general menace from without welded into one a diversity of hostile fragments, and discovered to them an unexpected identity of ideas. On a microscopic scale it was, in its results, the Franco-German war over again.

The men from the eastern coast, who had borne the first brunt of the invasion, had lost everything, including their headman. But they had found more than they had lost. They had found out that the western men were not necessarily their enemies, and that both they and the white men were ready to fight to the death to save the island from the grip of the yellow men.

They fully recognised that without the white men's help the marauders would have had their will, and matters would in all probability have gone very differently. In their way they were grateful, and by no means blind to the advantages of the white alliance. That their gratitude was based in no small degree on a sense of favours to come, in no way lessened its utility as a factor in the solution of political difficulties.

They too would share the benefits reaped by the western men from the white men's friendship, and when differences arose amongst them at once as to the choice of a headman, it was the most natural thing in the world to refer the rival claims to Blair, who might reasonably be expected to be without local bias in the matter.

The opportunity was too good to be lost. Blair was at pains to make clear to them the great advantages which would accrue from the union of all the communities under one head, and finally they argued the matter out among themselves and agreed to accept Ha'o as chief, with local headmen chosen by him and Blair.

They reaped their harvest at once and were content. Their houses were rebuilt, tools were given them, and they were initiated into the mysteries of the new foods and fruits introduced by the white men. A proper road was promised to further communication between the opposite sides of the island, and, so far, the descent of the Blackbirds made for good.

In another and quite unexpected direction also the invasion wrought in the direction of Blair's aims.

They were all sitting on the verandah of his house one night, watching the lightning play tremulously up and down the western sky, listening to the surf, and discussing matters generally. Captain Cathie, in the little leisure the refitting of the Torch afforded him, was much exercised in his mind as to what was to be done with the prisoners. Aunt Jannet had just expressed the opinion that it was a very great pity they had not all been scuttled.

"It does seem a pity you could not have made a clean sweep of them like Captain Cathie did, Kenneth," said she.

"Well, you see, we couldn't kill them in cold blood, Aunt Jannet."

"And now you've got them alive in cold blood what on earth are you going to do with them?"

"I see nothing for it but shipping them off home as soon as they are fit to travel. What do you say, Cathie?"

"I suppose there's nothing else for it," said Cathie gloomily. "We don't want them here, and yet I'm loth to turn them loose."

"I don't think they'll ever come back, after the reception they had this time."

"I don't know that they will, but they'll be at the same game somewhere else. I look on them as I do on mad dogs—best got rid of."

"Right!" said Aunt Jannet with emphasis.

"The trouble is that men are not dogs, you see—"

"That they're not. Dogs are mostly honest and good to look at," said Aunt Jannet again.

"We could put them on one of the schooners, and you could convoy them part way home," said Blair to Cathie. "I really don't think we have anything more to fear from them."

"I can do all that," said Cathie. "But all the same I'd as lieve they were none of them going home."

"Why?"

"Well, you never know. If ever they can do us a mischief you may take your davy they'll do it."

"I don't really see what they can do, captain."

But Cathie only shook his head. Perhaps his ideas were too vague to clothe in words.

Just then a shadowy figure slipped out of the darkness under the house, reached up, and rolled something softly along the platform towards them.

"Hello! What's this?" said Cathie.

"A present—for Aunt Jannet, I should say," laughed Blair. "Some dusky admirer bringing tribute."

"A thankoffering to the wounded warriors," said Evans.

"An unusually fine coco-nut," said Stuart, tipping it with his usable foot. "Carefully wrapped in leaves, too."

Captain Cathie picked it up, and began to open the bundle. Evans struck a match, and match and bundle fell suddenly with a dull, dead bump to the floor, and were followed by a quite involuntary and seamanlike oath from the captain.

"What is it?" cried the younger ladies in a breath.

"Come away!" said Aunt Jannet hastily, and set the example herself.

"It's a man's head," said Evans gravely, as he tried to light a lamp.

And when the lamp was lit, and the bundle lay open in their midst, they saw that he was right—it was the head of a man.

An exclamation burst from Blair as he bent over the ghastly offering, while the others wondered what it might mean.

Was it a challenge?—a defiance?—a threat?

None of these.

"It is the head of Ra'a," said Blair at last. "I wonder who it was that brought it? If we knew that, we might guess what it means."

There had been no fighting of late between Ha'o's people and Ra'a's. In fact, the quiescence of the latter during the other troubles had been cause for congratulation. And since then everything had been quiet in the villages—over-quiet, the quietness of repletion. Evans had indeed begun to fear ill results from the over-indulgence of savage appetites.

"What do you make of it, captain?" asked Blair at last, as of one more versed than the rest in heathen ways.

"Hanged if I know!" said the old man, with a puzzled frown.

"I take it, it is a sign of submission on the part of Ra'a's men," said Blair quietly. "Ra'a himself would never have come in of his own accord. His men have wanted to, and so they have brought him."

"I shouldn't wonder," said Cathie. "It's just the thing they might do."

And in the morning they sent up early for Ha'o, and showed him the message, and asked his opinion.

"Kenni is right," he said at last. "They submit."

And presently he went boldly up the mountain-side and in due course came back with Ra'a's followers in a straggling tail behind him.

He explained afterwards to Blair that Ra'a's men had wanted for a long time past to come in and enjoy all the benefits they saw the others receiving, but Ra'a had held them back, telling them that the whites were only tricking Ha'o and his people and would presently carry them away. They had seen the arrival of the Blackbird ships, had watched the fight at sea, and also that in the pass, and these had convinced them of the good intentions of the white men. Finally they had taken matters into their own hands and settled things their own way.

And so the divisions in the island were healed by blood, and that which had seemed like to wreck their hopes turned marvellously to their highest good.

CHAPTER XXIII

THE SCOURGE OF GOD

But there was trouble of a quite unexpected kind brewing.

The yellow men in their lives had slain a certain number of the brown. In their deaths they slew still more.

The whites had hoped that, with the introduction of new food supplies, the unnatural but deep-rooted native craving for human flesh would have disappeared. The final rites of the battlefield shocked them exceedingly, and words had so far failed to convince Ha'o and his people of the error of their ways.

"You eat pig," was Ha'o's blunt argument in reply, "and man is cleaner than pig."

There was, however, an argument in preparation for him with which the white men had nothing whatever to do, but which drove home conviction beyond dispute and in the most terrifying fashion.

Ever since the fighting, and the subsequent orgies, the villages had been unusually quiet. Even the wholesale submission of Ra'a's men produced little excitement among them.

"They are like snakes after a full meal," said Cathie. "They've eaten too much, and it'll take 'em all their time to digest it."

Evans, however, had his doubts. He hinted to Blair that he feared an outbreak of sickness, but as yet could form no opinion as to its character. The men had lost all their energy, the women were depressed, the children listless. It was as though the strenuous doings at One-Tree Pass had sucked all the life out of them. And Evans went in and out of the houses with a keen eye for symptoms.

It was about a fortnight after the fight that Blair, going up to the village, met him coming hastily from it, and was startled at the sight of his face.

"What is it, Evans?" he asked.

"It's come—I feared it, but could not be sure—smallpox."

"God help us! ... How has it got here?"

"I can only imagine," said Evans, with a quick, meaning look at him.

"Good God! How very horrible!"

"Yes. They'll have a lesson they'll never forget, and many of them will never have the chance to. What about our wives, Blair? Shall we send them away till it is over?"

Kenneth Blair's lips pinched tight at the thought of it all, and he walked heavily and in silence.

"We are in God's hands," he said at last. "I think it must be left to themselves to decide."

"Then they will stop," said Evans decisively.

"Yes, they will stop," said Blair. "God grant us a safe deliverance!"

"Amen!" said Evans, and they walked in the shadow of the coming death.

The ladies received the news with white faces but stout hearts, and did not hesitate one moment.

Their place was beside the men. They did not wait to count the cost, though in each one of them was the dull, dread knowledge of what that cost might be. Their duty was to these brown kinsfolk of their adoption, and they were British born.

Evans took charge of the defence with all the energy and skill that were in him, and, possessing their souls in God, they all went quietly into the fight, compared with which the battle of One-Tree Pass was veriest child's play.

The village was sheltered by the bush and the crowding palms. Every man was taken off the dismantled Torch, and set to work building a hospital on the beach, a long, open house of poles and palm-leaves, through which the fresh sea breezes could blow at will. Soft springy couches of palm-leaves were ranged inside, and the simple preparations were complete.

Not the smallest of the horrors and perplexities of the situation was the wholesale nature of the seizure. Springing from one identical cause, the results came all together. The hospital was filled before it was finished, and the builders could not keep pace with the demands for accommodation.

Not one of Ra'a's people suffered—clear indication of the ghastly origin of the evil. Blair induced them to return for the time being to their village on the hillside, and such of Ha'o's people as showed no signs of infection he camped temporarily on the opposite hill. Every house from which the sick were carried was promptly burned. The brown folk could not understand such radical measures, but they were scared by the sights they saw, and they did as they were told.

So suddenly had the catastrophe come upon them, and in so wholesale a fashion, that their thoughts had had no time to travel beyond their own immediate concerns. But when the work was steadily under way Blair bethought him suddenly of their new allies on the east coast, and he begged Captain Cathie to run round in the launch and see how matters were going with them.

Cathie returned in due course with a long face and the news that things were just as bad there, and Stuart and his wife promptly offered to go round and carry out the same measures as had been started at the home settlement. They were given half a dozen Torch men, whom they could ill spare. Evans promised to come round as soon as he possibly could, and the launch chuffed gallantly away to the relief of the still more necessitous on the other side of the island. Stuart could still only limp, and would have been better not to attempt even that, but the healing of his own wound was a small thing compared with that which had to be done. As a matter of fact he limped slightly for the rest of his life in consequence—a most honourable limp.

Then followed for all of them a time of patient endurance and endless self-sacrifice, which, trying as it was, still wrought mightily for and in them.

They went to and fro in that long open shed with quiet set faces, soothing and alleviating as far as these were possible, whispering hope to the hopeless, and insisting inflexibly on the observance of rules in which the only hope lay, rules the meaning of which these brown children could not understand, and which they broke at every opportunity.

Death sat grimly down before them and laid siege to them, and the little band of white-faced women and grim-faced men fought him day by day and life by life, losing heavily but refusing to be beaten.

They met one another with such cheerfulness as they could muster, and even with quiet strained smiles at times, but ever with keen apprehensive glances for what each feared any day to find in the other. A time for the trying of souls, with none of the glamour and activities of actual warfare, but with perils infinitely more appalling in their insidiousness and impalpability.

"Ech, Jean, my dear!" murmured Aunt Jannet Harvey one evening, as she and Jean and Alison Evans met outside for a few full draughts of sweet sea air. "It's terrible, terrible work. You're looking white; child. I wish you were back in London."

"I don't," said Jean cheerfully. "We're doing our appointed work, and I feel as if I'd never done anything worth doing at home. Kenneth says he believes this will be a corner-stone in the building up of the island."

"Ay, ay! Well, it's good to be able to take a hopeful view of things when they're about as bad as they can be. And I don't see that they could be much worse."

"Oh yes, they could," said Jean quickly. "Some of us might have taken it, which would be very much worse. We have to thank Mr. Evans for that, Alison."

"Charlie says he thinks we're through the worst," said Alison quietly.

"I wish I could see it," said Aunt Jannet.

"We have only had three deaths to-day, and most of the others are past the crisis. It's been a terrible clearance. There's that poor little baby crying again. I must go," and they separated to their various duties.

It was Nai's baby boy that cried, and it died in its mother's arms that night. She yielded it sorrowfully to those who took away the dead, and returned wearily to her husband's couch to keep the flies off him with a palm branch. Nai herself had been too much occupied with her baby to go with the others across the island after the fight, and she had not developed the disease. The baby had taken it, however, and Nai had nursed him and his father indefatigably, and now the boy was gone just as his father turned the corner, and the little mother was broken-hearted. They comforted her by telling her that Ha'o would live, and she fanned away wearily to the tune of her sobs that would not be kept in.

Jean, as she flitted noiselessly to and fro, with cold water for this one and medicine for that, and hopeful words for all, and special ones for Nai, thought now and again of the mighty change her marriage had wrought in her life, but never once regretted what she had done and all she had left. And more than once the dreadful thought came upon her—"Supposing Ken were to take the sickness and die and leave me alone!" Ah, then she felt as though her world would fall to pieces, and she prayed, as she had never prayed in her life before, that he might be spared, or that they might go together.

The one thing that wrought itself indelibly into all their memories was the contrast between their hospital work and its setting. Inside the long palm-thatched sheds—the moans and murmurs and restless movements of the sufferers; the ever-fluttering fans which kept off the plague of insects, and alleviated to some extent the pungency of the atmosphere; the irresistible depression induced by the close presence of insidious, crawling death. And outside—the implacable glare of the sunshine; the smooth, slow-heaving, blue mirror of the lagoon; the metronomic roar and long white flashes of the surge on the reef; the palms swinging slowly and solemnly with a sound like the patter of falling rain; and up above, the pale blue sky. Death in its most repulsive form, set in a picture of surpassing beauty, which yet had in it something of pitilessness from the very sharpness of the contrast. These things they never forgot.

They held no regular services at these times, for some were always on duty. But there was much prayer among them, and when the watches changed, the one in charge, Blair, Evans, or Cathie, would give his band of helpers a few brave words to carry with them—grateful thanks for perils past, hopeful prayers for safety in the hours to come. For they never knew but what the evil seeds might even then be working in any one of them, and they went with fear in their hearts though their faith and hope were strong, and their faces were tuned to quietness.

Evans wore himself thin with his ceaseless toils. As medical director the burden of the fight was on his shoulders, and he divided himself between the stricken camps in proportion to their needs. The going to and fro consumed much time, though he himself maintained that it did him good. But he showed the wear and tear so visibly at last that his wife, who had had a medical training at home, insisted on taking over the east coast hospital herself, and she joined Stuart and his wife there.

The epidemic ran its course, the dead were reverently wrapped in their mats, weighted with rocks, and towed out to sea on a small raft, and there committed to the deep. The convalescents began to creep about the beach and show a languid interest in life.

Ha'o was among the first to get into the sunshine. While none were neglected, Blair and Jean and Nai had nursed him as though all their lives depended on his recovery. And indeed, to Blair's thinking, very much more than their simple lives depended on Ha'o. He looked on him as the corner-stone of the work on Kapaa'a, and his death would have been a terrible blow to them all.

As Jean had said, he had great hopes that this sharp trial might also turn to good. He tackled Ha'o the very first day he judged him well enough for discussion.

"This has been a terrible time, Ha'o, my friend. Have you any idea why it came upon you?"

"It was your new God sent it, I suppose," said Ha'o gloomily, with the air of a child giving an expected answer with mental reservations of his own.

"God permits such things. If men will do wrong they must suffer. That is how they learn to do right. If you want to bang your head against this rock, God won't stop you. But the recollection of what you suffer may stop you doing the same again."

"What wrong did we do? You killed the yellow men too."

"But we did not eat them. Not one of us has been ill. Not one of Ra'a's people has been ill. They also kept apart."

Ha'o looked sombrely out over the lagoon. He was thinking of his boy.

"Kenni," he said presently, "I know you do not like us to eat men; but our fathers did so, and their fathers, and never have we had this crawling death before."

"Perhaps it was to teach you and your people. See, Ha'o! We want you to take your right place in the world. It was for that we came. It was for that we beat off the yellow men who would have carried you away. We are ready to give our lives to help you. But we must have the foundations firm or we cannot build. You do not build a house on running sand, nor a platform on cracking poles."

"What do you want me to do?"

"Promise me, here and now, that you will never eat man again, and that you will make it tabu to your people. They will do what you say. They are frightened. God never meant man to be eaten."

"How do you know, Kenni?"

"He forbade man even to kill man, but of the beasts He has provided He said, 'Kill and eat.'"

"You killed the yellow men," he said again.

"To save you from them."

"Then you did wrong too. Why did the crawling death not touch you?"

"It is not right to kill men, yet if a man attacks you, and in defending yourself he gets killed, the blame is his, not yours."

"You never tasted man, Kenni, did you?"

"No, never," said Blair, with an expression of disgust.

"Then you cannot know how good he is. My people think there is nothing equal to man—except woman or child, which are better still. But I will promise you never to eat yellow man again, Kenni."

"That is not enough. Unless you will give up eating man of any kind we must go. We have provided other food. You cannot go hungry. The pigs and the goats are all over the island. The paw-paws grow while you sleep. You have taro and bananas, and breadfruit and coco-nuts. You have the chance to become a nation, strong and powerful. You are sole chief on Kapaa'a now. I would have you chief of the other islands also. But if you prefer to eat man I can do nothing for you. It is the foundation of all the rest that you give up eating man."

"My little son did not eat of the yellow men, Kenni, but your God took him. Why?"

"It was the disease took him. It is the most terrible thing for passing from one to another. Could you stand the thought of your little son being eaten, Ha'o?"

"My son? No! I would have died sooner than let him be eaten."

"Yet you say other men's babies are good to eat."

Ha'o looked at him, and then lay looking out over the lagoon.

"See, Ha'o," said Blair at last, "if the thought of your little son will turn you from flesh-eating, he will have done more for Kapaa'a in the short time he lived than you have done in all your life, and we shall remember Ha'o's little son always as the beginning of the better times."

The brown man lay thinking a long time and one may not know his thoughts. But at last he said quietly—

"Twice you have saved my life and my people, Kenni. I am your man. You must not go away. For the thought of my little son who is dead I will give up eating man. I will become a nation."

"And you will answer for the rest?"

"I will answer for the rest. If any man eats man I will kill him."

Ha'o kept his word, and so, in the death of his little son, the foundations were laid in Kapaa'a, and the black cloud broke once more in blessing.

CHAPTER XXIV

GAIN OF LOSS

With a clean bill of health, and Ha'o as supreme chief anxious to become a nation, and therefore ready to follow the white men's ideas, matters began to progress rapidly.

The first thing to be done, as soon as the men could be spared from hospital work, was to get rid of the Blackbirders.

Captain Cathie, vehemently backed up by Aunt Jannet, would even now have made short work of them.

"Give 'em a fair trial and string 'em up," was his simple idea of the justice that would meet the case. And "Hear, hear!" said Aunt Jannet with energy.

"I really don't think they're likely ever to come back, after the lesson they've had this time," said Blair.

"They wouldn't if I had my way," said Cathie grimly. "Vermin like that is best stamped out when it's under your foot."

"We stamped pretty hard last time. They'll recognise that the game is not worth the candle."

So, in due course, the larger schooner, which was the older and poorer found of the two, was provisioned for the voyage, and the prisoners were brought over from the valley and put on board of her. Blair and Stuart and Cathie awaited them there, and, through Stuart, Blair told them very explicitly what would happen if they ever showed face in those waters again. Then the refitted Torch towed them out to the offing, and bade them make tracks for home, and followed them with dogged restraint for three days to see that they did it, and the island was once more purged of contamination.

When the captain got back, Blair laughingly asked him if they had got safely away, and Aunt Jannet eyed him with a spark of hope.

"They're gone," said Cathie, with a gloomy nod. "I'd have felt better if they'd gone by the shorter road."

"You ought to have scuttled them, captain," said Aunt Jannet.

Then followed many busy full days. First the village was rebuilt on a plan Blair had thought out during his hospital watches. The bush between the hills was all cleared away and burnt on the spot, leaving only the palms standing, and on this open space, with the shallow river brawling through the middle, the houses were built. Stereotyped lines, both as to design and location, were purposely avoided, and the result was eminently pleasing. Fresh plantations of taro and bananas were started, pawpaw trees and breadfruit were put in wherever space offered, and a close fence across the valley kept the pigs and goats from intruding.

The next great undertaking was the making of a decent road up to One-Tree Pass, for the benefit of the east coast community. And at all these works, brown men and white, Ha'o's people and the late rebels, the atoll men, and the east coasters, high and low without exception, toiled side by side, to the very great promotion of good feeling and mutual understanding. The ladies, meanwhile, fostered among the women and children all such imitative habits as were judged good for them, and after the stress and storm the peaceful times made for growth and enlightenment, and feelings of security and content such as Kapaa'a had never known before.

Of direct religious teaching there was no lack, though it still ran more to practice than to precept. Native habits and customs were interfered with as little as possible, save wherein they palpably ran counter to Nature's own laws and made for deterioration rather than uplifting.

The white men held their services regularly, and made them as simple as possible so that gleams of the light might penetrate dark hearts but by no means dark understandings. The brown men, at their work in the plantations, along the hillsides after the pigs and goats, and skimming along the combers on the other side of the ridge, chanted merry hymns whose meanings they understood not, but which did them no harm, and were very good to hear. The women learned many things in their own homes and in the mission houses, and the tubby, brown children rollicked nakedly in the school-house, learned games in which they delighted, and some of them were even beginning their ABC.

"Charles, my son," said Blair to Evans, as they were all sitting in usual conclave on the verandah one evening, "what do you say to vaccinating the whole community, lock, stock, and barrel? All, I mean, that did not have the plague. There may be some germs of it lurking in hidden corners yet."

"I'm willing, if you can bring them to it. I can take them in batches."

"I'll speak to Ha'o. He can make them do pretty well anything he pleases. I'm more and more thankful that he was spared to us."

"And Nai too," said Jean. "She is a great help. The women do whatever she tells them, and she's as bright as a needle. What do you think she came to ask for to-day, Ken?"

"No idea. Not a pair of shoes, I hope."

"No—some hairpins! She wanted to do her hair like ours."

"The eternal feminine," laughed Blair. "Well?"

"I assured her that it looked far nicer hanging loose with flowers stuck in it. But she was so disappointed that I had to give her the pins. You won't recognise the women in a day or two, I expect."

Blair explained the vaccination idea to Ha'o, and made it as clear as the limitations of language and understanding of so abstruse a matter permitted.

"You would give them a little crawling death to keep them from having it big?" said Ha'o, after much explanation.

"Yes, that is what it comes to."

"All those who did not have it before?"

"Yes."

"I will order it. It is right that Ra'a's people should taste it too."

Exactly what he told them they never learned, but in due course a batch of stalwart brown men came doubtfully into the compound, and watched Evans with apprehensive, white-eyed glances as he deftly pricked and bound up their arms, and sent them away looking doubtfully at their white bandages, in evident expectation of speedy and unique developments.

They were in fine healthy condition and the operation was prosperous. The bandage-wearers regarded them as badges of distinction. They looked upon their inoculation as a ceremonial necessary to full admission to the white alliance, and Blair was at once scandalised and amused by a crowd clamouring round the house next day for similar honours.

"Kenni," they cried, "make us Christians too! Prick our arms and give us our badges."

So their arms were pricked and they got their badges, and were no longer subject to the taunts of the favoured first batch, which had nearly led to friction in the village the night before.

CHAPTER XXV

THE LIFTING VEIL

Jean, and Alison Evans, and Mary Stuart found the tubby youngsters, and especially the little round, brown babies, irresistibly attractive. Such merry, mischievous little imps the former, and each newcomer such a wonder of soft, sleek, dimpled, black-velvet-eyed brownness, that their hearts went out to them, and the mothers laughed at their doting absorption and cackled strenuously and meaningly among themselves. And Aunt Jannet, never having had any children of her own, knew more about the rights and wrongs of their upbringing than any single mother ever knew in this world before, and had to be restrained by main force at times from putting some of her more strenuous theories into practice. But the good-natured brown women came to understand even Aunt Jannet's peculiarities in time, and to accept her efforts, so far as they accorded with their own ideas, with something like appreciation.

For educative purposes the children were, up to a certain age, left entirely to the care of the ladies, and it would have been hard to say whether pupils or teachers enjoyed most the time spent in nominal study in the wide, open schoolroom, or the still merrier jinks on the beach and river bank.

If Jean Blair's quondam friends in London could have seen her at play with her naked brown boys and girls on Kapaa'a front—well, in the first place they would not have known her, and when they did they would have renounced her acquaintance at once.

For the purpose of opening their little minds to better things than their fathers and mothers had known, she brought herself down to their level, became almost one of themselves, romped and played and danced with them, in the water and out of it, and captured all their hearts. And she enjoyed this partial and temporary reversion to nature as she had never enjoyed life before. The children learned many things without knowing that they were being taught, and Jean herself learned not a little also.

Aunt Jannet looked on with surprise, and spasms of doubt at times—it was all so different from her ideas of missionary work. But she had much to occupy her in connection with the other women, and as regards things generally she held an open mind, with a reserve of gentle sarcasm in case these extremely odd ways should turn out worse than she knew her own more precise methods would have done.

The men took the older boys in hand and employed ways quite as unconventional and with equally happy results, and the girls of size were well left to the care of Alison Evans and Mary Stuart, whose special training had fitted them excellently for the work.

In addition to the extraordinary curriculum of their school, the men were working hard at the new foundations of life in Kapaa'a.

It was a beginning of things such as Kenneth Blair's soul delighted in. He was at it night and day, and suffered no whit from all the hard work. For it was better even than recreation, since to all intents and purposes it was creation itself, the bringing of order out of chaos, the evolution of new life.

Ha'o, in the large hope of becoming a nation, worked with them hand to hand, and heart to heart. Savage born and all untutored, he was gifted with a sharp wit and a clear understanding, and he was a born ruler of men. He was tall in stature, and his bearing they had noted even in the hold of the Blackbirder. Of late his presence had seemed to increase in dignity, possibly from his own large belief in the future, possibly because they viewed him in the light of what they hoped to make him. Whatever it was, his own people noticed it also, and even the last returned prodigals never ventured to cross him.

His confidence in the wisdom and good faith of the white men was implicit. When he placed his hand in Blair's, the day they landed, and proclaimed himself his man, and again when they discussed the delicate subject of man-eating after his illness, he meant what he said and stuck to it loyally.

Not that he by any means assented at once to every suggestion they made. He could argue like an Old Bailey lawyer, and until a matter was explained to him so that he understood all the ins and outs, and the ultimate end and aim of it, and saw from his own point of view just how it would affect his people and himself, he would have none of it.

He would listen politely, follow with the most patient intentness, question till it was clear, argue-bargle occasionally, as Captain Cathie put it, and then,—"Kenni, it is good. It shall be,"—and some new brick was ready for the foundations.

They all enjoyed an argument with Ha'o. The turns of his quick mind were so odd and illuminating at times, that, as Evans said, it was actually educational.

Stuart especially delighted in him.

"He's an absolute revelation," he said, "And I'm more and more certain that there's more than ordinary savage blood in him. It's very queer to think of, you know, Blair. It's a clear case of reversion."

"And of evolution."

"I wonder now, if, by any conjunction of circumstances, we in Great Britain could ever go back like that."

"Impossible. The very suggestion is horrible."

"Nothing is impossible," said Evans. "The whole country might be devastated by a pestilence, and the few survivors might lapse into anything."

"Unless the whole earth were devastated in the same way, the survivors would have common sense enough to get back to their kind. But all this won't help Kapaa'a boys, so let's get to business."

They went very wisely to work, with the wisdom of long deliberation on other men's failures and successes. They imposed no restrictions save such as were absolutely necessary for the general well-being, and even these made for freedom. For the freedom of savagery is bondage worse than slavery.

They promulgated through Ha'o simple rules for the protection of life and property, and saw them carried out with the most rigid inflexibility. Any disputes, and there were many, were brought before the chief sitting in judgment on the verandah of his house on certain days, with the white men in attendance to assist his deliberations.

At first the Torch men acted as police when necessary, and carried out the orders of the court. But before long certain of the tribesmen, becoming distinguished above their fellows for their sobriety of conduct and general demeanour, were nominated to headships of sections, and did all that was necessary.

And Kapaa'a slept of a night, freed for ever from the stealthy terrors of the dark.

CHAPTER XXVI

THE GENTLE MARTYR

All these matters took time, and while their hands and hearts were full of them there came to them certain other little matters which filled both hands and hearts to overflowing.

To Kenneth and Jean Blair was born a son, and a month later to Charles and Alison Evans a daughter, and it is doubtful if anything in the history of Kapaa'a had ever stirred the feminine portion of the community to such a pitch of excitement and enthusiasm as did the arrival of these little white strangers.

"Now," said the brown women, with deeper lights in their lustrous eyes, as they gazed admiringly on the little pink-and-white squirmers, "you belong to us indeed, since you have borne children among us."

And every day they made pilgrimages to the two new shrines, and sat worshipfully, while the unconscious little saints performed their morning ablutions and then lay gazing placidly out of their blue eyes at the sights which no one else could see. Those striking blue eyes—the blue of the sky up above—completed the capture of the dark-eyed ones. There were blue eyes in plenty among the grown-up whites, but never were blue eyes like these, and the dark eyes never tired of gazing at them.

Of the rapturous joy of the two mothers, and the deep thankfulness of the fathers, there is no need to speak. For a time the new maternal cares monopolised the former, and the latter went into their island work with new high lights in their faces and with even greater vigour than before.

Aunt Harvey exulted in those babies as though she had had not a little to do with bringing them about, and Mary Stuart gloated over them with blushing cheeks and kindling eyes that told their own hopeful stories.

Every man of the Torch offered his services as nursemaid to carry them about the beach, and the numbers of small brothers and sisters they had all been in the habit of devoting their early years to was simply marvellous.

The christening ceremony—Kenneth Kapaa'a Blair and Alison Kaapa'a Evans—was an occasion of high festival throughout the islands, and Blair, with his life-work always large in his mind, turned it to account. Aunt Harvey was not present at that high ceremony, to her very great regret but more greatly to her honour. And this is how it came about.

Intercourse with the other islands had been constantly maintained by the regular visitations of the Torch and the quondam Blackbird schooner—renamed the Jean Arnot and captained by Jim Gregor, first officer of the Torch; but, compared with what had been done on Kapaa'a, the advances had been small.

Blair had, for a long while past, recognised the fact that the greatest object-lesson he could possibly offer the other chiefs was the sight of what was being done on Kapaa'a. But at the first suggestion of taking them over in the ship to see for themselves, their suspicions were in arms. That was an old trick of the white men's. They had all heard how the brown men were decoyed on board the white men's ships under wonderful promises, and never heard of again. They accepted all he gave them, they listened to all he had to say, but sail away in the big ship they would not.

Here was a chance not to be missed. Surely never in this world was there seen a younger pair of missionaries than Master Kenneth Kapaa'a Blair—Kenni-Kenni to the natives—and Miss Alison Kapaa'a Evans—Alivani—when they set out, in their frills and furbelows, to wile the hearts of the brown men and women of the outer islands.

Ha'o and Nai went with them, to add their persuasions and the argument of their presence to the rest, and Aunt Jannet went because she knew something untoward would happen to those babies unless her eye was on them.

Blair knew it would be no easy matter at best, and it was not.

At Kanele, the first island they came to, the largest of the group after Kapaa'a, about thirty miles away, the old chief Maru received them with the heartiest of welcomes, and his old wife and her daughter-in-law and all the other women went into raptures over the blue-eyed babies.

But when the subject of the visit was cautiously broached, the old man stiffened at once with his natural suspicion and declined the invitation on the spot, and nothing they could say would persuade him to it.

They stayed the night, however, and Ha'o had much talk with the old man's son, a bright stalwart fellow over six feet high whose name was Kahili. In the morning Kahili announced his intention of going with the white men. Whereupon loud lamentations from his father and mother and wife and children, who clung to him wherever they could grip, and expressed their intention of anchoring him to his native soil at cost of their lives. He reasoned with them good-humouredly at first, but finally began to get angry at the exhibition, and the more they tried to dissuade him the more determined was he to go.

Then, suddenly, the old chief surprised them all by proposing a bargain. If the white men would leave their grandmother—Aunt Jannet Harvey to wit—as pledge of their honourable intentions, both he and

Kahili his son would go in the big ship, and when they returned safe and sound the ship could take the grandmother away.

Blair laughed so much over the old fellow's 'cuteness that he came near to dispelling their suspicions. And the matter being explained to Aunt Jannet, without undue insistence upon the maturity of her new dignity, that good lady, with a somewhat forlorn attempt at nonchalance, accepted the offer on the spot, and said she would stop. And what it cost her no man may venture to say, for she had been looking forward to the christening of Jean's boy as a white stone day in her life.

"It's for the good of the work, Kenneth, so get away with them before I change my mind," said she, bravely enough.

"Oh, Aunt Jannet, I shall miss you so," from Jean, with a suspicion of tears in her voice.

"Not a bit, child. You'll have far too much to think of, and I'll be perfectly all right here."

"But—you—" for Jean knew all her longing in the matter.

"I'll chum up with Mrs. Maru, and we'll be as happy as—h'm"—with a glance at the native houses among the trees—"well, as things in a rug, you know. You shall tell me all about it when I get back. Don't let Ken forget to send for me."

She kissed the babies as though she knew in her own mind that she would never set eyes on them again, waved her adieus gallantly from the white shell beach, and when the Torch had swept out of sight round the corner she went up into a thicket of lemon hibiscus, and had it out all by herself there. Then she preened her ruffled plumes, and went down and rated Mrs. Maru for the untidiness of her dwelling-place, till the old lady regretted more than ever the exchange she had made. By degrees, however, Aunt Jannet's natural goodness and masterfulness overcame her disappointment. The two became capital friends, and talked away at one another, on a twenty-five per cent. basis of understanding, which left the most extraordinary views of the other's life on each of their minds.

Her self-sacrifice, however, bore excellent fruit. Old Maru and Kahili proved admirable bait for Blair's fishing. Persuaded themselves to a somewhat doubtful step, the step once taken they became most zealous partisans of their new cause. Assured, by the solid fact of Aunt Jannet's temporary residence on Kanele, of their own safety, they laughed to scorn the fears of others as doubtful in the matter as they themselves had originally been.

Their assured confidence amounted well-nigh to boastfulness.

"Look at us," they said, "we have no mistrust in going with the white men. Put away your fears, and come along."

The Torch made a most prosperous collection, and returned to Kapaa'a laden with dusky notables.

It would have been difficult to imagine anything less like a Christian martyr than Aunt Jannet Harvey, sitting opposite her hostess on Kanele, conscientiously eating away at the food with which they kept her supplied, wrestling strenuously with the intricacies of the Kanelese dialect, and an object of extreme curiosity to all the other women, and of wonderment to herself. But martyrs are found in the strangest guise, and Aunt Jannet wrought well for Kapaa'a when she consented to stop on Kanele that day.

The strangers viewed with amazement the changes in Kapaa'a. They had raided there aforetime, and fought more than one bloody battle on the white beach of the lagoon. For Kapaa'a, the largest of the islands and the richest, had always been an object of envy to the rest, and more than one warrior chief of the outer isles had cast longing eyes upon it, and had planned and schemed till he could attempt its conquest.

Now they found it richer and stronger than ever in the white men's alliance. They saw its comfortable homes, and large plantations of strange new grains and fruits. They were introduced to the pleasures of the chase. They ate piglet and wild goat, and found them good. They tasted still deeper of the novel atmosphere of law and order, and found these things also very good.

They watched the boys at cricket and football, and the men, brown and white, fencing and boxing as though their lives depended on it, and no harm done. They watched the cutlass drill, and tingled to do likewise. They saw the white men bowl over coco-nuts with their Winchesters at many times the distance they could hurl a spear, and do the same again quicker than they could wink, and for their benefit Long Tom bellowed his loudest, and they heard the roar of him clang to and fro among the hills. They compared the new Kapaa'a boats with their own, and they sat open-mouthed and listened to the last squeals of an ironwood tree from up the valley, as the circular saw cleft it into planks which they could not have imitated with weeks of hardest labour. And—they saw men sleep without weapons by their sides, and without fear. And these things wrought powerfully upon them, and set them thinking.

The christening feast of Kenni-Kenni and Alivani was long remembered in the Dark Islands. Aunt Jannet Harvey always professed regret at having missed it, but Kenneth Blair always assured her, with a great light in his face, that in missing it as she had done she had rendered service to the mission which no words could express.

Aunt Jannet's exile ran into a longer term than she had expected, and there were many anxious faces and apprehensive hearts in the island villages before the Torch came gliding quietly round the heads, and dropped her passengers at their homes.

They all came laden with presents, which already, before they landed, inclined them favourably towards similar trips in the future. But they brought with them also richer invisible freight of new ideas and new hopes, which kept their tongues wagging for weeks afterwards, and set their brains working.

For the visit had not by any means been confined to sight-seeing and enjoyment. The white men turned it to fullest account in the clear and definite explanation of their views and hopes for the whole group of islands, offering all an equal share in the new order of things on the sole condition of union and cohesion. The higher matters which lay closest to their hearts were touched on, but only lightly as yet. Blair had no faith in outward conversion born of a hankering after material good things. He had a firm belief in the advantages of hastening slowly. Get the savages out of their savagery, open the dark minds to the lower lights, and the higher would come in good time.

He suggested regular meetings of the headmen on Kapaa'a, and the idea was received with acclaim. Kapaa'a was a storehouse of good things. They desired no better than to come there often. And in that he saw the germ of a united nation. Ha'o, as the most advanced among them, would naturally preside.

Of Ha'o's loyalty and level-headedness he had no doubt. He was years ahead of the rest already. Blair believed his influence would grow, and in time make itself felt throughout the whole group, and through Ha'o he hoped to win them all to the higher life.

If on these highest matters of all he touched as yet but lightly, in others, concerning their material welfare, he gave them some very straight talk, by way of putting them on their guard against that which might come any day.

He told them that other white men would come offering to trade with them, to buy their land, to do great things for them, and of such he begged them to beware, and to allow him to deal with them.

He told them just what had happened in other places, where grasping white traders had pushed themselves in, bringing in with them drink, disease, and dispossession. He showed them how they, the heads of the communities, were responsible for their people. And he promised them every advantage these other men could offer them without any of the penalties.

"What do these traders come for?" he asked them, and answered himself, "To benefit themselves. And what do we come for? To benefit you. The time may be close at hand when you will have to choose between us. As you choose, so will your future be."

So the notables went back to their island homes with much to think about, and Aunt Jannet came back from Kanele, and Kenneth Blair and his friends had good reason for high hopes of the future.

It was a spring-time of hope for all of them. The work was prospering, and their hearts were full of gladness.

"Quite happy, Jean?" asked Blair, as he came up quietly and sat down beside her, where the sweet water ran into the salt, and the small waves of the lagoon creamed softly up the white sand.

"Happy, dear? Could any one possibly be happier? Look at that!"—Master Kenni-Kenni rolling gleefully on a white spread at her feet in a state of nudity, and gurgling paroxysms of happiness.

"He's a fine little fellow"—and he poked his son playfully in his fat little stomach, provoking fat-creased laughter and dimples and more gurgles.

"He's the finest little fellow in the whole world, and he's yours and mine, Ken. God has been very good to us, dear. I sometimes feel as if we had no right to be quite so happy while—"

"While?"

"One can't help thinking of the poor little souls in the slums and alleys at home. It really doesn't seem right, somehow. If we could only bring them all out here—"

"I wish it were possible, but it isn't. Meanwhile, this is our chosen work, and by God's grace it seems like to prosper. I am very grateful that you are content here, dear. After London—"

"London! I'd give the whole of London for one curl of Kenni-Kenni's hair. Isn't it beautiful? There never was any silk like it in this world."

"Never!" said Blair with conviction.

Then Alison Evans and Mary Stuart came across to them, Mary carrying Alivani.

"We have come to worship too," said Alison. "I wish you'd order Mary to give me my baby, Mr. Blair. I can hardly get touching her when she's about."

"Well, Jean won't let me have hers," laughed Mary in self-defence.

"Jean was just valuing the whole of London Town against one curl of that young man's hair. So you see what the whole of him's worth, Mary. Oh yes, you may touch him, if you'll promise not to spoil a hair of his head."

Mary laid Alivani down on the white spread by Kenni-Kenni, and the two gurgled and kicked in company, while she knelt over them with absorbed face and happy lights in her eyes.

"Jean was wishing she could bring all the poor children in London to kick on the beach here," said Blair.

"Yes. I often think how very much better off the children here are," said Alison Evans.

"In some respects."

"In all respects, I'm inclined to think. Their fathers and mothers almost worship them. Cruelty to children is unheard of. Bodily they are miles ahead—"

"And morally and spiritually?" he said, to draw her on.

"I have seen children at home, in Glasgow and Edinburgh, almost as benighted as these, and not half so pleasant to deal with. Now, with the chances we are giving them, I think these are infinitely the better off."

"Under the new order of things, perhaps. But hitherto you must remember that death dodged life round every corner here, and life broke off very short at times. However, we cannot clean up all the world; but, please God, we'll do our best with this little bit of it. And now," jumping up, "I must get back to work, or your masters will be calling me names. Don't kill those two infants with kindness, Mary."

He stood looking down upon them all for a moment, while the women all bent over the wrigglers on the white cloth.

"Is it possible that not one of you ever feels a longing for the fleshpots of Egypt?" he asked, with a smile.

"Do we ever show any symptoms?" asked Jean.

"You certainly do at the moment. You all three look as if you would like to devour those children on the spot," and he went away to grind out dialects with Matti and Ha'o.

CHAPTER XXVII

PEACE WITH A SPEAR

The work progressed favourably but not without occasional set-backs. On Kapaa'a, where its supervision was most constant, the advance was naturally greatest. On the outer islands the brown men and women were effusive in their promises—in expectation of largesse. Like the prodigals of all time, they were always ready to discount future benefits—which they did not very fully understand and considered somewhat problematic—for a trifle on account, which they understood extremely well. But the moment their preceptors' backs were turned, the promises were forgotten in immediate enjoyment of the reward.

All this was only what was to be expected, and in no way disconcerted the labourers in the field. Blair would rate the delinquents good-humouredly for their shortcomings, and they would acknowledge them like schoolboys, promise amendment, and break the promise before the Torch had rounded the Head. He felt himself in closer touch with them, however, on each visit, and was satisfied. His plans and hopes were very wide-reaching, and God's temples, natural, physical, or spiritual, do not rise in a day.

Occasionally there were more serious lapses, and these had to be dealt with firmly but delicately, so thin were the cords by which he held them.

Aia, the smallest island of the group, lay a short five miles beyond Kanele, sacred to the memory of Aunt Jannet Harvey. Aia had a population of about fifty. Kanele three times as many.

Blair and Jean and Kenni-Kenni landed on the latter one day, on one of the regular rounds of visitation, and received the usual expectant welcome from old Maru and Kahili and the rest. The women crowded enthusiastically round Jean and her boy, while Blair talked to the men and divided among them the things he had brought. They stopped on shore several hours and were regaled with fruits and coco-nuts. When they got into the boat the whole population lined the beach and waved them farewells.

"We really seem to be getting hold of them at last," said Blair, as they rolled along towards the Torch.

"They are very friendly and seem very glad to see us," said Jean, and they went on to Aia.

"Something wrong," said Captain Cathie, as the Torch drew in.

The village was not in its usual place. There were no people about.

They landed cautiously, Blair and Cathie and half a dozen men, and found the houses in ruins. With added caution they climbed the hill, and in time came upon the villagers lurking in holes and crannies.

Their story was simple. The very day after the Torch's last visit, the men of Kanele, headed by Maru and young Kahili, had come over in their canoes and demanded the goods they had received from the white men. These being refused, they proceeded to take them by force. The Aia men were outnumbered and beaten, their village burned, and several of them killed—and eaten. The rest had lived in the fear of death ever since.

Blair was a man of wrath that day. His first feeling was the same as Captain Cathie's, in whom the natural man always ran strong.

"Well, captain, what do you advise?" he asked.

"I'd like to give those Kanele men a right good skelping," said Cathie warmly. "Something they wouldn't forget in a hurry."

"So would I, but I'm not sure of the wisdom of it."

"Truckling beggars! Sweet as milk when we're there, and playing the devil the minute our back's turned. They need a lesson."

"We'll take the night over it. It's a serious matter."

They walked the deck far into the night, with the big stars swimming in the smooth black rollers, and the distant roar of the Aia surges, now to port and now to starboard, as they beat gently to and fro in default of anchorage.

"In the first place," said Blair, summing up their ideas, "these people are not safe here. Whatever we do or don't do, the Kanele men will take it out of them as soon as we're gone. We must do our best to persuade them to migrate to Kapaa'a. That will be a good thing for them and a good thing for us. As to the Kanele men, the difficulty is that we want to retain our hold on them. This affair only shows how great the need is. And if we take measures against them—any measures almost—we are like to weaken the small hold we have now."

"All the same," said Cathie bluntly, "it won't do to let 'em think they can carry on like this and nothing said about it. That'd be fair provoking them to do the same again."

"It's difficult to know just what to do," said Blair; and Jean down below, with Kenni-Kenni nestling close in her arms, heard the four feet tramping, tramping, slowly and heavily, to and fro, till she fell asleep. They seemed to be still tramping whenever the Torch gave a sudden kick and woke her. But there was a sense of guardianship in the very sound, and Kenni-Kenni's soft head against her heart was very comforting.

In the morning they set to work on the plans they had arrived at overnight.

Blair went ashore early, while Cathie prepared for his passengers.

It did not need five minutes' talk to show the Aia men how unsafe their position was. It was self-evident. But it took much talk and persuasion to induce them to migrate to Kapaa'a.

They saw the advantages. Some of them had been there already and seen for themselves; but the brown men cling to their own bits of coral or volcanic rock as strenuously as Highland crofter to his dripping heather, or Irish peasant to his patch of bog.

The women, however, had listened to those marvellous accounts of the unheard-of security of life and property on Kapaa'a, and now they joined forces with Blair and carried the day. By sunset they were all aboard the Torch with such belongings as the Kanele men had left them. The Torch beat to and fro again throughout the night, and not a native closed an eye for the strangeness of it all, and in the early morning Blair was ashore again on Kanele. He had assured Jean there was no danger; but he left Captain Cathie behind—to look after the crowd of brown men and women.

He walked boldly up to old Maru's house, and found it still asleep.

The old man started up wide awake at his call, and the look on his face was a matrix of Blair's—detected wrong quailing before righteous wrath.

"You know what I have come about, Maru," said Blair. "You have done ill by Aia. Why?"

"It was the young men. They desired more goods."

"Call the young men. I will speak to them."

But there was no need to call them. They had seen the Torch and were coming, and coming in expectation of possible trouble, for they all came armed.

"Yes, I see you know why I have come back," said Blair, as they thronged about the house. "You have done wrong, and you have got to answer for it. We came here to make life brighter by bringing peace—"

"We don't want peace. Fighting is very much better," growled one.

"Oh, you are brave men! How many men were there on Aia? Twenty-five at most. And how many of you went over? More than sixty. Oh yes, you like fighting when the others are weak. How will you like it when you are beaten and running for your lives into the hills? You have done ill, and you must answer for it. Maru and Kahili will come with me to Kapaa'a, and we will decide what shall be done."

"Not me!" said old Maru, or words to that effect, and drew from its hiding-place one of the axes Blair had given him, and began to swing it gently in his hand.

"If you do not come, we shall fetch you. It is for you to say. If we have to fetch you, it will make trouble."

Old Maru's axe swung gently to and fro, to and fro, as though hungering to bite, but doubtful.

"That would not serve you, Maru," said Blair quietly. "Though you cut me in pieces, the rest would come and you would suffer the more. The old times are past. We have come to give you better times. Peace you shall have, though we have to bring it with club and spear."

And just then Long Tom on the yacht bellowed his tremendous note, and the brown men looked round apprehensively.

"That is my big canoe speaking," said Blair. "But it is only a warning. It can strike as hard as it talks. Will you save trouble by coming, Maru?"

"I will not go."

"Then we shall come for you. I am sorry; but the wrong-doing is yours.... Let no man lift his hand, or worse will follow," he said, as a restless movement rustled among them. Then eyeing them steadily, he passed through, not sure at what moment axe or club might fall on his head. But so high was his look that no man, even of those he had passed, found courage for the blow, and he walked down to the beach alone.

"I'm mighty glad to see you back whole," said Cathie, as Blair swung up on deck. "I saw their clubs through the glass, and I misdoubted them. They wouldn't come?"

"No, they wouldn't come, so I promised to fetch them. Now we'll get on, captain. First to land our passengers on Kapaa'a, and then as we decided last night."

Ha'o and the rest were mightily surprised at the size of the Torch's company. But the chief jumped to Blair's views at once.

"You will soon become a nation at this rate, Ha'o."

"I will deal well with them," said Ha'o.

"And now as to the men of Kanele?"

"We will make an end of them."

"I want them as part of your nation, and dead men are no use. If we go in force enough, I do not think they will fight. But they have broken the peace, and they must have a lesson."

"We will teach them with the spear. It will be a lesson for the others also. When shall we start?"

"The sooner the better; but first we must see the newcomers housed."

That took two days, and then the Torch and the Jean Arnot sailed with larger crews than they were in the habit of carrying. First round the other islands, at each of which Blair and Ha'o landed and had a talk with the headmen and explained their ideas to them.

And much hard talking it took, in some cases, to carry their views. But they were set on it, and they prevailed.

From each village they enlisted the headman and certain of his followers, from six to ten, according to the population, and in due course came down on Kanele one hundred and fifty brown men and eighteen whites, with Long Tom in reserve, and great hopes that so large a display would suffice without any fighting.

All the boats on Kapaa'a had been requisitioned for the debarkation, and it was an imposing flotilla that drew in to Kanele beach that day to bring peace at the point of the spear. And, composed, as the gathering was, of the most discordant elements, it was yet all moulded to one purpose by the strong will of one man, and by the very differences that separated its units one from another. For each component felt itself but a part of the whole, and in a minority which left it no option but to work with the rest.

Not a soul was to be seen on shore, but they knew that black eyes watched stealthily from every cover.

"Maru! Kahili! We have come for you," shouted Blair. "Here are Ha'o of Kapaa'a, and Ruel of Anape—" and he recited all the names of the head-men. "We will give you till the shadows are smallest to come in. Then be it on your own heads!" and the great company sat down on the beach to pass the time.

"Will they come?" asked Blair of Ha'o.

"They will come," said Ha'o. "They would have no chance against us, and they are not fools."

Blair seized the opportunity for more talk with the leading men from the other islands. He showed them that none were safe if raiding were permitted, not even the strongest, for against the strongest combination might prevail. The only security was in union against illdoers; and he rubbed that lesson into them till they were not likely to forget it.

Before the wheeling shadows had shortened the slim black lines of the palms into their spreading crowns, a tumult broke out inland, and as they all stood expectant, a mob, in which were many women, came hurrying along, with old Maru and Kahili on its front like corks on a swelling tide.

"It is well," said Blair, as he went to meet them. "You have given us much trouble, but you have saved yourselves more. Do you understand, Maru, and you, Kahili, and all you men and women of Kanele, what this great company means? It means that the old times are gone for ever, and that the better times are come. If there is to be any fighting in future, we of Kapaa'a and the islands round about will have our say in the matter. Take those two to the boats," and at a sign from him a file of Torches led the prisoners away. "There are others among you who prefer war to peace," he said. "I want them also."

This caused a hubbub amongst them, and much hot discussion, but at last certain ones were evolved from the crowd, and pushed to the front protesting, and to the number of ten he had them marched down to the boats, amid the wailing of their women.

"Now, listen!" cried Blair, waving down their cries with a peremptory hand. "Is it to be peace or war henceforth?"

"Peace," wailed the women, and the men stood silent. "Then let the women bring here all the spears and clubs, for you will not need them."

This was touching them on the raw, for the brown man's weapons are his dearest possessions.

But this was to be a lesson once and for all, and not for the men of Kanele only.

"I must have them," said Blair. "If you will not bring them, we must get them ourselves. Which shall it be?"

The men stood, stubborn and sulky. Some of the women on the outskirts of the crowd began to trickle away.

Then old Maru's wife crept up downcastly from the side of the throng, carrying two long spears and a club, and cast them on the sand at Blair's feet.

"It is good, Maruaine," he said gently.

"You will not kill our men, Missi?" she asked piteously.

"I have come to make your lives happier, Maruaine. I will not hurt a hair of their heads. But they must learn, and this is the first lesson."

Kahili's wife followed, and one by one the other women came, with more spears and clubs, till the pile was a goodly one.

Then he had a fire kindled beneath them, and the brown men watched its easy lighting with a match with wonder, but twisted uneasily as the weapons were consumed.

"Now, listen!" said Blair, when the crackling died down. "Maru and Kahili, and the others we have taken will go with us to Kapaa'a for a time, and will live with us there. We intend them no harm. They will, I hope, learn many things amongst us, and then they will come back and tell you of them. We wish your good, only your good, always your good. But those who do ill, who break the peace, and rob their weaker neighbours, will have to answer to us for it. Ha'o of Kapaa'a has known us now a long time. He will tell you that we mean you well."

And Ha'o stood out before them, tall and brown, and said, in a voice that rang above the wash of the surf and the pattering of the palm fronds—

"Kenni is my brother. He has done great things for Kapaa'a. Twice he saved my life, and the lives of my people. Three times he risked his own life, and the lives of his people. His blood has run for us. What Kenni says and does is good. Any man who thinks otherwise I am ready to talk to him," and it was evident to all that Ha'o's talk would be strong, and to the point.

Blair said a word or two to him, and he added—

"While Maru and Kahili are living with us, Maru's wife will be your chief. She is a wise woman, and loves peace more than war. Has any one anything to say against it?"

No one at the moment desired to say anything against it, whatever they might think or feel.

"It is well," said Ha'o. "Let no man speak against it when we are not here. Now you will bring us food, and then we will go home."

Two very sober and thoughtful men were Maru and Kahili as Kanele sank into the sea astern. They were treated, however, with every consideration, and Blair was at much pains to explain his ideas to them so far as concerned themselves. For the rest, it was curious to notice how the men of each island kept themselves to themselves. There were differences of dialect, of course, which interfered somewhat with freedom of intercourse, but there were also lifelong memories of bloody feuds which kept them apart. It was a mighty step towards better times to see them there in peaceful toleration of one another's presence. The dividing lines were at once the mark of the past and the sign of the future. A year before they would have been at one another's throats.

On Kapaa'a the hostages received the same equal treatment with the rest. They were given houses and tools, and shown how to use them. They joined in the chase, and developed discriminating tastes in the matter of fresh-killed pig and goat cooked in paw-paw leaves. They were neither talked at nor preached at. They were simply allowed to absorb the new atmosphere of law and order, and found it good. And in due time they were returned to their own island new men, with the seeds of still larger knowledge within them.

CHAPTER XXVIII

NO THOROUGHFARE

It would be difficult to tell in words the exaltation of spirit which possessed Kenneth Blair at the brave show the new order of things was making in these Dark Islands of his choice. It was a beginning after his own heart, and he rejoiced in it greatly.

I can imagine what he must have looked like as he went about his Master's business—clad always in white from head to foot, and carrying always that high look of his, blazing with enthusiasm and the mighty joy of life, which caught the eye and held it. Kekera—White Fire—the brown men often called him, and he looked it to the life.

He felt things growing under his hand, and his heart was full. A beginning of beginnings and visible growth—what more could the soul of man desire?

Domestic concerns were prospering also. Mary Stuart had the satisfaction of her heart in a little son, and Kenni-Kenni and Alivani crawled neck and neck races on the white beach together. The schools were full, for the teaching was so sheer a delight that the wriggling brown bodies and glancing black eyes felt a day missed a day lost. If ever learning came without tears it did to these. They were actually beginning to use English words now and again in their talk and play—by way of showing off at first, indeed, but presently as a matter of course. And the larger children, their fathers and mothers, were imbibing new ideas of all kinds at a revolutionary rate. They were even beginning to put theirs into "Kown im!" and to show some knowledge of what the words meant.

And so far there had been no further disturbance from the outside; but they were always on the look-out for it, and it came, and in the expected shape.

The Dark Islands lie far out of the ordinary track of commerce. For that very reason, when once discovered, they offered unusual inducements to such as found the usual fields too small, and too hot, for their peculiar forms of immorality. The outposts of civilisation, such as it is, have not infrequently been pushed forward by individuals whom civilisation could no longer tolerate in its midst. It was such a one who came out of his way—and incidentally out of the way of some who ardently desired to lay hands on him—to bring the amenities of commerce and civilisation to the Dark Islands.

Old Maru, and his son Kahili, and the other hostages to law and order, had returned to their homes full to the brim of new ideas and great intentions, and Blair reposed great hopes in them.

He and Cathie, on one of their usual rounds of the islands in the Torch, came sailing round Kanele Head one day and were surprised to find a ship at anchor in the bay.

"Ah!" broke from them both at the sight.

"So that's come," said Cathie. "Bound to sooner or later. Nip it tight, sir, is my advice."

He gave some orders to the mate, and they went ashore.

A burly individual in sailorly garb came down the beach from Maru's house to meet them. He was stout and evil-faced, with small blue eyes and tangled hay-coloured beard and moustache, and the roll in his walk seemed too pronounced to come entirely from much walking of slippery decks.

"Morning," he said curtly. "Traders?"

"No, sir. Missionaries in charge."

"Gee-whilikins!"

"Yes, very much so," and Blair pulled out his watch. The man needed no investigation. His character was written all over him. "It is now nine o'clock. I will give you till half-past ten to clear out of here. If your anchor is not up by that time you will take the consequences. Understand?"

"Say, have you bought this island, mister?" gaped the other.

"Yes, from the devil and all his works, so you clear out. It is now two minutes past nine, and you've got eighty-eight minutes left."

"Well, I'm—"

"You will be if you don't stir your stumps."

"And suppos'n I say I'll be hanged if I go."

"I should consider it not unlikely. You certainly will if you stay."

"Well, I am—! Was it missionaries you said?"

"That's what I said."

"Very well, then," said the invader, pulling himself together, "I'll see you eternally annihilated first." That was not his exact expression, but it is printable and will suffice.

"Eighty-six minutes left," said Blair quietly.

Captain Cathie waved his hat three times to the Torch, and Long Tom's angry bellow rolled up into the hills and lined the side of the trader with curious faces.

"Missionaries! Well, I am—" and he looked at them, and then at the Torch with the cloud of blue-white smoke drifting slowly away from her deck, and then turned and humped his shoulders and went back the way he had come, and Blair and Cathie followed him.

They were all fast asleep at Maru's house, and not likely to waken in a hurry, if the empty rum bottles scattered about were anything to go by. There were some opened cases of trade lying about, and the scraps and remnants of a feast—in addition to the inert forms of old Maru and his wife, and Kahili and his wife, and some of their people.

"Eighty minutes!" said Blair grimly, as he looked round on this undoing of his work.

"Say, mister, couldn't we come to some arrangement?" began the trader.

"Certainly! The arrangement is that you up anchor and away inside—seventy-nine minutes," with a glance at his watch.

"I guess you'll pay for this 'fore you're done, mister. I'm an American citizen."

"Sorry to hear it."

"And an American citizen don't stand bein' fired out like this and no reasons given—not by a long sight!"

"There are our reasons," said Blair, pointing to the heavy sleepers, "and there are yours," and he pointed to the half-emptied case of rum. "Seventy-eight minutes more!"

The American citizen looked him over for a moment but found no hope of amelioration in his face.

"Well, I'm—" and he turned to the door and whistled shrilly to his ship, and presently a boat came slouchily across to the shore.

"Carry them things aboard," he ordered, and saw it done, and then followed his men into the boat.

Then he stood up in the stern and delivered himself luridly on missionaries in general, and on this new kind, as represented by Blair and Cathie, in particular.

"You'll hear of me again, my sons, sure as my name's Hartford Crawley. Yes, by thunder, you will, and don't you forget it!" was his valediction with threatening fist, and they could hear him cursing all the way to the ship.

Blair and Cathie returned to the Torch. At half-past ten Long Tom thundered a reminder to Mr. Crawley that his time was up, and before the echoes died away, the trader's anchor was apeak and his sails were dropping sulkily to the breeze.

He headed slowly out to sea, and was surprised to find the Torch do the same.

He took a notion towards the south. Long Tom barked angrily at him.

He tried a move towards the north. Long Tom barked again. Due west was his course, and they would permit him no other.

All day long the Torch followed him like a sheep dog, and at night drew in so close that they could hear Mr. Crawley still swearing at large. Fortunately, the moon was almost at the full, and he had no chance of slipping away in the dark. For three days they dogged him and kept him to his course. Then they ranged up within speaking distance and delivered their final word, "These islands are not open to traders. If you ever return you do so at your peril." Then they turned and laid their course for Kanele.

Arbitrary action, undoubtedly, but Kenneth Blair was the last man in the world to shirk what he deemed his duty from any fear of possible after consequences.

Maru and the rest were in their right minds when they got back to the island. They were full of excuses and explanations, but Blair said little to them beyond emphasising the fact that these were the men he had warned them against, and that their coming would make for evil times among them. And old Maru, in the keen recollection of the very bad head he had had the day after the trader's supper party was disposed to think he was right.

CHAPTER XXIX

THE ACT OF GOD

A full year of quiet progress left no monumental happenings to record.

The islands were rising rapidly out of their original darkness, and the hearts of the workers were as full as their hands.

Growth in the homes had necessitated ampler accommodation for scholars and worshippers outside. A church and two school-houses had been built to supply the absolute want, and were in full use.

The r and the capital H had got into "Crown Him!" and in some quarters a visible understanding of the meaning of the invocation.

Matters all round were progressing favourably. The bodily health of the islands was good, morally and spiritually it was improving. Law and order were striking slow roots into the shaky quagmire of custom and superstition, and Ha'o was in fair way to become a nation. For the headmen of the smaller islands came regularly to Kapaa'a for consultation—and gifts—and his influence over them grew steadily.

In all matters economic and politic Blair put Ha'o forward as head and front. For himself, he desired nothing but the good of the people, and he judged it best that the executive power should remain in native hands so long as they continued capable and trustworthy. In these matters Ha'o had justified him to the fullest, and had shown himself an apt, not to say an ambitious, pupil. Feuds were of rarer occurrence, and had even been brought to Kapaa'a for adjustment. Cannibalism was no longer openly indulged in, even in the outer islands, and they were hopeful that its day was past.

Evans and his wife had been resident for some months past on Kanele, Charles and Mary Stuart were on Anape, and the Jean Arnot had had a busy time going to and fro between the settlements. The Torch, with Captain Cathie on board, had made a voyage to Sydney, carrying letters home, and bringing back supplies and news. That was nearly twelve months ago, and was the only communication they had had with civilisation since they turned their backs on it.

Kenneth Blair and Jean and Aunt Jannet Harvey and Captain Cathie were sitting one evening on the platform of the mission house, enjoying the well-earned rest of busy workers. Master Kenni-Kenni was crawling about at their feet in light attire, with a strong band of knitted wool round his sturdy body, to which a thin rope and Aunt Jannet were attached, to keep him from falling overboard.

The sun was sinking, red and misty, into a bank of cloud which lay heavily across the western sky, though it still wanted an hour of sunset. The lagoon was sombre red, the spouts of foam on the reef gleamed dusty rose white, the hills behind were dull red bronze and the mouth of the valley was filling with purple shadows.

Cathie had been giving them the latest news of the Evanses and Stuarts, whom he had just been visiting in the Torch, which, with the Jean Arnot, now lay rolling sleepily over their own black shadows in the lagoon.

"Well," said Aunt Jannet, as she hauled Kenni-Kenni back from destruction and the edge of the platform, which for the moment was the limit of his ambition, "I've been hot in my life before, but to-day beats everything. It was like an oven."

"I had to start the engines to get home," said Cathie. "I came in by the lower entrance and there wasn't a breath of air. But we'll have a change soon, and a big one too if the barometer's anything to go by. I've been getting out double cables and kedges to the rocks for both the ships."

"We wondered what you were busy at," said Blair. "You expect a heavy blow?"

"You never can tell, and it's best to be on the safe side. We've been uncommonly lucky so far. But when the weather does get its back up here it sometimes gets it pretty high—Hel—lo!"

The arm of the hill which ran down into the water hid the seaward view on that side. As Cathie spoke, a trim black vessel, with a thin trail of smoke at its cream-coloured funnel, came silently round the point.

They all jumped up at so unusual a sight and stood watching eagerly.

"Service ship," said Cathie. "What on earth is she doing here?"

At sight of the two ships in the lagoon the stranger slowed down, and then her syren pealed shrilly across the water.

"We'd better go and see," said Blair, and the two sprang down off the platform and ran to the whale-boat drawn up on the beach. The Torch men and a crowd of curious natives were already there.

"Now, lads, show the navy men how you can row," was the captain's order, and in two minutes the white boat was bounding towards the opening in the reef. It leaped the rollers and presently drew in to the rows of bronzed faces which lined the side of the ship and looked on approvingly.

"This is Kapaa'a, I presume?" asked a tall man in a heavily-braided cap.

"This is Kapaa'a," said Blair.

"And is this Mr. Blair?"

"I am Kenneth Blair. This is Captain Cathie."

"Come on board, gentlemen." A ladder dropped over the side, and they swung up to the deck.

"Can we get inside there, captain?" asked the tall man. "And is there anchorage? I don't much like the look of the weather and the barometer is unusually low."

"Yes, sir, it's going to blow, or I'm much mistaken. You can get in all right. There's no bottom to that hole in the reef. But whether you'll be better inside or outside, if it blows hard, I wouldn't like to say. I've kedged both the schooners there, and I think they'll ride it out."

"And there's plenty of water and good holding?"

"Plenty water to within a couple of hundred yards of the shore. The shelf breaks there. Holding's fair. You'd better kedge same as we've done."

"Perhaps you'll con her in for us to what you consider a good position. We shall be here for some time, and it'll be pleasanter inside. You'll excuse me, Mr. Blair, for the moment. We'll have plenty of time to talk when we get ashore," and he went up on to the bridge with Cathie, and the big ship headed for the reef. She went weltering through the passage with the big rollers roaring at her stern, and crept up under lee of the southern ridge. Then the anchor went down with a plunge, and the boats dropped lightly into the water to carry the kedges and cables to the rocks.

Blair stood watching observantly. The ship he saw was H.M.S. Bonita. He casually asked one of the men, who happened to stand by him for a moment, where they were from, and was told "Australia," and the captain's name was Plantagenet Pym. Captain Pym had seemed a bit stiff in his manner, Blair thought, but that style, he knew, often went with a heavily-braided cap, and he thought no more of it.

Presently the two captains came down from the bridge and approached him.

"You will permit me to offer you such hospitality as the island affords, captain?" said Blair.

The other seemed to hesitate for a moment, then he replied, "Thank you, Mr. Blair, I shall have to be ashore part of the time so I will avail myself of your offer. I will accompany you in five minutes. Can I offer you any refreshment—a glass of wine?" and on their declining this he disappeared below.

He was up again inside the five minutes, and with a word or two to his senior lieutenant, descended the ladder into the whale-boat.

"Your crew does you credit, captain," he said to Cathie, as the proximity of the uniform braced every man of them to his best.

"Picked men, every one of them, sir, and good men all," said Cathie proudly, and every man felt himself a good inch taller.

The dull red glow had faded off the hills and out of the sky. The water of the lagoon was the colour of lead, with a sullen heave in it. The jets of foam on the reef looked like the fangs of wolves against the dark sky beyond. There were cold whispers in the air, and the palm-trees on shore shivered audibly. The white mission-houses and buildings gleamed chill white against the dark hill, but yet gave a touch of comfort and civilisation to the scene.

The crowding natives were greatly impressed by the sight of Captain Pym. Ha'o underwent the process of presentation with extreme dignity, and then Blair led the captain to his house.

"Why—Mr. Pym!" cried Aunt Jannet, who was nearest the steps and so met him first. "It is good of you just to drop in on us in this way," and she shook his hand with a warmth that almost succeeded in infusing the like into his response.

"Yes, I've come over six thousand miles to call on you, Mrs. Harvey. And how are you, Mrs. Blair? Still suffering exile with equanimity?"

"No exile, no suffering, Captain Pym," said Jean brightly. "We are all enjoying ourselves extremely, I assure you."

"Well, I suppose one can bring one's mind to anything."

"If it's the right kind of mind, you can," said Aunt Jannet heartily.

There was just a touch of implication in her tone and manner that some folks were not the happy possessors of that kind of mind. Captain Pym stiffened back into officiality somewhat.

"And you really experience no longings for London again, Mrs. Blair?" he asked, metaphorically turning his back on Aunt Jannet, who magnanimously went inside to see after supper.

"Not the very slightest."

"Marvellous!"

"You see I have here what I had not in London You shall see my boy in the morning. He's the finest little fellow in the world."

"Ah! ... I suppose that fills many a want."

"He fills our hearts so that there is no room for wants. Are you making a long stay?"

"That depends. A few days, at all events."

"We shall have heaps of things to show you. All our work here, and there's a wonderful valley down there with great stone gods that date back to about the time of the flood. Some ancient race that used to live here, they say. We will have a picnic there."

"If I have time I shall enjoy it."

In due course the time came, but Captain Pym enjoyed it less than he had anticipated.

"Now, good people, supper's ready, and you'll all catch your deaths if you sit out there any longer," called Aunt Jannet from the doorway. "We have been stewing with the heat all day," she added to Captain Pym, "and now it's gone to the other extreme. I think you must have brought a cold wind with you, captain."

"We haven't had a breath all day. It looks like a spell of dirty weather," said the captain.

The wind was coming off the sea in cold gusts. A weary half moon was bucketting through a rout of ragged clouds, which sped on over the mountains as if in haste to hide themselves from some unseen pursuer. In the gaps of the hurrying clouds the moon and a few stars shone wanly, and in their dim, ineffective light, the water of the lagoon tossed brokenly like a pan of boiling lead. The flying rags of cloud came from the dark bank in the west into which the sun had dropped. It was spreading upwards. The roar of the reef sounded harsher than usual and full of threatening. There was a strange uncanny look and feeling abroad.

"We're certainly in for something," said Captain Cathie, as he stood looking out to sea. "I've never seen it quite like this before. I shall go and sleep aboard the Torch"—which did not add to their cheerfulness.

"You'll have some supper first, captain?" said Aunt Jannet.

"Oh, yes, I'll make sure of some supper. If it's to be a fight I can fight better on a full stomach than an empty one."

So they went inside, and found it pleasant to close the door, which was a very unusual thing with them.

Captain Pym's manner during supper was still somewhat stiff and formal; but he unbent enough to give them the latest astonishing news of the outside world, the lack of which was the one thing they felt somewhat at times. But it was only when the pipes were alight afterwards that he disclosed himself.

"You are wondering, no doubt, what brings me here, Mr. Blair," he said.

"Well—yes, somewhat. You are the first visitor we have had."

"Not quite. And it is because of those others that I am here."

Blair looked at him in surprise. Captain Cathie nodded understandingly, as though in confirmation of his own thoughts.

"Certain complaints have been made to the Government concerning some of your doings here, and they have sent me to look into the matter."

"I—see. You refer to the kidnappers we put a stopper on—"

"That complaint comes from Peru. There is one also from the American government—"

"Ah, yes—Mr.—What-was-his-name?—Crawley, was it? He promised we should hear from him. Well, sir, we shall be glad to put our side of the case before you. You shall see what we have done here since we came, and no doubt you will appreciate our desire to safeguard our work in every possible way. We have done no single thing we in any way regret, and we would not hesitate to do the same again if occasion should arise."

"Ah," said Captain Pym, with a knowing official nod, "you gentlemen of the cloth, when you get right away from any authority but your own, sometimes go to extremes, and are perhaps tempted to magnify your office somewhat."

"That is quite impossible," said Blair quietly. "I consider my office the very highest in the world. As far as in me lies I have worked up to my ideal of it, and shall continue to do so. As to going to extremes, we have simply defended our work from spoliation. That also we shall continue to do."

"Hear, hear!" said Aunt Jannet energetically, and Captain Pym frowned officially at the pair of them.

"Supposing, Captain Pym," broke in Cathie, by way of lightning conductor, "you had an unarmed tender attached to your ship, and an enemy stole up in the night and carried her off, crew and all, you would consider yourself justified in following and bringing her back, and taking payment out of the other side."

"That's the way to put it," said Aunt Jannet.

"The cases are not parallel, sir. That would be a casus belli, and I should of course do my duty. You have no authority—"

"Oh yes, we have," said Blair warmly. "The very highest"—and as Captain Pym did not seem to appreciate that point, he added—"but, apart from that, we have the endorsement of Mr. Annesley, the Colonial Secretary. He and the Earl of Selsea were good enough to take very great interest in our intended work here. I laid all my plans before them, and they approved them. In fact, they spoke of a protectorate."

"The Earl of Selsea is dead, and Mr. Annesley retired from office twelve months ago."

"Ah, that may account for things. I am very sorry to hear that. However, we don't need the protectorate. Kapaa'a is almost on to its own feet, and can speak for itself."

"And what position does Mr. Blair occupy in the government?" asked Pym, with a cynical touch in his voice.

"None whatever, sir, and desires none. We have consistently worked through the chief Ha'o, whom you met on the beach. Nothing has been done without his approval. It is his elevation and his people's that we desire, not our own, and I think I may say he is as keen on it as we are."

"From all accounts, however, your work has by no means been confined entirely to the spiritual department, Mr. Blair; Long Toms and Winchesters hardly come within the strict bounds of the missionary calling."

"The shepherd may use his crook to keep the wolves off his flock. Our crooks consist, as you say, of Winchesters and a Long Tom. If we had not had them we should not be here—nor would our flock. My ideas of missionary duties may strike you as somewhat advanced, Captain Pym, but then, you see, I have the advantage of knowing all the requirements of the case. The very first essential to progress is peace, and you can't procure it with words when you're dealing with elementary facts."

"If we'd settled all those elementary facts at the start, as Captain Cathie and I advised, we would have heard no more about them," said Aunt Jannet, with a regretful shake of the head. "It's possible to be too conscientious for this world."

"We work for both, you see. I admit that a clean sweep would have saved much trouble. But I couldn't bring myself to hanging them, richly as they deserved it. As to the American citizen, his end and aim was to introduce the drink traffic, and that we won't have at any price. Not even under government orders."

Their talk had been so vital that the waxing of the gale outside had passed unnoticed, though the door was jerking at its latch and the windows buzzed like bees.

When the discussion came to a pause, Captain Cathie jumped up and went to the window.

"I'm off," he said quickly.

"If Mrs. Blair will excuse me for to-night, I will go too," said Pym. "If there is risk for the Torch there is risk for the Bonita, and I would sooner be on the spot."

"I hope there is no danger," said Jean. "We have had many a big storm, but the ships have never suffered."

"Barometer's lower than it's ever been since we came here," said Cathie, with a shake of the head; "and I've no doubt Captain Pym feels as I do, that when you don't know what's in the wind it's as well to be where you can find out."

"Quite so," said Captain Pym, and Blair went down with them to the boat.

They were nearly blown off their feet before they got to it, and the waves that swept up the white beach were such as they had never seen on it before. The rush of the wind in their ears dulled all other sounds. In the spasmodic gleams of the moon through the ragged clouds they could see the rollers sweeping over the barrier reef with unbroken crests, and the usually placid lagoon was in a turmoil.

"Can we manage it?" shouted Pym, in Cathie's ear.

"Under the lee of the ledge there," shouted Cathie, and pounded on the door of the men's house for his crew.

Blair helped them down with the boat, saw them all soaked through before they could get afloat, and then watched them toil away into the lee of the protecting ridge of rocks.

"They'll have their own to-do to get there," he said, when he got back to the house. "The waves are coming right in over the reef. I never saw anything like it."

"Is this man going to make trouble for us, Ken?" asked Jean anxiously.

"Oh, I don't think so. Don't worry about him, dear. He's a bit bumptious and unsympathetic, but I think we can show him that we could have done no less than we did. He doesn't trouble me in the slightest. Whatever he does, our work stands and tells its own tale."

In the morning it seemed to the unknowing as though the storm had blown itself out. The wind had fallen, but the sky was heavy; dark grey clouds boiled along close above mud-coloured waves, and the horizon lay just back of the reef. The sun made a faint fight for a show, but looked and felt out of place, and after pushing ghostly fingers through stray holes in the clouds, and peeping at the water below, went into retirement again.

The two captains came ashore after breakfast, but when Jean expressed satisfaction at the passing of the storm without any damage, Cathie only shook his head.

"Now, Captain Pym," said Blair, as they walked along towards the village, "let me remind you that less than two years ago these people were eating one another, and delighting in it. There has not been a man eaten on Kapaa'a for over twelve months now. Here is the boys' school. That is the girls'. As it is Sunday, they are all in church waiting for us. Perhaps you will stop for the service. It is very short and simple. Then we will go on and show you other evidences of our work."

The church was crowded, and when the brown men and women and children sang "Crown Him!" at the full stretch of their lungs, most of their black eyes were fixed on Captain Pym—to his great discomfort—as though they applied the hymn specifically to him, which possibly some of them did.

After service Blair conducted him to the village, and on to the plantations and taro fields, and even Captain Pym's official phlegm and preconceived notions had to acknowledge that, for a country three years ago buried in barbarism, the sights he saw were very striking.

He did not say much. His feelings were at strife. He had come to condemn, and he found himself forced to admit and admire.

The plantations had by degrees crept a considerable way up the valley. The party came back along the shoulder of Ra'a's hill, and as they came towards the open a furious gust of wind carried them almost off their feet.

And then they saw the most appalling sight of their lives, and one they never forgot.

Out of the dim grey curtain of the west there appeared a monstrous sinuous shape that reached from sky to sea, and came swirling towards the island with an easy voluptuous grace that was full at once of haphazard fortuity and most malign intention.

They stood frozen. Blair suddenly gripped Pym by the arm. He could not speak.

Behind the first monster came another, and another, and another, all reeling hither and thither like drunken demons, but all making straight for the island.

"Good God!" cried Pym, and instinctively put his hands to his mouth to shout a warning to his ship, a shout that could not have carried five inches.

Then he commenced to run down the hill as he had never run in his life before. His whole thought was for his ship and his men, Blair's and Cathie's for the people below.

Captain Pym reached the beach through a crowd of fugitives making for the hillside. The monsters had been sighted, and panic was afoot.

Blair and Cathie rushed down through the village, shouting—

"To the hills!" and sped on.

Jean and Aunt Jannet Harvey, busy in the house, had seen nothing. The two men dashed up the steps. Blair seized his boy under one arm, and dragged his wife by the other. Cathie laid hold of Aunt Jannet, and with a gasping word of explanation which only filled the women with fear, and explained nothing, they ran for the southern hill, whose arm ran out into the sea.

Only when they had got half-way up it did they dare to turn and look.

They saw Pym ramping alone on the beach like a madman.

They saw the first of the hideous whirling monsters hop lightly over the swollen reef without a pause and pirouette in the lagoon. Then a blast of smoke whirled from the deck of the Torch, and the dull sound of the gun went quickly past them. The monster writhed and broke, and the pendulous head of it swept inland. The ships pitched at their moorings till the kedge cables snapped and they seemed standing on their sterns. The waves of the lagoon churned up to the platforms of the mission-houses.

"Good lad! Good lad!" shouted Cathie.

Then the other three monsters, as though in answer to the challenge, as though endued with malignant understanding and most devilish determination, bent and swung and reeled over the reef and flung themselves towards the ships.

They saw Captain Pym suddenly throw up his hands above his head in a gesture of utter impotence and despair, and then turn and make for the hill.

The watchers crouched in a crevice of the hillside and gazed narrow-eyed, and their breaths came quick and short, not from the run but because their hearts were in their throats and choked their breathing.

It was a most terrible sight. The powers of all evil—death, destruction, and malignity—against the puny works of man.

The three awful whirling shapes danced and swung in the lagoon, showing off all their evil graces. Three ineffectual flashes broke from the gunboat, but they avoided them with an easy swing, as though they understood and were on their guard. They reeled towards one another and seemed to take evil counsel together. Then, as though moved by one mind, they swooped down straight on the ships.

"Oh, cruel! cruel!" moaned Jean, clasping her boy to her and hiding her face in him.

Captain Cathie groaned as he watched, and then burst into incoherent, and unusual, and most excusable blasphemies.

Aunt Jannet and Kenneth Blair stared in dreadful fascination.

For one of the whirling monsters reached the ships, picked them up, and smashed them and itself together in one dreadful destruction. When the wild welter settled down and permitted sight, the lagoon was bare save for scattered fragments and struggling figures.

Another of the awful things made for the opposite mountain side. They saw it strike and break there. The solid earth crumbled and splashed like mud, and palms and rocks slid down to the sea, while the swollen hanging top of it swung away along the hillside belching ragged torrents as it went.

The remaining one went roaring past them like a great wounded beast, and tore up the valley, breaking itself and scattering destruction broadcast. They heard the final crash of it away up among the hills, and a foaming torrent came sweeping down the valley carrying everything before it.

All this time the wind was blowing a hurricane, Such palms as were left standing whipped and writhed in vain agonies. Some snapped like carrots and lay still. The rain beat mercilessly on the fearful watchers and bit like whips. Blair bent over his wife and boy to shield them with his body. Aunt Jannet, dishevelled and grey, and haggard, still peered out at the horrors in front.

A sound from her, between a gasp and a groan, and a sudden terrified clutch at his arm, brought Blair's face up to the crowning horror.

There came a roaring from the sea the like of which was never heard before. A mighty wall of water came rushing on the land to overwhelm it. It leaped high over the ridge of rocks that lay like a protecting arm round the nearer curve of the lagoon. The jets of it went rocketting up to heaven, and the mighty ridged crest bristled like an avalanche.

Blair sprang upright instinctively, to face the danger standing, and dug his fingers deep into the cracks of the rocks in front of him.

The great wave broke on the solid earth with the crash of an earthquake. It was half-way up the hillside, and the opposite hill was suddenly shortened, and stood in the open sea. The valley was a boiling waterway of hideous and inexpressible confusion.

"It is the end of the world," gasped Aunt Jannet, and sank down, and looked no more.

"My God! My God!" groaned Cathie.

"God help us all!" said Blair, and the rain whipped his face till it seemed as hard and set as the neighbouring rocks.

They spent the night there in extremest misery, sodden through and through, chilled to the bone, faint with hunger. Even Kenni-Kenni was damp, though two protecting bodies did their best to shelter him. And all night long the only sounds in their ears were the hiss and rush and roar of many waters, as the terrible sea went back to its deeps, and the clouds discharged their ceaseless torrents, and the troubled land got rid of its torment.

And over and above the weariness of their bodies, their hearts were sick within them at thought of the destruction of all their work and all their hopes. For whether a soul besides themselves was left alive they knew not.

CHAPTER XXX

WIPED OUT

Jean and Aunt Jannet were dozing fitfully, fairly spent with the strain and misery of it all. Cathie's grey beard was on his chest, but whether he slept Blair could not tell.

He himself sat on his rock, chilled to the marrow of his bones, and watched with heavy eyes the slow birth of new life after the deadly horrors of the night. And his heart was as cold as his body.

He wrestled manfully with that which was in him, but surely man's faith and courage were rarely put to sorer test. He had striven so hard, and toiled so ceaselessly, at utmost stretch of hand and heart and brain, and here, just as the harvest was ripening, it was all dashed into nothing, as though by the stroke of an angry hand. Oh, it was hard, hard, hard!

But he fought out his fight singlehanded, and found himself—where steadfast faith and undaunted courage have always firm footing. And a spark of hope struggled up in him to meet the sun. The beginnings of things had always had a charm for him. And here must be a new beginning. They were back at first principles and the elementary facts of life. But, truly, there is a mighty difference between a beginning and a beginning again, and it calls for the best that is in a man to begin again with the heart with which he began before.

The rain ceased towards morning, the wind slackened, and when the sun rose behind the hills the western sky shone opalescent, and the sea below it was a cold, dark blue. The rollers were still of mighty size, but the reef was spouting foam again, and the lagoon was heaving within its usual bounds.

But everything else was changed—everything except the bare ridge on which they crouched.

The village—gone as though wiped with a sponge off a slate. The mission-houses, schools, church—not a plank left. And somewhere below the smiling face of the lagoon lay all that was left of the ships and the men who had been in them.

Not all below, after all, for from his perch he could see the beach strewn with fragments, human and otherwise. Right below him on the hillside, John MacNeil's waterwheel turned busily in fruitless labour, and its bare nakedness and useless fussiness added to the sense of desolation and discomfort.

Then the sun topped the hills, and cheered their chilled senses somewhat. Blair and Cathie straightened themselves wearily, but neither dared as yet look into the other's face, lest he should find there only confirmation of his own worst fears.

Kenni-Kenni, who had fared better than any of them, and was conscious of nothing more than bodily discomfort, gave a hungry cry which woke response in Cathie's breast.

"Let us go down," he said. "Maybe we'll find something to eat," and the two men scrambled down to the level, and walked over the soft mud where the houses had stood, and searched with anxious eyes for something that might stay their more pressing necessities.

Blair turned up towards the valley. Cathie, with more prescience, sought the beach, and presently a shout from him brought the two together again. When they met, the captain was carrying the body of a drowned kid under one arm, and a bundle of wood under the other.

"Here's breakfast," he said, and did not think it well to mention that he had found the kid lying between the bodies of two dead men, one brown, the other white.

The matches in their metal cases were all damp, but a few minutes' exposure to the sun put that right, and they soon had fire, and kid steaks grilling over it on pointed sticks. Then they helped the ladies down and were presently eating, though, in spite of their hunger, each one of them felt like choking at every mouthful. And there was no talk among them, for they were sitting on the grave of their hopes.

More than once Jean stopped feeding her boy and glanced questioningly at the men, and then, as they ate stolidly, weighted with their thoughts, she went on with her work.

It was only when they had all quite finished, and sat as though dreading what might come next, that she said—

"Are we all that are left, Ken? I thought I heard a cry just now."

"Did you, dear? It is possible. There must surely be others. We will go and see," and he and Cathie went off again towards the beach.

"How's it up the valley?" asked the captain briefly.

"Drowned out."

The beach was a pitiful sight. Every step spoke of the catastrophe. Bodies uncountable, white and brown, men, women, and children, pigs and goats, broken coco-nuts, bruised fruit, wreckage from the ships and plantations and houses.

"By God! Mr. Blair, I cannot understand it," broke out Cathie in a paroxysm, as he stood over the bodies of two of his men from the Torch. "What had we done to deserve this?"

"Cathie, Cathie! Come to your senses, man! This is no punishment of God's. Rather let us be thankful we are still alive."

"I'd almost as lieve be dead," said Cathie stubbornly. "Ships gone, men gone, everything gone, and all our work undone. Say what you will, Mr. Blair, it's bitter hard."

"These," said Blair, raising his hands reverently over the dead at their feet, "have gone home—beyond the reach of storms. The ships can be replaced. If there are any people left, the work can be rebuilt. If they are all gone, they are the better off, and they have gone further than if we had never come here."

"It's bitter hard, all the same—"

And then a faint, muffled cry reached them, apparently from the ragged hillside whose débris lay all over the beach, and they both ran towards it.

The cries were repeated, and led them at last to an out-jutting rock round which the sliding earth had flowed and settled.

"Where are you?" cried Blair.

"Here!" came from under their feet, and they spied a small hole in the earth, and set to work at once to enlarge it with their hands.

Cathie ran down to the beach and came back with some pieces of wood which made the work go quicker. The cries from the inside had ceased, and they worked the harder, and at last they had the hole large enough for Blair to get his head and shoulders in.

With his hand he felt the body of a man fallen in a heap, and by great exertions managed to drag it out through the hole.

It was the body of Captain Pym, white and senseless. They carried him down to the beach and dashed water in his face, and presently he came to, and lay for a minute looking dazedly up at them. Then he sat up.

"I apologise," he said, with an attempt at cheerfulness. "Been dead and buried all night—thought of coming to life again bowled me out. Saw you in the distance, and shouted and shouted—like being in a coffin—just room to stand, but couldn't move, and been holding up that hill all night. My God!" as it all came back on him. "What a horror it has been! Are you the only ones left?"

"I hope not," said Blair. "Can you walk? We've got a fire over there and something to eat."

"Bit shaky yet," said Pym, as he staggered along on their arms. "Never expected to walk again in this life."

"How was it?"

"When I saw that devilish thing smash the ships, and the other coming towards me, I made for the hill. I was just under that rock when it broke. It was like being under Niagara, only worse. It jammed me flat and beat the breath out of me. Then the earth came rolling down, and cased me in tight except a hand's space through which I could breathe. I've been seeing those ships go smash every minute since. God! It was awful!" and he hung slackly on their arms and glanced over the placid lagoon.

Jean and Aunt Jannet gave him quiet greeting, as one come back from the dead, and hastened to supply his wants. Blair and Cathie set off again up the valley with tight faces.

The havoc there was terrible. The cloud-burst and the great wave together had swept it bare. They went some distance up and stood looking round. It seemed incredible that so short a time could have wrought so woful a change.

The plantations were gone to the last stick and leaf. The very hillsides were almost cleared of trees. The smiling valley of yesterday was a stark empty pan, with deeply-scored sides and a sheet of shining mud caking slowly at the bottom.

"It will make good growing ground," said Blair.

"If we'd anything to grow and any one to grow it for," said Cathie gloomily.

"We shall find some of them in the hills, I hope. Let us get on."

And presently there was a shout up above on the hillside, and there came down, at a pace that risked their necks, Jim Gregor of the Jean Arnot and young Irvine, who was on the Torch when last they heard of him.

They whooped with joy and shook hands a dozen times with Blair and Cathie, and were quite incoherent for many minutes.

"We're right glad to see you, boys," said Blair, when they calmed down. "Are there any more up there?"

"Three more Torches, sir, and half a dozen Bonitas, and about a dozen islanders, men and women, and a couple of children. Have you got anything to eat?"

"Yes. Go on to the water-wheel. You'll find food there. Where are these others?"

"Right by yon rock. We'll go back with you. Some of them are badly bashed and can't walk without help."

So they all climbed up, and came on the forlorn little company crouching by the rock, and gave them new life by the very sight of them.

The sailors plucked up heart at once, but the brown men were very subdued and silent. Their eyes were still wide with terror when at last they sat under the southern ridge and ate the food Jean and Aunt Jannet found for them, supplemented by coco-nuts and bruised fruit from the beach.

All the men had strange stories to tell. Gregor and Irvine, and some of the others, asserted that when the waterspout struck the ships they were whirled up out of them and dropped into the lagoon some distance away. Then, before they could swim ashore, the great wave caught them and whirled them up into the valley, bruising them all more or less and breaking some. The brown men were mostly sound of limb. They had fled for the hills at the first sight of the spectral dangers outside.

"Have you seen signs of any others?" asked Blair.

Yes, they thought they had seen moving forms on the further hills, but too far away to distinguish clearly. On which Cathie set them to collecting driftwood from the shore, and piled it on the fire, with wet brush and tangle on top, till the smoke rose in a dense column.

"That'll bring them," he said, and in time they came dropping in, in small companies, from their various hiding-places, and last of all came one carrying a woman in his arms.

And at sight of him, toiling through the new soft mud where the village had stood, Blair sprang up and ran to meet him.

"Thank God, you are left to us, Ha'o!" he cried as they met, but Ha'o was as silent as the rest of his people. "Is Nai hurt? Let me help you."

Nai smiled wanly at him as he put his arms under her and took part of the weight, and then her face crumpled with pain.

They carried her gently to the fire, and laid her on the soft white sand, and Jean and Aunt Jannet knelt beside her and saw to her wants.

Captain Cathie, when he saw the increasing company, had made another visit to their only storehouse, the beach, and came back this time with a young pig and some bananas and coco-nuts, and some carefully-sought-out paw-paw leaves for the benefit of the too-fresh pork.

Ha'o was too weary and too hungry for talk, and Blair and Cathie called the militant members of the party to salvage work on the beach. Gruesome work too, and not calculated to raise their spirits even after a full meal, for every few steps brought them to the bodies of those they had known alive and well the day before.

These they drew up the sand for burial later. Meanwhile the orders were to save everything they could lay hands on. Where everything had been taken, the smallest find was of value.

Fruits and shrubs especially Blair commended to their attention, and he had a couple of dozen paw-paw trees and several rows of bananas planted before sunset.

Out of the piles of timber they secured, Cathie and Pym built lean-to shelters among the rocks sufficient for the whole party. With the coco-nuts and broken fruit, and the bodies of several pigs and goats, they had food for several days, if only they could keep it in eatable condition. By the time it was finished they would know more about their actual circumstances.

Jean informed her husband that Nai had an arm and leg broken, and he at once sought out slips of wood and strips of garments, and put the broken limbs into splints.

Ha'o, after eating, lay thoughtful for a time, and then went down to assist the salvage party. He dragged and carried in silence for some time, but finally gave voice to his thoughts.

"Kenni, why has this come upon us?"

"You have had storms before, Ha'o."

"But never a storm like this one, with whirling devils and waves like rushing mountains."

"I have heard of both before in other places, but I never saw them myself till now."

"Was it your God sent them, Kenni?"

"Only in the same way that He sends everything, Ha'o—light and wind and rain."

"Why did He send this when we were doing our best to please Him?"

"It came in the ordinary way of things. It was just a bigger storm than usual."

"We never had it like this before," said Ha'o, sticking stubbornly to his point. "My people are saying it is your God sent it. If He is that kind of a god we don't want Him."

"How do you train your young men, Ha'o? By treating them softly? By petting them, and giving them all things easy and pleasant?"

"Nay, we toughen them, so that they may endure."

"Exactly! Do you think that God knows less than you? He also wants men who can endure even when the fight goes against them."

That seemed to strike him. He went on stolidly hauling and carrying, and at last said, bitterly—

"If He had left my people alive, Kenni, and not broken Nai, I would have thought better of Him."

"Let us be grateful for what is left, my friend. Nai will get better. Many of our people are dead, but more are left than we think, perhaps."

But Ha'o shook his head gloomily, and went on hauling and carrying, and said no more.

CHAPTER XXXI

REVERSIONS

Captain Pym was in that state of mind in which every man who loses his ship finds himself, and from which his fellow in misfortune, Captain Cathie, was slowly emerging. No slightest blame attached to him in the matter, and he would have no difficulty in proving it. Nevertheless, he was suffering exceedingly. The burden of his thoughts kept sleep far from him, and, after tossing restlessly through the night on a by no means uncomfortable couch of dried palm fronds, he got up very early next morning to give his depressed spirits fresh air and wider space than the confinement of the lean-to afforded them. Blair and Cathie, worn out with hard work and anxieties, were still sleeping soundly.

As Pym walked along the beach, he saw with surprise a thin curl of smoke rising behind an angle of the hillside not far from the scene of his coffining.

When he came to the angle he stopped transfixed, and then set off at a run to the huts. He caught Blair by the shoulder and roughly shook him awake.

"Blair," he cried hoarsely, "your brown devils are eating our men," and Blair and Cathie were on their feet in a moment.

Blair was not very greatly surprised, though not a little disturbed. He had seen the upsetting the catastrophe had wrought in Ha'o, the most advanced of all, and he had wondered if the rest would stand the strain.

"It's a throw-back," he said, "but it's really not very surprising. Where's Ha'o? Cathie, will you call the men?"

He went quickly to the shed Ha'o had built for Nai, and found him there asleep, and was to that extent relieved. He woke him quietly, and told him what was going on.

"Food is scarce, and will be scarcer," said Ha'o, when he arrived at an understanding of the matter. "Everything is destroyed."

"Better starve than live so," said Blair vehemently. "But everything is not destroyed. We shall live somehow, and this has got to be stopped. Come on!"

He picked up a stick of wood from the drift, and set off at a run along the beach. The others armed themselves in like manner and followed him.

The brown men sprang up from their feast as they rounded the corner, some of them still gnawing at chunks of flesh in their hands.

Blair rushed at them like a blazing bolt. Several of them, for lack of clubs, snatched brands from the fire. He paid no heed to their weapons, but laid about him with his stick with such vigour that they gave way before him, and the others, following his lead with hearty good will, drove the brown men back, and finally put them to the run.

"Now," said Blair, as he leaned on his stick, "there is only one thing to be done. Pile all the rough wood you can find on to that fire. Keep out anything that may be useful. We must burn all those bodies. We can't take them out to sea, and if we bury them they'll dig them up."

It was obviously the best thing to do, and they set about the gruesome business at once.

They made a mighty pile of firing and laid the bodies reverently on it, and covered them with more wood, and more bodies and again more wood, till they had to wait till the pile burned down, because of the height of it and the heat. And their faces were pinched and their breaths shortened, as they carried to the pyre the bodies of those they had lived with in comradeship for so long, and they worked in silence.

The only sound that was heard beyond the crackle and fall of the burning wood, as the dense black smoke rolled up into the sky, was the voice of Blair, as he stood to windward and quietly recited portions of the service for the Burial of the Dead from time to time. And surely never did the solemn words sound more weighty and full of meaning.

"I am the resurrection and the life....

"Lord, Thou hast been our refuge: from one generation to another....

"Thou turnest man to destruction....

"They are even as a sleep: and fade away suddenly like the grass....

"In the evening it is cut down, dried up, and withered....

"For we consume away in Thy displeasure....

"Man that is born of woman hath but a short time to live.... He cometh up and is cut down, like a flower....

"In the midst of life we are in death....

"Ashes to ashes, dust to dust....

"Blessed are the dead which die in the Lord.... For they rest from their labours...."

None of them ever forgot that strange and somewhat ghastly service—the hungry lick of the flames, blue and green and yellow and red from the salt and tar, but almost unseen in the beams of the fully-risen sun; the rippling lagoon; the sparkling white beach; the foam-jets on the reef; the great blue sea beyond; the pitiful things the flames consumed; and the rolling clouds of smoke which spread like a pall along the scarred hillside.

Aunt Jannet Harvey came hurrying round the corner to see what they were at, and Cathie caught sight of her and sent her hurrying back surprised at his brusqueness. For this was one of the things that may be told but is better not seen.

Ha'o had taken no part in these doings. He had no desire for human flesh, but there was a doubtful look on his face, as though he thought the proceedings wasteful and possibly to be regretted later on.

The brown men stood in a clump at a distance and watched sullenly all that was done.

When the pile died down Blair went over to the chief.

"Ha'o," he said, "go and speak to your people. Tell them that things are as they were, and that flesh they shall not eat."

"They will starve."

"No, they will not starve. We will find them food."

Ha'o looked at him doubtfully, but not without expectation. The white men were so wonderful, that it was difficult to say what they could or could not do, and Kenni never lied.

Nevertheless, "Where, Kenni?" he asked.

"We shall not starve," said Blair emphatically.

The brown man looked searchingly at him for a full minute, and then turned and strode away towards the others.

CHAPTER XXXII

FROM THE BEGINNING

"Our brown folk have lost their heads for the time being," said Blair to his wife, as they all stood round the huts. "They have gone off to the hills. It is not very surprising. They will come back all right in time. Captain Cathie, I want you to make a raft and take the ladies and the sick—in fact, all but Gregor and Irvine—to the Happy Valley for a time, till things straighten out a bit. You will, I think, find food there, and the natives won't intrude on you."

"And you, Kenneth?" said Jean anxiously.

"I am going across to the other side of the island with Ha'o, to see how they fared there. If food is plentiful we will bring some back here for the women and children. They may have been washed out also. If so we must get food from the Valley. We will drop in on you from the upper end, but it is too rough a road for you and the sick men. Will you join us, Captain Pym, or will you go and take care of the ladies?"

"Captain Cathie is quite equal to that, I am sure, Mr. Blair. With your permission I will join you."

"Can you induce Nai to go with the ladies, Ha'o?"

"She will go," said Ha'o tersely.

He was in a gloomy frame of mind through all these strange happenings and the defection of his people.

"Then the sooner we get to it the better." And under Cathie's directions they all set to work on a raft. Timber and rope were not wanting.

"Take all you can, and especially what we can use for boat-building later on," said Blair. "We shall have to get out of our hole ourselves, and that, I think, is the way out."

The brown women and children he set to collecting for themselves all the food they could find along the shore. He also gave them some lengths of rope, and bade them untwist it for fishing-lines and then start fishing from the ledge with splinters for hooks.

"You will probably find the bottom of the valley scoured out, Cathie," he said; "but there should be both fruit and animals on the hillsides. We may have to replenish the island from there."

When the work was well forward, he set out with his little band to cross the island by One-Tree Pass, and found the passage extremely difficult. For the cloud seemed to have finally broken on the saddle of the hills, and in many places the road they had built with such labour and difficulty was washed completely away, and in other places it was buried deep under slides of broken rock.

They found their way over the ridge, however, and saw at once that the deluge had wrought heavily on the further side also. The long slope was deeply scored and furrowed, but there were houses and palm-trees still standing down below, and they went on quickly to see how the brown folk had fared.

The villagers welcomed them heartily and received their news with amazement. The storm above and the storm below had terrified them. The water had come down the hill in cascades, but the long stretch had dissipated much of its force before it reached them. Then the great wave had swept across the beach and carried away all their boats. Their palms and plantations had suffered heavily, and they had picked up a number of dead pigs and goats, but otherwise there had been no loss of life. They had not overmuch food, but what they had they were quite willing to share with the others who had none. And Blair's heart, still sore over the defection of the western men, was comforted somewhat by their simple kindliness.

They stayed the night, and Blair explained more fully the disasters on the other side of the island and the temporary aberration of Ha'o's people, and begged them, if there should be any attempt at raiding, to treat the others as reasonably as might be, remembering what they had gone through.

They set off again very early in the morning, carrying such burden of food as was possible on the rough road they had to travel, and reached the huts by the sea before midday. The brown men had taken possession and received them in sulky silence.

Blair gave the food to the women and children, and to the men some bits of his mind in his own special way. He acknowledged the direness of the catastrophe, but bade them remember that the white men had suffered equally and yet had not lost their heads or their heart. He told them to be grateful for their lives, and assured them that there was no need for despair.

Blair's high spirits in the face of all difficulties, his forethought and far-reaching grip of the necessities of the case, made a deep impression even on Captain Pym's habitual and official phlegm. Under stress of circumstance he found himself under the necessity of rearranging his preconceived ideas. He became decidedly more human, and perhaps more of a man, than he had been for many a year.

He sounded Blair as to his hopes and intentions, and they discussed matters freely. In furtherance of them, when they had rested, they all set to work making another raft, and if the Bonita men could have seen their spick and span, stiff and starched captain, hauling and lashing, with his coat off and his trousers up to the knee, it is certain they would not have known him.

They paddled their raft across the lagoon to the place where the ships had lain before the storm, and after some searching found where the Torch and Jean Arnot were lying. The great wave had probably washed them inshore but the return had carried them out again. The Bonita had disappeared completely. She had probably been carried over the edge of the shelf and lay in unfathomable depths. They could see the other two dimly through the clear water, with the many-coloured fishes darting in and out of their battered sides and broken raffle, and Captain Pym's face pinched at the sight and at thought of it all.

Ha'o was the most expert swimmer of the party, and had long since shown that he could remain under water twice as long as any of the white men. On him therefore the burden of discovery lay, and he appreciated with the rest how much depended on his efforts. They had timber in quantity from the broken boats and ships, but without tools they could turn it all to no account. There were tools below there in the ships. Ha'o was going down to find them. With tools in their hands the door of deliverance would be at all events ajar.

"You will most likely find them in the front part of our ship, Ha'o, underneath where the big gun was," Blair told him. "If the gun has fallen through, so much the better. It will help you," and Ha'o nodded, and shot down through the clear water like a brown streak.

He was up again presently and hung panting to the raft. The big gun had gone out of sight through the side and bottom of the ship. He would get inside next time.

But it took many visits before he discovered anything, and then a ringing cheer went up as he came to the surface with a saw in his hand, and flung it on to the raft.

"There are more things, but they are scattered," he told them, when he had got his breath, and next time he took down with him one end of a thin cord they had unravelled out of rope, and presently sent up by it a heavy hammer, and came up himself with a chisel. It took many hours' hard work, but at last they had enough to go on with, and Ha'o lay panting on the raft, while the others paddled it slowly down the lagoon to the Happy Valley.

CHAPTER XXXIII

SALT OF THE EARTH

The effect of the great wave in the Valley had been extraordinary.

When last they were there the whole place was a tangle of luxuriant undergrowth, ferns, mosses, lichens, pandanus, hibiscus, paw-paws, with stately palms waving gracefully above.

Now the bed of the Valley was bare. The growths and the undergrowths had been torn off and swept away, and the newcomers were led wonderingly through the uncovered ruins of the city built by the men who set up the stone gods—along a wide street paved with stone blocks, which ran up the middle of the Valley with the stream flowing through it; past the foundations of great buildings; into an immense square where the denudation had been less complete. A certain amount of mud had silted down again on to the ruins. Nature was already at work covering up the scar of her latest wound. And the great stone gods sat gazing expectantly out to sea, as they had gazed when the city below still teemed with busy life; as they had gazed through all the long years since, while the ruins of the city slowly disappeared beneath the touch of the healing hand.

The first party had found strange quarters in the uncovered basement of a building, which, from its size, had probably been a temple. It was a great quadrangle, and the head of the wide roadway that led from the sea ran right into it, and ended there. The upper end of the enclosure rose ten feet or more above the level, and was composed of great chiselled blocks of stone, and in this were cavernous square openings, the entrances of which now served as houses for these houseless strangers. They had appropriated four adjacent holes, and had made themselves as comfortable as circumstances permitted.

The whole place had been covered in with wild growth, but the great wave foaming up the valley had swept it all bare. The apartments were not uncomfortable except in one respect. They ran so far back into the hillside that the ends of them had not yet been discovered. "And," said Aunt Jannet, peering into the shadows which the firelight quickened into ghostly life, "I'm always expecting something will come out, and either frighten us to death or eat us alive."

Ha'o stood it for one night, with crumpled face and quick-glancing eyes, but next day he carried up some boards from the beach, and built a tiny lean-to outside for himself and Nai, and they found life more tolerable.

Nothing ever came out of those mysterious passages for their undoing. What dark uses they may have served in the bygone times they could only surmise. One passage they followed till it issued in the cliffs behind the stone gods. The others ran straight into the heart of the mountain, with cross cuts leading round towards the city, and the uses they might have been put to in the hands of a priestly oligarchy were apparent.

Captain Pym was fired with thoughts of hidden treasure, and spent many odd hours searching for it. Blair laughed at the idea, and begged him to keep it to himself, lest the men should catch the infection, and waste on it valuable time which might be used to much better advantage.

"Treasure is unlikely," he said. "If, as we suppose, these pioneers were accidentally blown across, or fled for reasons, they would not be likely to bring much with them."

"All the same, they built mightily," argued Pym, and went on with his search. All that he ever found, however, was a few flat beaten plates of gold, and some golden ornaments, of no great value save as curiosities.

Captain Cathie reported a fair amount of fruit and palms still standing on the hillsides, and pigs and goats enough to re-stock the island, in time and with protection. Most of the other animals had disappeared completely.

"I'll take the men back to-morrow over the hill," said Cathie, in excellent spirits at the prospect of the opening door, "and we'll bring back another raft of timber. With the tools you've got we can make a start anyway, and we can fish up more by degrees. There's timber enough in the lagoon to build a new schooner."

"Build us something that will float as far as the Marquesas or Paumotus, and we'll soon have a new schooner, captain. But the first thing I want is to get to Kanele and Anape to see how Evans and Stuart have fared. If they came through pretty well we can get fresh stock from them, both animals and plants."

"I've got a lot of paw-paws for you on the beach, and some bananas and plantains. Where will you plant, Mr. Blair?"

"For the present in the mud of the old fields. It'll make splendid growing ground. Later on, when we rebuild, we must get higher up. We're not likely to have another deluge just yet, but what has been may be, and we must take all precautions. When your boat is ready, and we've had a trip round the islands, my idea is for you to run across to the Marquesas and buy a schooner there, if you can lay hands on one, and send her back by Gregor for our use while you're away. Then you go on to Sydney and buy a new Torch and everything we need, Long Tom, Winchesters and all"—with a quizzical glance at Pym. "You know just what we want, and you can have all the money you require."

Captain Pym listened with surprise. His ideas of missionaries were crystallising rapidly from the solution of scepticism into concrete beliefs and admirations. He was not a man given to admiration of other men, but he recognised in Kenneth Blair a master mind and an indomitable spirit. He said little but thought much.

Every one was at work soon after daylight. Cathie produced drowned meat from an adjacent passage way, which he used as cold storage. Jean and Aunt Jannet prepared the morning meal. Blair had planted two rows of paw-paws and a number of bananas before breakfast, and Ha'o had built his lean-to for Nai and brought in some fruit.

Then Cathie built a small raft, and in due course Aunt Jannet Harvey was seated on it with many startled exclamations, and wafted herself uncouthly out into the lagoon. She was provided with two fishing lines and a supply of bait, and a rope to the shore lest she should disappear entirely from human ken, and she had instructions to catch all the fish she could for the amplification of the larder.

And Blair, when he had made sure of her safety, and turned to go up the valley to cross the hills, could hardly contain himself at sight of her face, in which determination to catch struggled desperately with horror at thought of pulling the hooks out of what she caught.

"This is a change from Kensington, Aunt Jannet, isn't it? You're quite sure you won't tumble overboard?" had been his jovial parting word.

"I'll t—try not, Kenneth. D—do you think it hurts them much to have the hooks pulled out?"

"If you leave them for a few minutes they'll die quite comfortably. Then it won't hurt them. Anyway, you see we need them."

So Aunt Jannet pursed her lips valiantly, and cast in the lines he had baited for her, and watched him and Captain Cathie with one eye, while the other waited on her lines in fear and expectation.

They waved her an adieu at the turn of the valley, and in her attempt to reply to it she frightened away a swarm of eager nibblers and nearly fell overboard herself.

"Yes," she said to herself, "it's a great change from Kensington. But if that child Jean can stand it, I can. And she seems as happy as a lark. That's partly Kenni-Kenni, of course. Oh dear, I've caught something! Whatever am I to do now?"

She looked wildly round for assistance, but the men were climbing the hill, laden with provisions for the brown folk. So she tightened her lips and hauled in her line, and at last drew her first fish on to the raft. And then, after a pitiful look at its changing colours, she turned her head away as far as she could, suppressed a strong inclination to throw her victim back into the water, and waited for the poor thing to die comfortably.

When Jean and Kenni-Kenni came down to inquire how she was getting on, she was quite herself again.

"I've got a dozen or so," she cried. "I hope they are all fit to eat. It's really quite interesting when you get used to it. If you like to try your hand at it, Jean, haul me in and I'll take care of Kenni-Kenni for a bit."

The men were back before nightfall, very tired, but rich in timber, and in high spirits at the recovery of more tools, and all with appetites that disposed of Aunt Jannet's fish in a very much shorter time than it had taken that good lady to catch them.

Next day they laid the keel of their forlorn hope, and when that ceremony was over, Blair and Ha'o started off again across the hills to the old village, to endeavour to get the brown men to make a start on their own buildings and plantings. Characteristically, they were inclined to lie down under misfortune and let things take their chance, and Blair, characteristically also, stated his intention of stopping there till they got to work. He exhorted them to better heart both by word and example, and Ha'o lent the weight of his authority, and, where that failed, added the still weightier impulsion of physical force. Authority weakens under disaster, but a bold heart and a heavy hand are strong arguments, and, disaster or no disaster, Ha'o had no intention of abating one jot of his seigneurial rights. He was chief still and he let them feel it.

"What is the good of planting?" said the brown men. "We shall be dead before the fruit comes."

"Oh no, you won't!" said Blair cheerfully. "There is fruit in the Valley and fruit on the other side of One-Tree Pass, but in future you'll have to go and get it for yourselves, and you can have all the fish you want for the catching."

"But we don't care for fish every day."

"There are many things I don't care for myself, my sons, but when I can't do better I put up with them. You must learn to be men."

The actively mutinous spirit, which the opportunity of the day after the storm had kindled in them, had passed with the passing of that which had excited it. It had vanished in the smoke of the funeral pyre, and Blair was grateful, for things might have been very different. Instead of fighting the lethargy of despair they might have had to defend themselves against its fury, and he was well content.

He tried hard to get them to come over into the Valley, but that they would not do. They would come to the hill top for such fruits as might be brought there for them, and they would go over One-Tree Pass, but into the valley of the stone gods not one of them would set so much as a toe, and Ha'o himself could not make them.

With all hands working heartily and at high pressure,—from Captain Pym, who dropped the last remnants of his starch in the process, to Aunt Jannet who, in the intervals of her other duties, picked oakum as if she had been undergoing a term of imprisonment,—the boat building made famous progress, and four weeks from the day the keel was laid the Kenni-Kenni was launched—prevailed upon, at all events, and apparently much against her will, to quit mother earth and take to the water. And if she looked, as Captain Cathie admitted, something of a cross between a washtub and a patchwork quilt, she was undoubtedly built strong and would stand a good deal of knocking about. As to her sailing qualities, they might have been better and they might have been worse, and, as Cathie said, they had not started out to build a cup-winner—which was perhaps just as well.

There was an old candle-nut tree in a corner at the head of the Valley, and they set out to stain the little ship dark red with a decoction of its bark, but as the supply ran short the result was not altogether happy. However, she floated on an even keel and was as tight as a drum, forty feet over all, ten feet beam, decked all over and yawl rigged. Spars and sails they had in plenty from the treasure trove of the beach, and Captain Cathie undertook to take her all the way to Sydney if need be. He also expressed the explicit intention of overhauling the first ship or island he came across for a supply of paint, all of one colour, sufficient to go all round her.

Nevertheless, and in spite of her lack in such minor details, their hearts were very full as they lined the beach, with their eyes on the little ship, and in their ears Blair's voice ringing strong and true with gratitude and hope, as he prayed God's blessing on the accomplished work of their hands, and on the work she had still to do.

When the ceremony was over, and Blair happened to be standing for a moment alone, Captain Pym came up to him and wrung his hand heartily.

"Blair," he said, and his old shipmates on the Bonita would not have known either his voice or the look on his face, "I'm glad I came here. But for my poor fellows who are gone, I could almost say I'm glad I was wrecked here. I have learnt a great deal," and Blair answered him with a cordial grip and a beaming smile.

On the morrow, Blair and Pym and Cathie and a crew of six, three Torches, and three Bonitas, took leave of the rest and sailed for Kanele.

Jean felt this parting terribly, the little ship looked so small, so uncouth, so unequal to emergencies. But she kept a brave face, and waved her farewells from the shore with a fervent prayer for their safety, and then went quietly about her work, with her own Kenni-Kenni clinging to her skirts, while his namesake carried his father away across the seas to possible dangers, to possible— Nay, she would have faith in that protecting hand which had brought them through so many difficulties before, and to fear was to doubt.

So her heart sang valiantly, "God's in His heaven, all's well!" and after that first hour her face was calm and hopeful, and she was counting the days to their return.

The secret passages of the old temple made capital homes. The men had snatched odd moments from their other labours, and material from their abundant stores, and had boarded off the interior darknesses and ghostly possibilities, and had knocked together some rough tables and stools. They had food enough, though they were all tiring somewhat of fish, fish again, and always fish. Blair had laughingly assured them it was good for the brain, and Aunt Jannet asserted that she was getting so brainy that, unless a change of diet came soon, she would not answer for consequences. But in reality there was very little to complain of. The health of the whole party had been excellent, and Blair's high spirits had permitted no one else's to droop for a moment.

Jean had more than once suggested their return to their work among the brown men and women. But, in view of this first trip round the islands, to which he had been looking forward with much eagerness, Blair judged it best for them to remain where they were.

"As soon as we're rid of Captain Pym and Cathie and the rest, we'll go back and tackle the work," he said. "The brown folks are getting on all right in the meantime. They're actually beginning to learn how to help themselves."

"Jean, my dear," said Aunt Jannet, one day after the Kenni-Kenni sailed, "it's just wonderful the way you stand it all."

"Stand it, Aunt Jannet? Why, what do you mean? What is there to stand?"

"Why—heaps. Look at your dress, for instance. And when one remembers that you've got £10,000 a year or so!—yes, I say, it's just wonderful."

"I've done my best with it, and it's very rude to comment on people's clothes before their faces. Besides, your own is no better, and the needle Captain Cathie made for you out of that fishbone was very much better than mine."

"Well, well," laughed Aunt Jannet. "It wasn't your dress I was meaning, child—"

"You're getting fish on the brain, dear. Isn't that enough to make any woman happy?"

That, of course, was Kenni-Kenni, whose great delight it was at this time to rush through and through the shining stream that babbled across the temple floor, kicking up diamond showers with his pink toes and squealing with delight as the sparkling drops played round him.

"Yes, it does one good just to look at him," said Aunt Jannet. "But I do wish you could get him to wear some more clothes. He's—"

"Clothes!" said Jean scornfully. "What does a boy like that want with clothes?"

Kenni-Kenni was developing rapidly. He had one day thrown a stone at a little black pig which sought his acquaintance. And when the piglet fled Kenni-Kenni came suddenly to the knowledge of his prowess and thereafter became a mighty hunter of small pigs whenever chance offered.

He had also, after considerable hesitation, thrown a pebble at one of the stone gods, of which he had hither-to stood in much awe. And as no ill results followed he had become bold and warlike, and thought nothing of challenging the bearded sailormen to mortal combat. And they delighted in him exceedingly, and had promised to teach him to box and to swim as soon as the boat was finished.

Nai was getting about again and would soon be as well as ever. The broken arm and leg were mending, and never was invalid more tenderly ministered to, or more grateful to her nurses. It was upon Ha'o that the catastrophe seemed to have had the most lasting effect, and that, after all, was perhaps not unnatural. The country was his, and the people were his, and they had suffered terribly. His faith in Kenneth Blair underwent no visible eclipse, however, and he laboured at the boat-building with the rest.

The days passed very slowly for those left behind, and when the limit allowed for the voyage was exceeded by one day, two days, three days, Jean's anxieties began to show head again.

"Don't worry, child!" said Aunt Jannet. "That boat has probably proved even slower than they expected. My only wonder was that it would sail at all. Not one of them ever built a boat in his life before, and I'm sure it looked a deal more like a big washtub with a cover on than a ship. They'll turn up all right in time. If they'd been meant to be drowned they'd every chance when all the rest were."

And surely enough, on the eleventh day, the Kenni-Kenni came wafting slowly down the lagoon, having come in by the upper entrance and made a short call on the brown men in the old quarters.

They were all well and brought a full cargo of news and stock and plants, and Blair himself was in the highest of spirits and hungry to get to work on the new plantations.

The other islands had suffered somewhat from the big wave, chiefly in the matter of boats. The news of the dire happenings on Kapaa'a had filled them with amazement. The Evanses and Stuarts, and all their works and belongings, were flourishing mightily. They sent endless condolences to Jean and Aunt Jannet and Nai and Ha'o, and had been for embarking at once to their consolation. But as the Kenni-Kenni was to start on her longer journey as soon as she could be provisioned, that was out of the question, as it would have been impossible for them to get back home again.

"Yes," acknowledged Captain Cathie, in reply to a pointed question of Aunt Jannet's respecting the sailorly qualities of his boat, "I'm bound to say she's not exactly what you might call a fast boat. But she's sure, and if you give her wind enough and time enough she gets there all right."

They had a busy three days preparing for the long voyage. Captain Cathie reckoned they might make the Marquesas in twelve days with good weather. So they made provision for twenty, out of the stores they had brought from Kanele and Anape. He had borrowed Evans's pocket compass, but vowed he could find his way without it.

"If we go west with a touch of south in it we're bound to hit either the Marquesas or Paumotus," he said cheerfully. "You may look for that schooner here in six weeks from to-day—that is, if there's one to be had, and if I can find a trader who'll negotiate the drafts."

Jean had been racking her brains as to how they were to get hold of some of the money waiting to be used in London, for all her papers had disappeared in the deluge. But Blair had thought the whole matter out, and had brought over paper and pens and a bottle of ink. And among them they drew up a number of documents which, with Captain Pym's verification of the circumstances, would, they thought, procure for Captain Cathie all the money he needed as soon as he reached Sydney, and possibly before that.

And a very busy man would Captain Cathie be, if ever he reached Sydney. For he had to buy a new Torch and a multitudinous cargo; engage new hands—to a limited extent, however, this time, for henceforth they hoped to utilise largely the services of the brown men; and last, but by no means least, to provide, so far as money could do it, adequate recompense for the families of the men whose lives had been given in the service of the Dark Islands. So far as forethought and hard thinking could do it they had attended to everything, and Captain Cathie's programme might have daunted a less valiant man.

And so, very early one morning, before the sun had topped the hills behind, though the outer sea danced and sparkled merrily, there was a great leave-taking on the white beach at the mouth of the valley where the old village used to stand. The Kenni-Kenni had brought them all up the day before, with all their belongings, in a couple of trips, and they were among their own brown people once more, ready and anxious to be at their work again.

The last hearty handshakes had been given and the last words said. The shallop they had built for use with the larger boat, and which was to be left behind, had just put Captain Pym and Captain Cathie on board. The sails ran up, and the Kenni-Kenni's nose turned determinedly for the passage and the long journey westward.

Kenneth Blair and his wife Jean, and Aunt Jannet Harvey stood in the centre of a line of brown folk and waved the farewells and benedictions their voices could no longer carry, and little Kenni-Kenni waved and shouted because the others did. His namesake bobbed and rose to the swell of the passage and was lost to sight behind the spouting jets of the reef.

The line of watchers on the beach climbed the hillside behind them, and watched and waved till the white sails alone were visible, till they became a tiny white speck, till they disappeared.

Then Kenneth Blair kissed his wife very tenderly, for his heart was very full. And he turned to the brown folk, and said—

"We will ask God's blessing on their journeying, for it means much to us all, and then we will get to our work. Let us pray!" and the brown folk bent their heads.

On the little ship, Captain Cathie had given the helm to Jim Gregor, and stood looking back at the peaks of the little land where he had spent so many full days.

And to him came Captain Pym, and said—

"That is one of the finest men I ever met, Captain Cathie. I count it a privilege to have known him. He will do great things yet."

"Yes, sir," said Cathie quietly, for the parting was still on him. "The brown men call him White Fire, and so he is, and his wife's another, and so is Mrs. Harvey. Salt of the earth, sir, every one of them. If there were more like them the world would be a sight better to live in than it is."

John Oxenham – A Concise Bibliography

God's Prisoner (1898)
A Princess of Vascovy (1899)
Under the Iron Flail (1902)
Barbe of Grand Bayou (1903)
Bondman Free (1903)
Hearts in Exile (1904)
John of Gerisau (1904)
A Weaver of Webs (1904)
White Fire (1905)
Giant Circumstance (1906)
Profit and Loss (1906)
The Long Road (1907)
Carette of Sark (1907)
In Christ There Is No East or West (1908)
Pearl of Pearl Island (1908)
The Song of Hyacinth (1908)
My Lady of Shadows (1909)
Great Heart Gillian (1909)
A Maid of the Silver Sea (1910)
The Coil of Carne (1911)
The Quest of the Golden Rose (1912)
The Gate of the Desert (1912)
Bees in Amber (1913)
Broken Shackles (1914)
The King's High-Way (1916)
All's Well (1916)
The Fiery Cross (1917)
The Vision Splendid (1917)
High Altars (1918)
Hearts Courageous (1919)
The Wonder of Lourdes: what it is and what it means (1924)
The Hidden Years' (1927)
Gentlemen - the King! (1928)
God's Candle (1929)
Hearts in Exile (1930)

The Splendour of the Dawn (1930)
The Man Who Would Save the World (1930)
The Pageant of the King's Children (1930) (with his son Roderick Dunkerley)
Cross-Roads: The Story of Four Meetings (1931)
A Saint in the Making (1931)
Christ and the Third Wise Man (1934)